OPERATION INTERSTELLAR

By
GEORGE O. SMITH

ARMCHAIR FICTION
PO Box 4369, Medford, Oregon 97504

For more information about Armchair Books and products, visit our website at…

www.armchairfiction.com

Or email us at…

armchairfiction@yahoo.com

RADIO WAVES ACROSS THE GALAXY

For years men had struggled with the linking up of real-time planetary communications. They said the theory wasn't sound. It seemed impossible. But Paul Grayson had been working with the Z-wave in the hope of establishing the legitimacy of his own theories.

But so far, success had eluded him. No one would give him a chance to test his findings. The closer he came to proving the validity of his theories, the harder multiple political factions worked against him...including his own boss!

Veteran sci-fi author George O. Smith concocts a tale riddled with intrigue, murder, and good old-fashioned space opera in this classic tale from the golden years of science fiction.

FOR A COMPLETE SECOND NOVEL, TURN TO PAGE 151

CAST OF CHARACTERS

PAUL GRAYSON
His work in interplanetary communications was ground-breaking. But he didn't expect to be accused of murder because of it!

NORA PHILLIPS
She was an incredible beauty who played her part well and betrayal was one thing that came easy to her.

DR. HAEDAECKER
He had worked hard for power and adulation. But just how far would he go to keep it?

JOHN STACEY
His needed to find answers surrounding the mysterious Nora Phillips—little did he know of the deadly game being played!

CHARLES HOAGLAND
He had strong political interests. Unfortunately, Paul Grayson stood in the way.

FRANKLIN HUSTON
His desire to help Grayson wasn't wholly political; it had become personal, and it involved the entire galaxy's future!

CHAPTER ONE

PAUL GRAYSON walked the city street slowly. He was sauntering towards the spaceport, but he was in no hurry. He had allowed himself plenty of time to breathe the fresh spring air, to listen to the myriad of sounds made by his fellow men, and to revel in the grand freedom that being out in the open gave him. Soon enough he would be breathing canned air, pungent with the odor of compressor oil and the tang of the greenery used to replenish the oxygen, unable to walk freely more than a few dozen steps, and unable to see what lies beyond his viewports.

Occasionally his eyes looked along the low southern sky towards Alpha Centauri. Proxima, of course, could not be resolved by the naked eye, much less the stinking little overheated mote that rotated about Proxima. Obviously unfit for human life and patently incapable of spawning life of its own, it was Paul Grayson's destination, and would be his home for a few days or a few weeks depending entirely upon whether things went good or bad.

Only during the last four out of two thousand millions of years of its life had this planet been useful. Man needed a place to stand, not to move the earth with Archimedes's lever but to survey the galaxy. Proxima Centauri I was the only planet in the trinary and as bad as it was, it was useful for a space station.

In an hour, Paul Grayson would be locked in a capsule of metal hurling himself through space towards Proxima I. He was looking forward to ten days cooped up in a spacecraft of the type furnished by the Bureau of Astrogation to its engineers, which was a far cry from the sumptuous craft run by the Big Brass. His confines would be lined with functional scientific equipment; his air supply would be medically acceptable but aesthetically horrible; and his vision limited to the cabin, for beyond the viewports would be only the formless, endless, abysmal blackness of absolutely nothing while the ship mounted into multiples of the speed of light.

Then days in a building filled to the dome with power equipment and radio gear; timing mechanism and recorders; and a refrigerator set-up that struggled with the awesome heat poured into Proxima I by its close-by luminary but which succeeded only in lowering the temperature to the point where the potting compound in the transformers did not run out, where the calibrating resistors would not change their values, where the recording machines would still make a record.

And then again more days in the ship before it returned to earth. Call it thirty days and understand why Paul Grayson sauntered along killing time in the fresh air before taking off.

Paul grinned. Four years ago he had arrived a full hour early and wasted the hour in the smelly ship instead of filling his lungs with clean fresh air. Never again. He would arrive a full five minutes before check-in time.

He heard some radio music, its tone stripped of high frequencies from its passage through the slit of a partially opened window. He sniffed the air and laughed because someone was cooking corned beef and cabbage. Then he was out of the range of the radio music. Paul liked music. He hummed a tune as he walked, and then as the fancy struck him, he started to sing. It was faint singing; it would not have carried more than a few feet, but it sufficed for Paul. It was a refrain from an early atomic-age ballad:

"Round and round and round go the deuterons
Round and round the magnet swings them
Round and round and round go the deuterons
Smack! In the target goes the ion beam!"

Paul stopped his song because the interesting click of high heels on the sidewalk pointed to the approach of someone who might view a *cappella* singing as an indication of inebriation.

She was coming towards him, walking on the same side of the sidewalk. Her step was quick and lithe, and the slight breeze outlined her frock against her body, revealing and at the same time concealing just enough to quicken the pulse and awaken the interest. Paul was thirty and unmarried, and experienced enough to catalogue her shrewdly.

No crude attempt at pick-up would work on this woman.

She was sure of herself and obviously could not want for admirers. It would take careful strategy over a period of time to get to first base with a woman like her; an inept campaigner would be called out on strikes. And Paul Grayson had to be on the way to Centauri within the hour, which automatically eliminated the initial step in any plausible scheme to wrangle an introduction.

Paul Grayson grinned ruefully. It seemed to him that when he had hours to spend and nothing to do, the streets were barren of presentable women while the most interesting specimens of womanhood smiled and offered their charms when he was en route towards some schedule that could not be delayed.

This was woman enough to make a man forget his timetables—almost.

She came forward, her face lighted by the street lamp that Paul had just passed. Blue-eyed and fair-skinned, her hurried route was on collision course with his and with a minute shake of his head because he had neither the time nor the inclination to attempt anything as crude as striking up an acquaintance by barring her path, Paul angled his course aside.

She angled to.

"Hello," she said brightly. "I thought you'd be along sooner."

Paul Grayson gulped. Obviously she mistook him for someone else and a faint feeling of jealousy ran through him for the lucky man who owned her affections. The street lamp behind him must have cast heavy shadows across his face making identification difficult. He opened his mouth to explain away the mistake, but the girl came up to him, hardly slackening her pace until the last possible moment. Then instead of speaking, Paul found his parted mouth met by hers. Her lips were warm. Her arms came around him in a quick embrace, and his arms instinctively closed about her waist.

Paul kissed back, cheerfully accepting the pleasure of the error with a sort of devilish glee.

Then he stepped back.

"I'm sorry," he said, "that I am not the guy you thought I was."

She looked up at him with a blink. Her expression changed to surprise, and then her mouth opened in a scream as her eyes flicked away from him and centered over his left shoulder.

Paul started to whirl, but someone dropped the north pole on the back of his skull. It chilled him completely. Her scream rang in his ears as he fell forward. Vaguely he felt the silk of her dress against his outstretched hands, and then against his cheek just before the sidewalk rose up to grind against his face. Something pulled at his coat.

Then he felt nothing more. Only the frightened scream of the woman that rang in his ears, shrill, angry, fearful, and never ending—

—until Paul realized that the siren wail was not her scream but the ringing of his own ears, and that the girl was sitting a-sprawl on the sidewalk with his head between her thighs. She was rubbing the nape of his neck with her fingertips, quietly erasing the pain bit by bit.

The threshold of ringing in his ears diminished and his field of vision increased as the darting lights went away, and Paul Grayson then could hear the sound of running feet and the babble of voices.

"What happened?"

"This man was clipped—by a thug."

"You saw it?" came the voices in a mad garble of scrambled speeches.

"Right in front of my eyes."

The babble broke into many and varied subjects. Curiosity, both morbid and Samaritan; anger both righteous and superficial, but both directed at the things that make such happenings possible; suggestions both sensible and absurd, and offers both welcome and ridiculous.

Paul groaned and tried to lift his hand to the raw spot on his chin where the sidewalk had removed some hide.

The woman looked down at him and smiled in a wan, apprehensive manner. "You're all right?"

Paul struggled to sit up and made it with her help. The wave of pain rose and localized in his head at about forty degrees right latitude. It made him want to carry his head at an angle with his neck ducked down below the level of the knot of pain. Hands helped him to his feet, led him across the sidewalk while he became stronger by the moment.

He shook his head to clear it and winced as the motion caused the knot of pain to vibrate nastily. "What happened?" he asked in a quavering voice. It sounded like someone else's voice to him, and surprised at the sound of it he repeated the question. It still sounded like someone else's voice and while he was wondering if his voice would sound like that for the rest of his life, the girl explained what had happened.

Paul missed most of it, but then asked another question: "Did you see him?"

"No," she said. Her voice was regretful, yet tinted with a dash of amusement. "He sort of rose out of the shadow behind you— you're a tall man, you know. All I saw was a ragged silhouette. He hit you. You fell. I screamed. He grabbed at your wallet —" Her voice trailed away unhappily.

Paul smiled. "Nothing in it but personal papers all replaceable. Not more than a few dollars. I'd have handed it over rather than get this clip on the skull. Too bad you couldn't see him."

The touch of amusement came again. "I had my eyes closed, sort of."

Paul smiled again. Inwardly he was welcoming the footpad to the contents of his wallet and accepting the bop on the bean as the price to pay for an introduction to the girl.

Someone in the crowd said: "You'd better come inside until you feel all right."

Paul shook his head and was happy to find that the knot inside had diminished to a faint pinpoint. His voice was sounding more like his own, too. "I've got to go," he said.

"But—"

The wail of sirens came and a police car dashed to the curb.

It spilled policemen from all doors, who came warily. "What's going on here?" demanded the sergeant.

Paul explained.

"You'd better come to the station and lodge a complaint." Paul shook his head. "I'm Paul Grayson of the Bureau of Astrogation," he said. "I could prove it but the crook has my identification papers. "I'm due to take off for space within…" Paul looked at his watch. "…within forty minutes," he finished.

"We'll require a complaint."

"Can't you take it?" pleaded Paul. "Good Lord, man, I can't identify a criminal that clipped me from behind. Hell, the only contact I had with him was hitting the back of my head against his black jack."

The sergeant looked at the woman. "You can't help?"

"Not much more. He was just a blurred shadow to me, he looked like any other man wearing dark clothing—which can be changed all too easily."

The sergeant went to the police car and spoke to the main office over the radio. He returned in a moment. "The lieutenant says we're to run you over to the spaceport and take depositions en route. That'll save time for you, and it will get the dope for our records that we must have. You too, Miss—?"

"I'm Nora Phillips. I'll go along, of course. Will you have one of your men keep an eye out for a tall man who should have been passing here by now. He's overdue. He will be Tommy Morgan; we had a date but I came out to meet him on his way to my home. Tell him what happened and explain that I'll return home as soon as this matter is taken care of."

The sergeant smiled. "Toby, you take this stand and ask everybody that comes along if he's Mr. Morgan. Then explain."

"Right."

The ride, so far as official information went, was strictly a waste of time. Paul made a mental note of Nora Phillips' address and telephone number and decided that the incident called for good reason to renew the acquaintance. The sergeant made it easy by telling them: "When you return from your trip, Mr. Grayson, I'll ask you to come in to the station and make a formal complaint. You'll be there too, Miss Phillips."

"I'll be glad to help," she told them. Then she turned to Paul. "You're with Astrogation?"

He nodded.

"But why Proxima? I've heard it was a completely useless place."

Paul shook his head. "We want to measure the distance to better accuracy than heliocentric parallax will permit us," he said. "We know the speed of light to a fine decimal, and we can measure time to even a finer degree. So we started a radio beam towards Centauri four years ago, and it will be arriving in not-too-long a time. Then we'll have the distance to a nice detail of perfection."

Nora thought for a moment. "I suppose you're ultimately aiming at NeoSol," she suggested.

"That's the idea."

"But NeoSol is a hundred light years away—"

"One hundred and forty-three at the last count," Paul corrected.

"So it will take a hundred and forty—"

"No," he smiled. "Less than three years from now. You see, seven light-years is the greatest distance that separates the stars between here and NeoSol. We've got a nice network of radio beams criss-crossing the pathway between here and NeoSol. Oh," he admitted with a smile, "the triangulation beams will be arriving from now until a hundred years from now, but they're mostly check-beams, and the final beam from Earth to Neoterra will take the full time. But in the meantime we can refine our space charts using the network of beams once they start to arrive. And each time one of the triangulation check-beams gets home, we'll be able to refine the charts even more. But there's no sense in waiting for a century and a half."

The sergeant looked at Paul. "You're certain you can fly with that bump on the head?"

"Sure."

"Why not let someone else take it."

Paul shook his head. "It's my job," he said quickly.

"But there must be someone else that can do it. What if you died?"

"Oh, there are others trained in this sort of job in that case."

"Why not let one of them take it, then?"

Paul shook his head again. "I'm all right," he said. He realized that his insistence was too vigorous and that his reasons were too lame. But he could not let them know why it was so important that Paul Grayson go in person. If Haedaecker got wind of what Paul carried in his spacecraft, there would be hell to pay. He thought of a plausible excuse. "Most of them aren't on earth right now."

"Couldn't you call one of them?"

Paul smiled ruefully. "They're outside of the solar system."

The sergeant nodded. "The Z-wave can't cross interstellar space," he said. It was a statement thrown in to display his knowledge to the technician from the Bureau of Astrogation, and also a leader for more conversation.

Paul did not bite.

"That's Haedaecker's Theory," added the sergeant. "Isn't it?" he added after another moment of silence.

"Haedaecker's Theory is that the Z-wave propagates only in a region under the influence of solar activity," explained Paul. He looked out of the police car and saw the spaceport only a few moments away. Then he talked volubly to fill in the time so that he could be off without further questioning. Haedaecker had plenty of evidence to support his theory, but they all were missing one point that was as plain as the nose on Haedaecker's face.

"We can talk with ease from the Zero Laboratory on Pluto to the Solar Lab on Mercury, to the boys who are working in the poisonous atmosphere of Jupiter, to the extra-terran paleon-tologists who are combing Venus," said Paul. "And the Radiation Laboratory sent a gang to try the five planets of Sirius. Again they got the Z-wave working after a bit of fiddling with the tuning. But we've not been able to get so much as a whisper from Sol to Proxima Centauri via Z-wave. What started Haedaecker thinking was the experiment they tried about ten years ago." Paul went on before anybody could interrupt.

"No one can measure the velocity of the Z-wave, you know. So they started a spacecraft running right away from Sol. So long as they were within a fair radius, the Z-wave went both ways easily. But once they went into superdrive and raced away from Sol and got out beyond the orbit of Pluto by quite a bit, they lost contact completely. They made some measurements but these were quite unsuccessful. All we know is that we can use the Z-wave for speech for a long distance beyond the orbit of Pluto, but beyond some distance that might lie between ten times that orbit and—I think they tried it at a light month—the Z-wave dies out abruptly. It falls off like a cliff, you know. There's no apparent attenuation of the Z-wave so long as it is strong enough to get there. Beyond that, there is not even the whisper of a signal. It's a peculiar thing, but we know very little about the Z-wave, and—"

The driver brought the police car to a screeching halt. "Here you are, folks," he chirped.

Paul got out of the car quickly. "I'll be back," he told the sergeant. "I'll call you." And then to Nora Phillips he added, "I'll call you, too."

"Do," she said pointedly. "I'd like to know more about the Z-wave."

Paul nodded amiably. He did not voice his inner thought: *So would I, baby!*

CHAPTER TWO

THE POLICE CAR U-turned in the broad roadway and headed off to return Nora Phillips to her home and to pick up the officer set to sentry duty. Paul waved them off and then started to walk up the pavement towards the administration building.

He was feeling better. Everything pleased him vastly. The knot inside of his head was gone, he had made the acquaintance of a very delectable armful of femininity, and now he had been chauffeured to the spaceport by none other than the City Police Department, complete with siren.

On his way up the sidewalk, Paul planned the retort perfect. Anticipating some humorous sarcasm on the mode of his arrival, Paul hoped to crush any verbal volley with unanswerable repartee. Usually Paul's fount of boundless wit ran just a trifle slow, following the definition of a bon mot: Something you think of on the way home. This time he was going to be prepared.

He swung the door airily and strode in, his tongue poised over a few words of terse wit.

The guard looked at him and swallowed a large lump. "How in hell did you get out?" he gasped.

This was not according to plan; unfortunately, the guard had not read Paul's script, and the prepared answer would not fit the question. "I was never in," said Paul lamely, again wishing he had a tongue full of ready wit instead of fumbling for a prepared speech.

"The hell you weren't."

Paul took it from there, ignoring the fact that the guard had not followed Paul's mental conversation. "That was a car reserved for very important personages," he said. "From now on you can call me Viper."

The guard bypassed this. "But how did you get out?" he asked. His voice was almost a plea. "You didn't pass me."

"Were you guarding the jail too?" chuckled Paul. "Fast man, no?"

"You came in a taxicab the first time."

"Ah yes. But that was years ago before people knew of my brilliance, importance, and high station. Now—"

"Years ago, my eye. Less than fifteen minutes ago—"

"I did not."

"You did."

"Not me." Paul's feeling of airy well being came down a few thousand feet and mired in a cumulus cloud.

"Look, Grayson, you came in a taxicab and breezed in here about fifteen minutes ago as though you had only a minute to spare."

"You're thinking of someone else."

"Your picture said Paul Grayson, and so did your identification. How else would I be knowing you?"

"You've seen me often enough."

"Maybe. But don't forget that I see a few thousand people every day. And I know you only well enough to know that you do own bona fide credentials. You've got 'em?"

"I—" Paul blinked. A great searing light was starting to cut through the cobwebs of his brain. The airy feeling of wellbeing dropped below the cumulus cloud and made a one-point landing on strictly solid ground. "Look," he said soberly. "You claim a man came through here a few minutes ago, resembling me?"

"Unless you ain't who you are, he was you."

"He wasn't me. My papers were stolen less than an hour ago. He must have—"

The guard was no imbecile. He turned in a flash and hit a button on the desk beside him. An alarm bell rang in some inner room and four more guards came tumbling out of a doorway, alert and ready for trouble.

"Tommy," snapped the guard at the door, "go check Paul Grayson's ship, that's number—"

"BurAst 33-P.G.1."

The guard looked at Paul carefully. "You're a dead ringer for the other guy that came through here," he said. "But you happen to know Paul Grayson's BurAst number. Anybody could memorize it."

Paul watched the other guards tumble out of the building and head off across the spaceport on a dead run, drawing pistols as they went. He started to follow them.

The guard barred his way.

"No you don't!"

"But that guy is stealing—"

"Maybe your name is Grayson and maybe the other guy is Grayson. You look alike and he had identification. I don't know Paul Grayson well enough to accept or deny you—or him. But until you show me credentials entitling you to roam this spaceport, you stay outside!"

"But—"

"The boys I sent out there are capable. Don't get in their way. They might shoot the wrong Paul Grayson."

"But—"

"Get your credentials. Get some sort of identification."

Paul looked at the big standard clock on the wall. "But I've got less than eight minutes until take-off time."

"There's always tomorrow. You'll get cleared first or no entry! And that's final."

"Hell's Eternal Bells!" exploded Paul. "The cops that brought me here did so because I was clipped on the bean and robbed."

"It's my job," explained the guard quietly. "I don't want to be any more of a bastard than I have to be. If you're Paul Grayson and the cops know you were robbed, there's the telephone."

Paul grabbed the phone and started to dial, fuming at the delay. First there was a few seconds until the dial tone came, then Paul dialed the outside line. Another few seconds of delay until he could dial the number of the municipal police department. Then a bored voice asked:

"Police headquarters, who's calling please."

"This is Paul Grayson at the Municipal Spaceport."

"What's the trouble out there?"

"A crook stole my identification."

"We'll send a man out to investigate."

"No!" yelled Paul to prevent the telephone operator from cutting off the line on the assumption that the call was closed. "You don't understand. I'm supposed to take off in—ah—seven minutes."

"We can't get a man there that quickly. You'll have to wait."

"Look," said Paul hurriedly, "there's a squad car that just dropped me here. I was clipped on Talman Avenue and they went there to investigate, they brought me here. Why not call them and ask them to come back and explain to the guards here what happened?"

"I'll check that and take action," promised the voice in a completely bored tone.

Paul fumed.

There was the sound of a shot outside, followed instantly by the shrill, whining song of a ricochet, probably a glance from the hard metal flank of a parked spacecraft.

The telephone went dead and a second later came the dial tone again. Paul hung it up reluctantly.

And that made it worse. Other hands were not as imbued with the importance of the project. To other hands it was a routine bit of trouble, not the matter of life and death that it was to Paul Grayson; yet he to whom this thing was vastly important must sit with folded hands while men handled the matter in ponderous routine.

The clock continued to turn inexorably. Paul's mathematically inclined mind went to work; it was less than two minutes since the police car left. Give them a minute to check up, and a minute to make sure, then a minute to call the car. That was three of the precious seven minutes gone to hell. If it took them as long to return as it took them to get where they now were, throw another two minutes down the drain and that left two minutes in which to let the sergeant explain to the guard, clear Paul Grayson on a pro tem basis, get him across the spaceport to his ship, in, up, and away.

He groaned.

He wished frantically for some means of knowing what was going on; what measures were being made in his behalf. He

16

wanted desperately to listen to the radio in the police car. He wanted to get on the radio himself and roar out explanations, to exhort them to greater effort—

The siren wail of the police car cut into his thoughts and Paul raced to the door to fling it open. The car slid to the curb and the siren whined down the scale as the driver turned it off. They got out of the car and came up the walk briskly.

"Hurry!" he called.

He cast a glance over his shoulder at the standard clock. He had three minutes.

"Tell 'em who I am!" he exploded breathlessly.

The sergeant blinked. "But I don't know who you are."

"But I've told you."

"Hell," grunted the guard. "You've told me, too." To the sergeant, the guard said: "Do you know anything about all this?"

"We got a call that this man had been clipped and robbed. He was." The sergeant looked at Nora Phillips. "Can you identify this man?"

Nora bit her lip. "He's Paul Grayson."

The guard speared Nora with a cold look. "Do you know that or is it just what he said?"

"Why I've—"

"She's never met him otherwise," put in the sergeant.

"That's true, but I think—"

"Thinking ain't good enough."

Nora looked at Paul. "Haven't you anything to show?"

Paul shook his head. "Nothing that would cut any ice. Belt buckle with initial G. A few laundry marks and cleaners' marks. A checkbook in my hip pocket but no name printed in it. I might check the balance against the bank, but that would be tomorrow morning. We might call Doctor Haedaecker, but by the time we arrived on some means of personal identification, take-off time would be gone and past."

Paul paused, breathless, his whole body poised tense and his head bent to listen. There came the patter of feet outside.

The standard clock was swinging towards the hour, two minutes remained, enough if all went quick and well.

17

One of the guards burst in. He took a quick look around and spotted the police sergeant. "Good," he said, breathing heavily. "We've just shot a man out there. You're needed."

"Was it the man who passed himself off as me?" shouted Paul Grayson.

"As we came up to BurAst 33-P.G.1 this guy jumped from the airlock and started to run. We gave chase and lost him in the dark beyond a group of parked spacecraft. We called for him to halt. We found him again on the far side of the ships and Joe fired a shot.

"It must have missed him because he kept running, and then we all started shooting, losing him behind another ship parked by the fence. You know old Mupol 3316? The way the guts are parked all over the spaceport and left to rust? A derelict if I ever saw one, and after this I'd say it was about time we cleaned up that old wreck—"

"—Please hurry," blurted Paul.

"—we got to the fence where he'd climbed out over some junk stacked behind Mupol 3316. We went after him, and then guess what?"

"What?"

"We found this character flat on his face in the road, as dead a corpse as ever died."

Paul exploded again. "That proves it," he said. "Now—"

The spaceport guard shook his head. This shake was echoed by the sergeant of police.

"But I've work to do—"

The sergeant smiled unhappily. "We've work to do too, son. I'll call you Grayson for the benefit of the doubt. There is not much doubt that something is highly rotten here, but we've got to be certain. There's been one slugging and robbery, the attempted theft of spacecraft, and now a man killed by armed guards in performance of their duty. This is going to require clearing up before we let you go."

"But you know where to find me. I'm due on Proxima Centauri I to check the arrival of the Bureau of Astrogation survey beam. I'm to take off—"

"IF you are Paul Grayson."

"If the other guy was Paul Grayson, would he have run from cops?"

The sergeant laughed bitterly. "This may come as a shock to you, son. But you have no idea of how many of our Nicest People, Pillars of Society, and Solid Citizens have secrets in their daily lives that make them shun Law and Order when Law and Order comes toward them with a drawn pistol, a subpoena, or a warrant for arrest.

The loudspeaker came to life at that moment. "BurAst 33-P.G.1 taking off for Proxima Centauri I. Timing signal for synchronization first check..." the voice died to be replaced by a series of clicks, one second apart.

"That's my notice—"

The guard snapped a switch. "Master Control," he said quietly. "This is Edwards, guard at the main gate, hold the flight."

"Hold the flight?" answered the speaker.

"Hold the flight. We've had trouble here."

"Is that what the shooting was all about?" The timing clicks died in the background. "What's the trouble?"

"We've got two Paul Graysons wanting to take off."

"Tell 'em to draw straws. This is costing money."

"One of them—"

"Dammit!" yelled Paul. "I'm Paul Grayson and I've—"

"That you'll have to prove, son," said the sergeant.

"—is dead," finished the guard.

"Dead?" gasped the speaker. "Which one?"

"It ain't funny," said the guard seriously. "Just hold the flight."

"Okay, sport. But—"

Paul spoke up, "Can you get the Elecalc free for a course for tomorrow night?"

"Who's this speaking?"

"I'm Paul Grayson."

"The live one, huh?" chuckled the unimpressed voice from the speaker. His bantering tone made Paul want to rip out his larynx with a crooked thumb and shove it down his throat. "Okay. We'll have the electronic calculator figure out a course for Proxima I for tomorrow night. Doubtless *someone* will take the flight."

"Oh damn!" groaned Paul. "Why does this have to happen to me?"

The sergeant smiled. "If this were the first attempt to steal a spacecraft, I'd be surprised."

The guard shook his head. "It's more than that," he added sagely. "If the other guy was a thief bent on swiping a BurAst ship, he could have gone off in it ten minutes before the second Paul Grayson arrived. He didn't. He was waiting for the take-off signal; and if he were a crook, he hoped to fill in the real Paul Grayson's place. If he was the real Grayson, we've killed a frightened Bureau man, and this bird here—"

Paul looked at the standard clock. It was now moving past the precise second marked for take-off. He sighed resignedly and relaxed. "For the moment we'll assume that I am Paul Grayson," he said quietly. "So soon as we can find someone to corroborate me, the second part of your supposition will have no grounds."

The sergeant shook his head. "I think we'd all best head for the station and wait this thing out."

Paul gulped. "You're going to jug me?"

"Both of you."

"But you can't arrest me—"

"Five will get you eight," chuckled the sergeant.

Nora Phillips came forward until she stood between Paul and the sergeant. "Why am I being arrested?" she demanded.

The sergeant smiled affably. "No one is being arrested."

"Why am I being detained, held, or otherwise prevented from enjoying my rights of freedom?" she snapped.

Paul shrugged. "I've missed my take-off," he said. "I'll have to wait until tomorrow anyway. And I can get identification in an hour or so without any trouble. In fact, I'll gladly go along with you if you'll permit me the telephone. They can bring my stuff down there and we can settle this quickly. But there is no reason to hold Miss Phillips."

The sergeant turned to the woman and bowed deferentially. "Forgive a harried policeman his habits," he said quietly. "As a shoe salesman will mentally catalog the shoes of the people sitting opposite to him on the street car, and a physician will mentally diagnose the ills of his fellow-spectators at a baseball game, a policeman habitually views the acts of his contemporaries with one eye toward their motives."

"Meaning what?" demanded Paul Grayson.

The policeman faced Paul and said with a level voice: "So far as every bit of evidence goes, you are Paul Grayson. You behave as a man might behave when placed in the position you appear to be in. On the other hand, if you were a smart man, you would behave as you are now behaving even though you had reasons most dire to execute as soon as you leave the watchful eye of law and order. This is a bit too trite. A stolen wallet containing only a few bucks and a whale of a lot of identification, complete with a witness to the crime, makes fine story material to use in establishing a false identity. Motive can come later—if any. If you are Paul Grayson, I will make abject apology. If your tale is not true, there will be some tall explaining to make."

"How about Miss Phillips' boy friend?"

"Now that's a nice thought, but not necessarily conclusive proof. He might easily and sensibly be included to give any story an air of veracity. However, we can check with Toby Reed as soon as we get back to the patrol car."

CHAPTER THREE

PAUL GRAYSON AWOKE the following morning to the tune of the telephone beside his bed. "This is Sergeant Hollowell," said the other man. "I've just called to apologize once more and to tell you that everything is OK. We'll even give you a guard if you want it."

Paul stretched and said, sleepily: "Thanks, Sergeant. I guess everything will come out all right without a guard."

"Okay. I'm glad for all concerned. For your information and not to be repeated, the character we got last night is—was—a petty crook with a record as long as your arm. A plain case of theft. Interrupted luckily. We call it closed."

"Thanks again. And the ship?"

"It's there as it was last night. So far as we and the BurAst guards know, no one but the crook was near it, and no one will be permitted to go near it until you come to take it up."

Paul breathed easier. "Okay, see you later."

"Your wallet, intact, will be delivered to your apartment within the hour. That closes that case, too." The policeman's voice sounded well pleased with himself and the night's work. Paul hung up and sprawled back in bed, thinking.

There was no point in arousing the policeman's suspicions again. A howl of 'Why?' might delay Paul Grayson; might cause another technician to be sent to Proxima I to check the arrival of the radio beam. Paul had all the reason in the galaxy for wanting to be there himself, and an equally large quantity of reasons for not wanting someone else running his ship.

But there *was* more to this than met the eye.

Paul reached for a cigarette and laid back in bed blowing smoke at the ceiling. A smile touched his lips. Aside from the annoyance at being delayed for twenty-four hours, it had been one large evening.

Then his grin died and he reached out one quick arm and picked up the telephone again. He dialed a number and waited until the ringing was answered.

"Stacey?"

"This is Stacey's office."

"Is he there?"

"Who's calling, please?"

"Tell him Paul Grayson—if he's up yet."

"He's up," came the cheerfully amused voice at the other end. "But he's still grumpy."

"I'll cheer him up," promised Paul. There was the click of a connection made and one quick burr from the ringing of the distant telephone.

"Stacey," came the reply.

"Paul Grayson."

"Hell's Eternal—I thought you were on your way to Proxima."

"Got delayed a day."

Stacey was silent for a moment; Paul imagined that he could hear the clicking of the other man's mind as it started to analyze the situation. Then Stacey said: "What's on the technical mind, Paul? You didn't call me at this outrageous hour just to pass the time of day."

"John, how much will it cost me to have a matter looked into?"

"Normal charge is twenty-five a day and expenses. I think I owe you a few favors. Make it expenses if it isn't too involved."

"It might be."

"Then we'll make some arrangement as soon as we know how involved it is. But gawd, Paul, what brings you to the employment of a detective?"

"Someone tried to steal my spacecraft last night."

"Nuts. Call the coppers."

"Nope. There's more to this than meets the eye."

"What, for instance?"

"I'll be over to tell you about it."

"Big?"

"I don't know. Bothersome, anyway."

"I'll wait. Make it quick."

Paul hung up, and then went into a whirlwind of action. He dressed and shaved and gulped a glass of orange juice. He eschewed breakfast, promising his stomach that food would come in due time. He took his car from the garage where he had parked it for a month the evening before, and within a few minutes after hanging up the telephone, Paul Grayson was heading towards Stacey's office.

It was a small office. Stacey's secretary knew Paul by sight if not by telephone voice, and she nodded him in to the inner office. Stacey's inner office was as small as the outer office because file cabinets lined the room. The detective sat with his chin in his hand, poring over some pages of writing. He looked up at once and greeted Paul with a smile.

"So someone tried to swipe your ship?" he blurted. "And why isn't that a case for the cops?"

"John, how would you go about stealing a ship?"

"Get into the spaceport on some pretext, get into the ship by some means, and then take off like I had to make Messier 31 by mid-afternoon—or whatever place happened to be aligned at the time."

"That's what I've been thinking."

"So—?"

"You wouldn't worry about the dispersion factor. You wouldn't worry about course. Your main interest would lie in getting the hell out of there before someone came along and decided that you were intent upon theft."

"Naturally."

Paul nodded. Then he explained as well as he knew, and as well as he could remember, everything that had taken place on the previous evening. He finished up with: "So I've met a gorgeous gal, kissed her by accident and found it fun; was clipped by a footpad and sort of nursed back to the conscious level by the same luscious dame; had two rides in a police patrol car; one trip to the hoosegow; cleared of all suspicion by an official courier arriving with officially sealed pouch of identification; was escorted home in style."

"Go on. There's more to this than that."

"Remember what Sergeant Hollowell said: That a stolen wallet and a witness were fine dovetails towards the establishment of a false identity?"

"Yeah."

"What better way to louse Paul Grayson up than to decoy him with a flagrantly beautiful woman; a dame possessed of self assurance and poise, yet incredibly feminine enough to betray a warm, human passionate hunger for some one man. Natural male concupiscence would draw any man into the game of trying to divert her affection towards himself."

"Speak for yourself, wolf."

Paul grinned at Stacey. He stood up. "Maybe I'd better look into this thing myself. Set Stacey on the trail of a glam-amorous female and—"

"Siddown. I'm a married man."

"I was thinking of your poor, deluded wife and daughter."

"Gloria knows all about your natural male concupiscence, and Ginny will know you as a doddering old man by the time she discovers that you can tell a man from a woman without looking at their clothing."

Paul sat down again. He had not intended to leave anyway. "So," he said, "what better way to divert Paul Grayson than to bait him with a gorgeous dame?"

Stacey grunted. "To divert you long enough to clip you, to steal your papers, to enter your ship—for what purpose?"

"That's where the mystery comes in. The guy had plenty of time to fire up the drivers and grab an armful of sky. The galaxy makes a fine hiding place, John. They scoured the stellar systems of a hundred and more suns before they found that NeoSol had a planet that was capable of harboring Terran life without difficulty. Lord knows, no man hunting for a place to live would wait and head for Proxima I. Yet that seems to be what the crook had tried to do."

Stacey shook his head. "You are supposing that Nora Phillips was mingled in some sort of plot to steal a spacecraft. Granting that, Paul, explain me one thing. Just why would a person intent upon delaying you go so far towards helping you?"

"Huh?"

"She did sort of rub your skull, didn't she?"

"And a fine job she did of it, too."

"Professional?"

"Seemed as if. If not professional, at least experienced."

"So she brought you out of the unconscious, painful dark in time to intercept the criminal at his business?"

"Uh—"

"And Nora Phillips strode up and kissed you with warm, mad passion on the street, thus immobilizing your skull long enough for the enterprising sharpshooter to take a stance and perfect his backswing."

"So you don't think so?"

Stacey thought for a moment. "This does not smack of simple theft," he said at length.

"Hell," growled Grayson. "That's what I've been trying to tell you."

"Um. I see—"

"So someone looks like me. He tried to swipe my ship, it would appear. But they didn't need a dame to distract me; I could have been pushed off by a gunman. Frankly, I am of the type that will gladly hand over my wallet, my shoes, and/or my worldly goods rather than to have a hole drilled through my dinner. So, John, here is Nora Phillips' address. You can get the name of the defunct crook from the police, I'm sure. See what connection they might have had."

Stacey looked at Paul with a smile. "You're not making uranium out of broken pop bottles are you?"

"Nope. I'm just a guy working for the Bureau of Astrogation."

"Uh-huh. But with a secret under his hat large enough to keep him from yelping too loud."

"You know the reason for that."

"And how many others?"

"Damned few. Less than six, I'd guess."

Stacey shook his head again. "They don't clip screwballs for having a half-baked idea crammed in their simple skulls. So far as I can see it, you've got nothing to conceal, nothing to steal, and nothing much worth hiding."

"If Haedaecker knew what I had—"

Stacey grunted. "If Haedaecker wanted to stop you he would not have to hire a bunch of phony actors to do it," he said succinctly.

"But what else?"

"My life of crime," chuckled Stacey, "tells me that there are as many motives for crime as there are men with ambition, avarice, and ability. The trouble is that there are more motives for crime than there are varieties of crime. If there is a motive for this cockeyed affair—and I've yet to see a crime without a motive, however involved or simple—you must know it."

"Aside from spacecraft stealing—"

"That's ruled out."

"Then I'll be eternally relegated to the nether regions if I know what it is."

Stacey nodded. "Maybe you know it and don't recognize it."

"Maybe I should visit my family psychiatrist?"

"He might be able to ferret out the hidden secret. But I'd waste no time on it. Just proceed and see what happens."

"Like another busted head?"

"As I recall, it's hard enough."

Paul laughed. One could hardly be sour in Stacey's presence. Nothing appeared serious to the detective; he managed to make everything sound quite cheerful and amusing, even the threat of further depredations. It was a trait disliked by many people, which was probably the main reason why Stacey was a small time operator instead of being the mainspring of a worldwide agency.

It took a long acquaintanceship with Stacey before people realized that the light banter was only a false front used to keep Stacey's own spirits from bogging down in the world of trouble. A sympathetic sort himself, Stacey forced himself to treat every case as impersonally as he could because only a man uninvolved emotionally can make clear decisions based on fact and not feelings. Newcomers meeting Stacey resented the fact that the detective obviously treated their troubles as less than the most important thing in the world.

But Paul Grayson knew Stacey well and he was willing to let the detective handle the case completely from this point, knowing that Stacey would do it honestly and quickly, friend or not. Paul waved goodbye at the door and drove towards home. He went in and sat down, ticking things off on the fingers of his hand.

One, identification cleared.

Two, wallet returned.

Three, puzzle-solution started.

Four—

Grayson went to the telephone and called the spaceport, was connected with the calculations department.

"Grayson," he said. "How's for my course this evening?"

"Sure you want to go?" came the dry retort.

"Absolutely."

"Want to bet?"

"Look," grunted Grayson, no longer angry at the voice, "you've got a fine calculating gadget there. Why not have it figure out the betting possibilities and make book on me?"

"We tried to make it pick horses for us once but the answer came back as 'Data incomplete, factors uncertain.' The Elecalc does not like horses."

"But I'm not a horse."

"I hear there's a woman tied up in this thing. That's the predictably unpredictable factor, that men, the imbeciles, will get involved with women—even as you and I. Anyway, Grayson, we'll have you a course. It won't be as cold turkey as last nights, but it will serve in a way."

"In what way?" asked Paul.

"We can't set the spotter ship. Not enough time. You'll have to aim the ship visually. It'll make the dispersion-factor somewhat large."

"I don't mind."

"Good thing you don't," came the glum reply.

Both of them knew that the job of aiming a stellar ship was accepted by the public as one of the things that had to be done; few of them knew what went into the job. All stars are but pinpoints in the sky, there is no quick way to tell a close-by star from a distant star by visual inspection. To the untrained, even the solar planets blend with the interstellar reaches. Only the trained eye can tell planets from the stars by the lack of twinkle.

The true distances between the stars is too vast to be comprehended. Men speak of light years. Yet even the learned must indulge in quite a bit of cerebration to understand the length of a year, the velocity of light presents figures too extreme for comprehension. Light travels at 328 yards per millionth of a second, 328 yards can be grasped, as a distance of three football fields, but a millionth of a second cannot be grasped readily; 186,000 miles per second offers only one factor capable of being understood. One can count "Ten-Hundred-One" and realize that a second has passed. But the mind is incapable of grasping the fact that during that time of counting, a beam of light traverses 186,000 miles.

Proxima Centauri is four light years away. Using the longest base that the solar system provided, the beginning and the end of the aimed course was like trying to hit a match head at ten thousand yards with a snub-barreled pistol. A misalignment too minute for the eye to see meant a probable target dispersion as broad as the outer orbits of the solar system.

Aim a ship at a target four light years away across aiming points a couple of light hours apart. At a velocity within a couple of percent of precise, multiplied by a number of seconds mounting into five or six figures, you can establish the volume which will contain the spacecraft on its arrival. A volume of probabilities— far, far from the layman's idea of a precise science.

Heading as he was for Proxima Centauri, that tiny star would be the focus of his aim. But Proxima is a tiny star, one of a trinary, and the other two magnificent stars overwhelmed the feeble light of Proxima. So the system of Alpha Centauri would lie on the cross hairs of Paul's telescope.

And the cross hairs of the telescope would be displaced from the axis of drive by a small angle. It was this angle that required the use of the electronic calculator.

Not only because Proxima lies a smidgen of space apart from the more brilliant pair, but because Alpha Centauri drifts along in the galactic swing, and Sol moves as well. The eye sees Alpha Centauri where it was four years ago. Any trip across space, lasting ten days, must bring the traveler down out of super-velocity and into the realm of visibility at the position where Alpha will be ten days after take-off—not where Alpha was four years ago.

This was a problem not yet licked. Like the 'sighting-in' of a brand new pistol, each shot fired added to the knowledge of the correction factor that must be applied.

For the same reasons of inward anxiety that makes a man who has missed a train on Monday turn up two hours early on Tuesday. Paul turned up at the spaceport early. The guard greeted him with a cynical smile but checked the identification carefully before waving him through the gate.

Paul went to the Elecalc office to get his folder of course-data. The usual procedure was to have the course calculated as early as possible before the date of takeoff, so that the busy department could sandwich course-data in between the longer range jobs. This was different, undoubtedly some long-range job had been stopped in mid-calc so that Paul's course could be run off. He was not too surprised to have the man at the desk smile and point a finger at the Superintendent's Office and say:

"It's in there. Go on in, he's expecting you."

Paul went to the door, opened it, and then swallowed a lump as large as his fist.

The man sitting quietly behind the desk, huge hands folded in his lap was Chadwick Haedaecker.

CHAPTER FOUR

CHADWICK HAEDAECKER was the kind of man who collected college degrees, both earned and honorary, and had them lettered on his office door like a collection of trophies. He had enough ability and ambition to get to the top of his particular heap, and once he got there he had garnered enough additional power to stay there. He was a tall man with piercing eyes and an indomitable nature and he used both to quell any objectors to his plans, projects, ideas, and theories. Twenty years of authority in a position where no man was permitted to doubt his word or argue with his self-assured proclamations had completely erased any trace or humility he ever had.

But whether Haedaecker was a prince among men or a jackal among jackals depended entirely upon the beholder. When Haedaecker believed in your idea, he was a stanch supporter, throwing all he had—and he had plenty—behind your idea. His whip cracked just as hard in your behalf as it lashed against your back when Haedaecker was not convinced of the soundness of your idea.

Since Haedaecker was head of the Bureau, his presence here made Paul blink.

While Paul tried to think of something clever to say. Haedaecker smiled and nodded, finally speaking after he knew the state of discomfiture of his employee.

"You've had quite a time, haven't you?" asked Haedaecker.

Paul nodded ruefully.

"Just what happened?"

Paul explained, carefully, completely. He would have preferred to answer Haedaecker with nods or grunts or shakes of the head on the theory that opening the mouth is the first step towards spilling the whole tale, or at least enough of it to give a man as cagey as Haedaecker to think that there was more equipment in the BurAst spacecraft than radio beacon checking gear. Haedaecker was not the kind of man to come forth to console a man; especially one that apparently came out of the deal with nothing lost. Haedaecker's principle was to get 'em off balance and keep 'em off balance, because when they're off balance they cannot get set to swing. Paul knew that he would have to play this interview with the same finesse that a mouse should use to escape the cat's corner.

"Have any ideas about this?" asked Haedaecker.

Paul's ideas were all confused ones but he did not say so. "The police accept it as a plain case of attempted theft," he said.

"And you?"

Paul spread his hands in a universal gesture. "I can't make more out of it than the police," he said.

Haedaecker speared Paul Grayson with those piercing eyes. "You're not mixed up in anything, are you?"

"Lord no!"

Haedaecker's glare lessened. "I don't mean anything lawless or underhanded."

Paul looked at Haedaecker coldly. "Then what else?"

Haedaecker smiled blandly. "You are an ambitious young man. You are idealistic. You are enthusiastic and energetic. You are also determined."

"Are those unfavorable traits?" asked Paul with a slight edge to his voice. He hated this baiting; knew that he should take the sting of Haedaecker's acid tongue without flaring back. Haedaecker had Paul over the proverbial barrel, from which position there is little chance for counterattack.

"Listen to me," snapped Haedaecker. "You were twenty four when you came to this department. Two years later you came to me with an idea. You hoped to link the stars by voice. An ideal. A magnificent hope and plan for mankind on earth and upon NeoSol. For years everybody who has had a touch of space has been trying, testing, and experimenting towards that end. Men of learning, both abstract and concrete; men who have spent years studying that very idea."

"What has that idea got to do with my getting a lump on the head?" queried Paul.

"Only this. As a member of this department, you were given a job to do. You have proceeded well and executed this job proficiently. Four years ago, Grayson, I told you that the experiments you suggested had been tried. I was patient. I explained that there was a certain appropriation set aside for communications research;

that the appropriation intended for this galactic survey was under no circumstances to be used for communications."

"I remember that. I also claim that my experiments have never been tried."

"Nonsense. I accepted your theory and have had other scientists check your reasoning. They state that there is no relation such as you claim. Now, to get back to the correlation between that crack you got on the head and my presence here, it goes as follows:

"Until last evening I let you alone. I knew that you continued to hold that mad theory despite arguments against it. But a man can have his dreams, and so I permitted you to dream. I assumed you to be honest. I believed that you would not defy orders and employ funds for Z-wave research. But when a man who has no great wealth, no vengeful enemies, no polygonal love affairs, and no power to dispute or usurp gets involved in a tangle as well-contrived as this, there is but one thing left: I am convinced that you are planning to test the Z-wave!"

Paul laughed bitterly. "Just why do you assume that this is some sort of plot? Why not accept it as attempted theft as the police do?"

"If I were a thief," said Haedaecker softly, "and managed to break into the spaceport, I would not wait until the guards came after me, then to drop from my stolen spacecraft and run! A thief does not need the spotter craft to lay his course. He takes off for anywhere so long as it is off and away. A man contrived to resemble you closely enough to pass superficial inspection follows you before the takeoff, clips you on the skull, and steals your wallet. You are the traditional technician, Grayson. You do not dress like Beau Brummel, nor do you show evidence of affluence. Any footpad would look for a more wealthy client. He knew you, Grayson. He clipped you for your credentials!"

"So?"

"Why?"

"I don't know."

"I can suggest a theory. Because he knew that you were going to try the Z-wave."

Haedaecker smiled with a wolfish serenity. "Can you think of any reason why any man would want to put a monkey wrench into our plans to survey the galaxy?"

"No—"

"Then it must be for your wild schemes."

"But just the same question, Doctor Haedaecker: if I were going against orders and attempting to test the Z-wave, why would a man attempt to stop me?"

"You are an idealistic simpleton," snapped Haedaecker. "You have a manner of convincing people of the worth of whatever idea you happen to hold dear. Despite the reams of evidence to the contrary, you have the enthusiasm necessary to convince people who have not the truth at their fingertips of the validity of your ideas.

"Piling supposition upon supposition," smiled Paul, cynically, "if that has been done, I fail to see any reason why any man would not want to be linked to NeoSol by voice."

"You have a lot to learn about human nature, Grayson. You'll find as you grow older that whenever someone proposes a plan for the benefit of mankind, there are violent factions that will work hard to circumvent it. How many leagues of united nations have failed throughout history because of jealousy, aggrandization, megalomania. Both personal and national. In one instance after the Bomb convinced all men that uniting as one was the smart, safe, sensible thing to do, people hailed with joy the creation of a new sovereign state apart from its neighbors. Another nation blocked amity became of an ideology. A third nation presented a territorial possession with its freedom and at the same time contemplated the addition of two new states to its union. Grayson, once a man rises above his daily job and tries to set up something beneficial to mankind, he will find other men who see that plan as a threat to their own ambitions."

Paul leaned forward over the desk. "Why not let me try?" he asked eagerly.

Haedaecker leaned back wearily. "We've been all through that."

"But why?"

"I will not have one of my own men involved in an experiment as ridiculous as yours!"

Paul eyed Haedaecker quietly. "But—"

Haedaecker shook his head. "You are not to attempt this." He eyed Paul angrily.

"Who says I am?" demanded Paul.

"Reason and logic. And," said Haedaecker coldly, "excepting for one thing, I'd go out and inspect that ship of yours for Z-wave gear. But Paul Grayson is smart enough to smuggle the Z-wave gear on earlier trips, not leaving his evidence for the last attempt, so I would find nothing at this time."

Paul felt his heart pound thrice and then settle down again. The one thing that he was trying to avoid was not going to come off.

But Haedaecker glared at Paul once again. "I absolutely forbid you to do this."

Paul glared back. "What have we to lose?"

"I'll not have the ridicule attendant to such an abortive experiment pinned onto my department."

Paul laughed sarcastically. "It seems to me that a man in your position might like to have the name of being willing to have himself proven wrong."

"What do you mean?" demanded Haedaecker.

"Can your own personal ambition be great enough to block and forestall the linking of Sol and NeoSol by Z-wave?"

"You young puppy—"

"Your position is due to the proposal of Haedaecker's Theory," said Paul. "I am not attempting to insult you, Doctor Haedaecker, I want you to view this in another light. According to all of the evidence at hand, Haedaecker's Theory is correct and we cannot communicate with the Z-wave across interstellar space. The proposition of that theory and its math have made you a famous man. Perhaps you fear that if Haedaecker's Theory is shown to be incorrect, you will lose your position. This is not so. Men have always been on the side of a great man who was humble enough to doubt his own theories occasionally, who was willing to see them attacked. It means a lot to mankind; show mankind that your personal ambition is not so great as to prevent them from having the benefits of—"

"You're talking as though you knew that your plan would be successful," sneered Haedaecker.

"I believe it will be if I am given the opportunity to try."

"I tell you that it will not, and I forbid you to try." Haedaecker speared Paul with a glance from the icy eyes. "You understand, whether or not the experiment might be successful, if I hear of your trying it, you will be subjected to every bit of punitive action that the law permits."

Paul leaned back easily. "Now," he said with cool candor, "you're assuming that I have all intention of attempting it without official permission."

"I would not put it past you. In fact I believe you are."

"All predicated upon the fact that a footpad belted me and swiped my wallet?"

"Yes. For what other reason?"

"Theft is usually done for—"

Haedaecker stood up angrily. "I've heard enough," he snapped.

Haedaecker strode to the door and hurled it open with one swing of a powerful arm.

What happened next was not too remote a coincidence. It has happened to everybody, several times. Someone with the intention of entering a room will brace themselves, turn the doorknob, and thrust, only to have the door opened from the other side. The net result is that the muscular effort, tensed to strive against the mass and inertia of the door, will find its force expended against no resistance. Doors are pulled from one side and pushed from the other. If the shover pushes first, the would-be puller gets slapped in the hand with the doorknob, sometimes resulting in a broken finger or thumb. But if the puller pulls first, the shover finds himself catapulted forward by his own muscular effort. The results of this latter can be both comic or tragic.

In this case the result was a flurry of splash-printed silk, a bare white arm, a fine length of well-filled nylon, and the frightened cry of a woman.

Paul gulped.

Haedaecker's reflexes worked fast. He caught Nora Phillips before the girl went headlong to the floor and he stood her up, retaining a light grip on her waist until she got her bearings and her breath.

"Young woman," stormed Haedaecker angrily, "are you used to busting into closed conferences?"

Nora looked at Haedaecker with eyes large, luminous, and fetching. "I didn't know it was a closed conference," she said in her cool contralto. "I'm most sorry."

"Miss Phillips, Doctor Haedaecker. She is the woman I met last night, Doctor Haedaecker."

"What are you doing here?" demanded Haedaecker.

"I did not know this was any kind of conference," she explained. "I came to see Mister Grayson, and the guard said he was in this room, talking."

"Why didn't you wait?" stormed Haedaecker.

Nora smiled, wanly. "I was excited," she said. "It may have occurred to you, too, that the man who tried to steal Mister Grayson's spacecraft last night was not playing a game. Everything seemed wrong. He was not smart. I got to wondering why he just didn't get into the ship and take off.

"Well, less than fifteen minutes ago a flash came over the air. Among the news was the statement that the criminal killed last night in attempted spacecraft theft was Joel Walsh. He was an escapee from penitentiary in Antarctica. That explained it."

"How?" demanded Haedaecker, "does that explain anything?"

"Of course it does," said Nora. "He was in jail for ten years. He must have been sent away when he was about twenty. How many men are competent space pilots at that age?"

"Not many," agreed Paul.

"And being in jail for the last ten years, it's natural that he did not know how to run the ship."

"Um," grumbled Haedaecker.

"He probably wanted to stowaway," said Nora. "Once he did that, he could hold a gun at the pilot's head and make the pilot do his bidding until he learned how to run the ship."

There was one very fine flaw in Nora's reasoning, but Paul did not want to belabor this point at this moment. He had not intended to push Haedaecker to the point of firing him for impertinence, insubordination, or rank carelessness. For on the "BurAst 33.P.G.1" was the Z-wave gear that Haedaecker's vindictive nature accused him of stowing away.

Paul laughed. "So much for your intrigue," he said.

Haedaecker glared at Paul angrily. "Your intrigue," he said with heavy emphasis on the first word. "Just let me find you trying it!"

Paul smiled crookedly and looked Haedaecker in the eye coldly. "Doctor Haedaecker," he said in a level voice, "if I ever try it and fail, no one will know of my failure. If I try and succeed, I assure you that you will be able to do nothing to me."

Haedaecker nodded, his manner as cold as Paul's voice had been. The gage had been hurled, the swords measured and weighed. So far it was stalemate. But only until Paul Grayson really did something against the rules, large enough to let Haedaecker really clip him deep, lasting, and legally justifiable.

Haedaecker left and Paul turned to Nora Phillips. She smiled at him and asked: "What is this intrigue business, or is it a top secret?"

Paul shook his head. "I'd prefer to tell you after I return."

"Do that," she said. "I'd like to hear about it."

Paul pondered briefly. The obvious thing was to offer her a chance to look over his ship. He could do that, now that he had all of his credentials and papers back. But the Z-wave gear was evidence against him, and even though it was parked in a convenient locker, certain hunks of cable-endings and associated bits of equipment were a dead giveaway; the same sort of evidence in the shape of capped pipes will tell the observer that plumbing once existed in a certain room. Paul had no intention of trusting anybody at this moment.

Mayhap Nora's timely information about the deceased thief were true. Still, there was a hole in her tale. If the thief wanted only to stowaway until take-off time, he would pick another spacecraft than the BurAst P.C.33-1. The registry number glowed in luminescent paint a yard high, and matched the numbers on his identification card. Certainly no half-idiot would try to stowaway in an official ship that was almost certain to be investigated as soon as the hue-and-cry was heard.

He suspected Haedaecker's hand in this, anything to keep Haedaecker's Theory in high gear, to keep Haedaecker top man in his field. He might as well suspect Nora, too. At least until motive or innocence could be shown.

He decided to lie glibly. "Normally I could take you aboard and show you the crate," he said. "But this is an experimental run and subject to security, though I'll not be able to explain why they think it so."

Nora laughed and shook her head. "Space ships are cold, powerful, and dangerous things to me," she said. "I'd feel uncomfortable on one of them."

"Then let me show you the Elecalc."

"What?"

"Elecalc. Short word for electronic calculator. I'm here to get an aiming point for my trip tonight."

"Now that I would like to see," said Nora, hooking an arm in Paul's.

CHAPTER FIVE

"I'M POINTING FOR Alpha Centauri," said Paul. "And so that's what we calculate for."

Nora looked at the bays of neat equipment and shook her head. "Why not aim at it and run?" she asked. "Surely you do not need this billion dollars worth of stuff to point out your destination."

"We do," objected Paul. "You see, if I took off with my telescope pointed along the axis of drive with the cross hairs pointing at Alpha Centauri, I'd be heading for the star where it was four years ago. I intend to be on the way for nine days. So I'll want to point the nose of the ship at the spot where Alpha will be nine days in the future instead of four years in the past. Since Sol and Alpha drift in space, the motion and velocities of both systems must be taken into account, a correction-angle found, and then used to aim my ship. My telescope will angle away from the ship's axis by that correction-angle. Add to that the fact that I am taking off from earth, which will give me some angular velocity and some rotational velocity differing from an hypothetical take-off from Sol itself. Furthermore, I want Proxima Centauri instead of Alpha, and that must be taken into consideration too.

"Then there is the question of velocity and time. We cannot see when we are exceeding the velocity of light. We must run at so many light-velocities for so many seconds. A minor error in timing or velocity will create a rather gross error in position at the end of the run."

"Oh," said Nora, but her tone indicated a lack of comprehension.

Paul smiled. "One second of error at one light-velocity equals a hundred and eighty-six thousand miles of error. One second of error at a hundred times the velocity of light equals eighteen millions of miles error. Not much as cosmic distance goes, but a long way to walk."

Nora understood that, and said so.

Grayson's data had been handed to him by Haedaecker. But apparently the long-range calculations that had been temporarily halted were still halted, for the operator was taking this opportunity of feeding some future flight-constant information to the big machine.

It was not a complex calculation as some computations may go, but there were a myriad of factors. Terran latitude and longitude, the instant of take-off as applied to the day and the year, an averaging of previous dispersion-factors noted from previous trips, velocities, vector angles, momentum, and others, all obtained from tables and ended in the machine before the start lever was pulled. The machine mulled the information over, tossed electrons back and forth, chewed and digested a ream of binary digits, and handed forth a strip of paper printed with an entire set of coordinates in decimal angles.

Paul showed Nora his folder of data. "The rest," he said, "is up to me."

He led Nora from the computation room, intending to hit the dining room for coffee. Halfway across the lobby of the administration building he was hailed by the autocall. He went to the telephone.

It was Stacey.

"I've a couple of things to let you think over," said Stacey.

"So?"

"I've been on the job. I haven't much, but there are a few items you might mull over."

"Shoot."

"One. Your deceased thief was an ex-convict, escaped from the penal colony on Antarctica."

"This I've heard."

"Then I suppose you know that the guy was cashiered from the Neoterra run for smuggling."

"Huh?" blurted Paul.

"An ex-pilot, tossed out on his right ear for conduct hardly becoming a safecracker and a thief, let alone an officer and a gentleman."

"That I didn't know. How long ago?"

"Five years, almost."

It was not quite the ten that Nora had claimed.

"Well, that makes it—"

"That ain't all," came Stacey's voice. "The weapons carried by the Spaceport guards are regulation Police Positives. Our erstwhile felon was shot once, right between the eyes, with a forty-five, which according to all of the expert opinion, came from an automatic at a distance of three feet, plus or minus six inches. Know what that means?"

"I'm just digesting the information now. You tell me."

"It means that the ex-crook was killed by a party or parties unknown, someone other than one of the guards. Furthermore, he was facing his executioner, not taking it on the lam. How do you make that?"

"It doesn't make good sense."

"Sure it does. It keystones nicely. Men of that calibre are often chilled because they fumble a job and the mainspring doesn't enjoy the prospect of having a fumbler running around with information that might lead to the capture, arrest, conviction, and/or demise of aforementioned mainspring. They made one error. They should have used a thirty-eight revolver instead of a forty-five automatic. The forty-five is a gangster's weapon. And they should have drilled their ex-companion from behind between the scapulae to make it look as though the guards were better shots than they really are."

"That's food for thought," said Paul.

"That isn't all," said Stacey. "Here's one more bit of information that may be either juicy or full of sawdust depending upon how you taste it. Your girl friend, Nora Phillips was born and raised on Neoterra."

"You're certain of that?"

"So the Bureau of Vital Statistics claims."

"But how——?"

"Negative evidence, my fine scientist. Negative evidence. I offer you two alternatives. Either she was born on Neoterra, or she is employing an alias, pseudonym, or nom de jour." Stacey's French lacked a certain vocabulary, but it was none the less to the point. "She is certainly not born Nora Phillips of Terra. I'll let you pick your choice. But enough of that. A couple of hours ago she received a telephone call. Nice position she must have. She chinned for about three minutes and then leaped to her feet and took off like jet propelled. Didn't bother to say anything to the management of the joint at all. Then——"

"Where does she work?" asked Paul.

"Timothy, McBride, and Webster. Attorneys-at-Law. We couldn't tap their telephone, but we had a lip-reader peering at her through a telescope from a room in the building opposite hers."

"What did he catch?"

"Nothing, she just listened, and then took off. And can that dame drive! If we didn't have an idea of where she was going after the first few minutes, my man would have lost her for certain. She with you now?"

"Uh-huh."

Paul thought fast. Just what unearthly reason why people would try to stop his plans for creating voice-fast communications with NeoSol, Paul could not fathom. Obviously there was one faction working against him. But how had they——

Paul paled.

Had the criminal hoped to lay Paul low enough to keep him quiet until the criminal could take off in Paul's place? True identification would be impossible once the crook were in space. But what could he accomplish? Certainly——

Suppose the thief that clipped him intended to place Paul in a position where he could be captured easily. To take Paul's place to perform certain acts in Paul's name, while Paul was held captive. Then, once these acts were consummated Paul could be found in the wreck of a spacecraft or the ruin of a radio beacon on Proxima Centauri I.

But why? Columbus had been kicked around for having screwy ideas, and the Brothers Wright had been thoroughly laughed-at. But people did not try to murder characters who had cockeyed ideas. Of course, there was Galileo, but Galileo had publicized his screwy ideas, whereas Paul Grayson's theories were known to very few.

But Nora Phillips could not be held as part of that particular mob. It seemed to Paul that the woman had done a fine job towards keeping Paul hale, hearty, healthy, and imbued with ideas available only to a man in the finest of health of mind and body. If Nora belonged to some group intent on stopping Paul Grayson, she was working against them, too. For she had done a fine job of smoothing the headache out of his skull with fingers that acted with experience and practice.

On the other hand, Nora Phillips had behaved as though she wanted Paul to succeed, and she acted—if this were an act—as though she enjoyed her work.

So what had really happened last night when Paul Grayson was clipped unconscious?

Had Nora forestalled them—*them?*

Nora was quite a woman. Her loveliness was not of the un-touchable, fragile, bandbox variety; perfection that must not be marred by a misplaced hair or a wrinkle in the frock—or a clue of rouge, printed offset from her own ripe lips to her own smooth cheek by Paul. Nora was all-desirable woman, and neither complete deshabille nor minor imperfection would mar her appeal. Paul recalled the lithe slenderness of her body. Her sculptured arms were molded with the smooth, well-balanced muscle of fine tonus. Her waist was slender but not too soft—

"Hey! Are you there?"

"Yeah, Stacey. I was thinking."

"Don't think so hard."

"Look, Stacey. Can you tell me whether the man who clipped me turned up with scratches on his face?"

"I don't know. Why?"

"Just a loose end."

"I might be able to find out."

"Take a swing at it; but it's not too important."

"Okay, Paul. Have I given you something to think about?"

"More than," said Paul soberly. He hung up, turned, and saw the guard of the previous evening standing near by, about to go on duty. Paul went over and asked: "Hi!"

"Hello. Say, I'm sorry about last night—"

"Forget it, you were doing your duty. But can you tell me: Did the guy who used my identification last night have any scratches on his face?"

The guard frowned in thought. "All he had was some well applied make-up, and a fine job it was, too. He looked me right in the eye."

"No marks?"

"Not a trace."

Paul smiled and went back to Nora, thinking furiously. Something must have interfered with their little plan. He looked at Nora, lissome, lovely, as lithe as a tiger. All desirable—

But maybe it might be a good idea for him to learn her desires, to ascertain her limit before he took any liberties with her beautiful white body. Intelligent women did not scream or faint these days, nor did they rake their attacker with fingernails. They employed Judo.

Now, if Nora Phillips knew Judo, it was plausible that the erstwhile footpad instead of finding an inert victim and an hysterical woman, discovered that the woman was capable of defending her outraged dignity, revenging their cowardly attack, and thwarting any further plans the criminal held for them both. It would explain in part why the criminal's little idea did not culminate as expected.

If Nora Phillips knew Judo...

Paul smiled faintly. He had not changed his mind about Nora Phillips; she was still the type of woman that would react unfavorably to any crude attempt at approach.

Regardless of whether her interest in him were an act, swift passion, or the awakening of tender love, Paul knew that she would not employ the punishing Judo holds upon him, if she knew Judo. On the other hand, Paul believed that instinct might react faster than intellect, and that her first instinctive move would give her away.

So Paul took her hand as he came close to her. He drew her forward, his free arm gliding towards her waist and around it.

Nora's free hand moved forward, upward, touched his cheek, and then went on around his neck. The hand that he held came free and joined the other. She was warm and supple in his arms and her lips were soft and clinging.

It was a satisfying emotional experience. Intellectually it proved nothing that had not been empirical knowledge for a couple of millions of years.

Paul would never learn whether Nora knew Judo by that method. He abandoned his primary intrigue for the moment and indulged in one of his favorite indoor sports.

Then she moved back a bit, and Paul's hands slipped to either side of her waist. "I could learn to like this sort of thing," he said.

Nora looked up into his eyes. Her own eyes were a trifle dreamy, but a trace of smile lurked in the deep corners of her mouth. "But how do I know you'll be true to me?" she asked him in a voice that sounded like pure soap opera. "In space—"

"I've a dame in every port," he told her. "I'm true to 'em all."

"But why so many?" chuckled Nora.

"Variety." Paul let go of Nora's waist and she stepped back a bit. He turned around and started leading her the rest of the way towards the coffee shop. "I've a couple of hours left," he said. "I'd prefer to soak up some dinner in candlelight, with music, et al. But Ptomaine Joe's is handy. I've hit so many snags so far that I'm inclined to find me an advantage and then sit on it until I'm safe in space."

Nora shuddered a bit. "Safe in space," she said softly. "That's a strange thing to say."

"Why?" he asked.

"So far out there, away from the friendly earth; nothing solid to stand upon, nothing to—"

Paul laughed. "No footpads to raise lumps on the skull, no taxicabs to dodge, no—"

"No women to kiss?"

"You've convinced me! But I'm baffled by you. What kind of job do you hold?"

"Why?"

"It isn't everybody that can pick up and leave their work for an idle afternoon."

"Oh," and her laugh was genuine. "I'm librarian for a large office of lawyers. I can get away because of polite contusion. No matter who misses me, he assumes that I am looking up a batch of stuff for one of the others. There are so many of them that they couldn't possibly get their heads together close enough to check up. Actually I'm doing just that often enough so that I can play hooky once in a while and not get caught."

Paul laughed with Nora. He felt at ease with her and her presence made him forget all of the niggling little questions that bothered him. Time passed swiftly enough to surprise them both when the announcer called the time and number of Paul's spaceflight.

"This is it," he said ruefully.

"So it is," she agreed. "There's another day."

"I'll call for it when I get back."

"Do that," she said. It was not a tone of command. It was more a tone of absolute agreement. It pleased him.

"Raging Vegan Gorgons couldn't stop me," he chuckled. He reached for her and she went into his arms forward for a goodbye kiss. Paul made the most of it; gave it all he knew how to give, and for his efforts he received a pleasant promise for the future in return.

Nora leaned back in his arms, took his hands from around her waist, and turned him to face the spaceport door.

"It's that way," she said in a throaty voice. She gave him a gentle shove. He went through the door and out upon the spacefield, walking across the sandy floor towards the spacecraft numbered BurAst P.G.1.

Actually, the spacecraft was quite close to the shape of a hen's egg. It stood upon its smaller end, supported by four heavy vanes that held the drivers. Above them, the bulge of the hull swelled out in the gentle curve, and about the place where the soft-boiled-egg gourmet cuts the top off of his breakfast food, the hard metal stopped and the upper curving dome of the spacecraft was made of window. Not a clear expanse of glass, but more like the greenhouse roof. Small facets set between rigid girders in a neat and efficient pattern. The girders were reasonably heavy, because each one held shutter flaps that would snap closed if the pane of glass beside it became pierced because of contact with cosmic detritus.

At the very top of this dome the glass was a smooth sheet, polished and unbroken. This section, a full ten feet in diameter, was optically perfect. For through this dome of glass the spacecraft was aimed.

If the stars actually were where they looked to be to the eye, there would have been something less of a problem. A set of precision cross hairs set along the axis of ship's drive could be used as a line-of-sight aiming point. Like a ship near the shore the bow could be aimed at the pier, the power set, and then the rest would take care of itself.

But stars move in their heavenly way. A poor ten to fifty miles per second can become a rather awesome gulf after four years. Alpha Centauri is a little more than four light years away. That means that the star as seen by the naked eye will be quite some distance from where it really is. Students of trigonometry will understand; a second of arc will subtend a cosmic sine at the end of four light years.

To help the pilot, the spotter was used. The spotter was a tender spacecraft that roamed the solar system far out from Sol. Two light hours away it was. When one of the star ships was scheduled to fly, the Elecalc would compute the course and the big telescopes would direct the spotter spacecraft via the Z-wave until the distant ship was directly in the line of aim between Terra and the calculated spot in the heavens where the distant star would be at the end of the ship's flying time. Once the spotter was properly located, two hours before the take-off time the spotter would emit an atomic spotlight for a half-hour.

Two hours later the light from this immense searchlight would arrive at Terra to provide an aiming point for the space pilot. The ship could take off on this line of sight, aiming for it directly. Of course, by the time the space travelling ship reached the spot, the spotter craft would have moved aside; the light would have ceased, and the star ship was heading for deep space with nothing to impede its course.

Paul was handicapped. The spotter was not available. Lacking the spotter to use as a point of aim, Paul was forced to choose the aiming telescope in the dome instead of the more precise cross hairs on the optical-glass. This added to the error, and to add once more to that error was the fact that spacecraft in flight tend to revolve along their driving axis so that the angle between the true line of flight and the aiming point changed in angle. Paul would have to use Alpha Centauri itself as a point-of-aim. The correction-angle was supplied by the observatory and applied to the aiming telescope in the dome.

A lot of minute errors that added up to a gross at the end of flight. Basically, the job of the galactic survey would remove one of the errors: That of the crude measurement of distance between the stars themselves.

Paul was a good pilot. He cut the aiming-star close and watched it in the scope until it disappeared. He was now in that blackness that surrounded every ship during the faster-than-light speed. He was on his way. Nothing to do for two weeks but wait for the course to end. Nothing to do but to sit and think, and plan, and dream. To think of Haedaecker and the Z-wave; to plan for the future when his discoveries brought him fame and fortune; to dream of Nora Phillips.

Paul began to hum, and after a moment or two the humming broke out into a full-throated, but dubious baritone:

*"Round and round and round go the deuterons
Round and round the magnet swings 'em
Round and round and round go the deuterons
SMACK! in the target go the micro amps!"*

CHAPTER SIX

BURIED IN THE LOOSE, powdery dust that covered Proxima Centauri I, a spacecraft lay concealed. Ten miles across the blazing flatlands of dust, Galactic Survey Station 1 was clearly visible. From the station the spacecraft blended so well with the dust that it could not be seen. Only a sharp observer who knew where to look and what to look for could have seen the turret of the spacecraft lofting above the dusty plains. The long-barreled machine rifle would have been invisible to the sharpest of eye.

Several miles to the other side of the Survey Station there were a group of furrows kicked-up in the plain where test-bursts from the machine rifle had landed.

A television detector was set upon the area between the concrete landing deck and the main spacelock of the Survey Station so that any erect, moving object that intersected the detector-line would cause the machine rifle to fire so that its projectiles would pass through the moving object.

The man in the hidden spacecraft had been playing solitaire for day upon day; the record of his score on the wall of the ship was long—and not too honest.

Eventually the detector-alarm rang and he dropped his cards. He ran to shut off all of the detecting equipment because detecting equipment itself could be in turn detected and he wanted no reprisals. He set his eye to the telescope and watched the new arrival.

Paul Grayson landed his ship on the concrete apron and donned space attire for his walk across the airless planet to the Station. He came from his ship—and though he had seen it countless times before—Paul paused to view the beauty of the airless midnight sky. He looked for Sol, hidden in the starry curtain. He looked at Proxima, a tiny star but utterly brilliant at this distance. It blinded him; luckily the beautiful binary of Alpha Centauri was behind the little planet and he was saved the hurt of looking at that brilliance.

With the same thrill of anticipation he had enjoyed for day upon day now, Paul turned from his ship and started to walk toward the Station. What he might learn there would change the thinking of the galaxy. It was the culmination of years of thought and experimentation; it was the crux of the matter, the final evidence that would give Paul the weight and the conviction. From here he could go on and up; here, now, at any rate soon, was the incontrovertible truth.

He checked his gear thoroughly, but it was force of habit caused by the desire of his own safety. He had planned well. He had forgotten nothing.

He chuckled happily.

He had forgotten nothing. The lissome sweetness of Nora Phillips and the promise of complete fulfillment was sweet recollection.

When Paul returned to Terra he would have the world in the palm of his hand—to hold tightly and give to Nora.

His eye caught a bit of glitter in the dust of Proxima I and he stooped to pick it up because Nora might like a crystal from a far planet.

He did not hear the passage of bullets over his bent back because Proxima I possessed no air to carry their sound.

He could not hear the cursing of the man in the spacecraft hidden ten miles across the dusty plain, nor could he see the frantic effort to readjust the sighting mechanism of the machine rifle. Five thousand feet per second was the muzzle velocity of the rifle in space and because there was no impeding air, the bullets had taken two seconds to travel from gun to target position. In those two seconds Paul bent over, causing the burst of fire to miss.

There was no second fusillade. The enemy had had too little time to readjust his sights. The enemy had also been overconfident, so had not prepared for a miss.

* * *

The radio was silent. Only the crackle of cosmic static came from the speaker to show that it was alive. The Z-wave was even more silent for there was no interfering cosmic energies to make Z-wave static.

Paul set up the test equipment and checked both. They were obviously 'hot' and awaiting the arrival of some signal in order to burst into full-throated life.

Then he settled back to wait. How long, Paul could not tell. Actually, the measurement of this matter was the basic reason for Paul's being here. The books set Alpha Centauri at 4.3 light years from Sol. Ergo a beam of light or a radio wave should take 4.3

years from transmission to reception. Ten percent error would cause a variable of almost five months; an error of one percent adds up to two weeks.

The observatories had admitted an error of one percent as a maximum and considerable space travel between Proxima I and Terra had diminished this error to an absolute of about three days plus or minus the nominal. Paul had been gratified to discover that despite his delayed take-off; he had arrived at Proxima before the radio signal arrived from Terra.

Paul had been worried about his delay and he had driven his ship hard. Not during the days of faster-than-light travel, of course, but after Paul had come down out of the blackness and could set a course by inspection. He had been either lucky or proficient. Even using a not too precise method of aiming his ship, he had still emerged from the blackness less than five million miles from Proxima, which was very good aiming indeed.

Pilots always aimed for their target on the nose. For one thing, the dispersion was huge because the slightest irregularity in any phase of the maneuver would throw off the point of aim by millions of miles. In years and years of spaceflight, the first direct hit upon target had yet to be recorded. In fact, five million miles was considered brilliant piloting—or as is more possible, it was brilliant luck!

Then as Paul found his landing-spot, he had pushed the BurAst P.G.1 hard enough to make her plates creak and Paul had descended at a full four gravities all the way to the ground. He had arrived before the radio signal had reached the planet and that was all he cared about.

So he settled back to wait. There was little to do but sit and think, and to watch the occasional meteor shower land on the dusty ground.

There had been an extensive shower about ten miles from the station shortly alter his arrival. The impact was, of course, both invisible and inaudible. But upon impact the dust spurted upwards, billowing and flowing like the column in miniature that came from an atom bomb explosion. Since there was no air on Proxima I, the billowing dust rose and spread apart until the individual dust mote lost its energy and fell back to Proxima I by gravitational attraction.

He would have liked to inspect that particular spot because the shower had been spectacular. A number of meteors in a close-knit group had landed, sending forth a series of dusty columns—some of the larger of which were still visible when the radio chattered into life three days after his arrival.

It came all at once and its sound dinned his ears and re-echoed from the smooth walls of the Station. The sound snapped Paul from his place by the window-dome. It grated on his ears until he could rush downstairs to the radio room to turn the volume-gain control down so that the audio signal fell below the overload point.

From a raucous, nerve-tingling screech, the volume fell until distortion no longer fouled up the filtered purity of the signal-note broadcast from far-off Terra four years ago. Paul measured the signal strength and found it entirely satisfactory. He coupled the recorders to the gear, and then settled back to await the arrival of the modulated timing signals that were transmitted after an interval of straight tone, the first period to be used for establishing contact before the actual timing of the transmission-time began.

Once the radio signal was coming in perfectly, Paul turned his attention to the Z-wave receiver.

He tuned it gingerly, cautiously. And then it came to life!

Paul cried in exultation. His was success! True, it was a weakling signal that faded and died at times, but it came in strong and clear enough for recording in the periods of good reception. A bit of work and research, and the construction of a real interstellar Z-wave station would remove this fading.

Paul snapped the extra recorder on, and then began to dream his dream again, this time more strong than ever before.

He had connected the Z-wave equipment at Terra's Z-wave central to the big interstellar radio transmitter, lacking a Z-wave transmitter for his own use. So that now he was hearing the Terran end of conversation. It was a woman's voice that talked from Terra to someone currently on one of the planetary outposts of Sol.

"…but it won't be long, my dear…Of course, it seems so… Do that, by all means… In a month, you say? …I'm very happy about that…" Here the signal faded for a full minute. It returned again,

"Terry said so... How do I know? ...By all means, my dear..."
And here again the signal faded.

But it was enough.

Exultation filled Paul. This was proof. This was the door, opening for life upon everything he ever hoped to gain, everything he hoped to be. It gave him what he wanted to offer life, and by happy circumstance, he had found the one he wanted to offer it to. He could go to Nora, not as a technician in the Bureau of Astrogation but with a grand future of success and opportunity to build ever upward and ever onward to real fame and fortune. Not the real success in his hand, for when the final success in life comes, ambition and desire begin to wane. But far more exhilarating was the hope of success, the chance to work for a magnificent future together.

He gloated for hours, measuring the radio signal as few radio transmissions have ever been measured before.

Then with his work finished, Paul packed up to leave. The glittering stone he held in his hand was nice, but tiny now, compared to his tale of success. A bright rock from a far-off planet, not much more than a seashell from a distant beach.

With a chuckle, he tossed the stone aside and broke out the sand-jeep. Nora might like a meteorite from far Proxima I. At least, it was a souvenir to be quite in evidence wherever it might end up.

He headed for the meteor shower of three days before, and found it after an hour of running across the featureless sands.

The area was small, which in itself was strange, for meteor showers cover miles of area, not square yards. The sands were pocked with small craters, and Paul looked at them until he found a crater of medium size where the rock was still showing. He hefted the stone from the sky and carried it to the sand-jeep. On his way back to the little buggy, he caught sight of a glitter less than fifty feet away.

He dropped the stone in the back of the jeep and strode over to see what could be glittering this brightly in Proxima's veritable sea of bland, yellow sand.

Then he stood dumbfounded, for the glitter came from the circular disc of glass, the eyepiece of a space suit, which was buried in the sand. A crater of irregular shape surrounded it, and the meteorite was lying in half-exposed view. Paul hopped into the crater and lifted the stone, to disclose a nauseous clot of brownish blood, the remnant of space suit, and contained in it, the remains of a man. Mostly buried by the impact, the man's body stood almost upright, the headpiece at ground level while the rest of the body was curved brokenly backwards down in the crater, driven into the sand instantly by the meteor.

Paul shrugged and removed the helmet.

The face was vaguely familiar. The man wore clothing under the suit, but there was no sign of identification in it. The face bothered Paul, however. He believed he had seen it somewhere.

Not only that, but just exactly why any man possessed of sane mind would be on Proxima I (save Paul, who had business there) was mystery at its best.

Paul stood up and looked around the plain.

He caught another glitter, and got into his jeep to investigate.

It was the semi-submerged spacecraft, and Paul wondered at it. It was smashed flat by a gigantic meteor, ruined beyond any hope of reconstruction. Paul tried to enter to inspect it. It had been too badly wrecked by the meteor.

Abandoning the spacecraft as a hopeless job for immediate identification, Paul went back to the lone victim. There was still something vaguely familiar about the man's face. The difference was not because the vacuum of Proxima had distorted the face, for the suit had been sealed at the break by the meteor and the sand and there was no distortion.

Paul pondered. Identification might be possible by dental means, by prints, by iris-matching, if the face distorted on his way back. There was his refrigerating gear aboard the ship, Paul could stick the corpse in there and hope that some light could be shed on this mystery.

Paul folded the lower, ruined portion of the space suit to preserve whatever minute bit of air it contained, and packed it onto the jeep. He shoved the body into the freezing cold of the storage bin with a grimace of distaste and determined to dine on canned beans for the duration. It annoyed him to hurl several pounds of fine, well-hung tenderloin steak onto the bald sands or Proxima I to make room for all un-hung corpse. But it had to be done.

Then, with the mystery still gnawing at his mind, Paul fixed the drive-scope on Sol, made a few adjustments, and set his autodrive and microtimer according to the data supplied before his departure from Terra. It was a corrected-for-duration course, the reverse of his approaching orbit.

Paul clicked the drive and headed for Sol. When the ship dropped into invisibility, he relaxed. Busy all the time of his stay on Proxima I, he felt seedy. While still pondering the problem, Paul shucked his clothing and showered. Water, both hot and then chilled, did not help his memory any. Nor was it the memory of Nora Phillips that made him lather his face and shave. Not entirely. For the three-day beard made his face uncomfortable and it was personal comfort rather than White Man's Burden that prompted Paul to reap his beard. Like most men, shaving was not a pleasant occupation, and when no matter of personal appearance insisted upon a smooth face, shaving was postponed and indulged in only when the factors of discomfort balanced one another equally and in diametrically opposite directions.

Paul grinned at his clean face in the mirror. "Y'know," he said to himself in the glass, "you're vaguely familiar, too."

The idea hit him hard, then.

One of the reasons why a picture of one's self does not resemble one's familiar appearance in a mirror is due to the lack of facial symmetry. The left side of a mirror image is the right side of the face on a photograph and the two seldom match.

Paul gulped and dressed quickly. Then he went to the freeze--locker and hauled out the dead man.

It would take a third observer to tell. But so far as Paul Grayson could tell, this man from Proxima I was his double!

"And that," he said in address to the corpse, "makes two of you!"

CHAPTER SEVEN

TEN DAYS LATER when Paul's ship dropped out of the realm of invisibility, he was no nearer to the problem's solution.

He did have a course of action formulated, however. So his first telephone call was not to Nora Phillips. It was to John Stacey, the detective.

"I'm back."

"Glad to hear it. Wha' hoppen?"

"I've got a corpse on my ship."

"Friend of yours?"

"Nope."

"Look," came the cheerful reply, "if you want to murder someone, go ahead. But there's no sense in putting yourself in jeopardy by carrying the mortal remains around with you. Why didn't you dump the thing out in space?"

"I want it identified."

"Now, for the first time in years, you make sense."

"Thanks.

"But look," said Stacey suddenly, "just what kind of mess have you gotten yourself into?"

"I don't know. I hope to find out."

"Well, it's thick."

Paul blinked. "I know it. But why?"

"You answer that one, it's your question."

"What's new?"

"Nora Phillips is missing."

"Missing?" exploded Paul. "Where did she go?"

"I haven't been able to find out yet."

"What do you know?" demanded Paul.

"Damned little. She left you on your departure day and started to drive back to town. Instead of returning to her office or going home, she turned off on Bridge Street and stopped at a mansion. Number 7111, to be exact. Drove her car into the garage as though she were expected. Hasn't come out since."

"You haven't kept a man watching the place for all this time?"

"No, but I've had a gent prowl the joint at least once a day for the last two weeks, and the car is still in the garage. You can see it through the windows of the door."

"Didn't she come out?"

"Garage is connected to the house. She could have gone into the house without breathing fresh air."

"That's 7111 Bridge Street?"

"Check."

"How about her job?"

"By careful enquiry, we've learned that she resigned. By letter."

"How did you get that?"

"Well, law outfits seldom take kindly to characters asking leading questions. But an advertisement appeared for a librarian and I had Milly fill it. She pored through the personnel files and found a typed letter of resignation. Terse; disappointingly uninformative."

"Her apartment?"

"She ran a three-room job alone. A man appeared, armed with a letter from her. He packed up her stuff and it was removed from the premises by the Howdaille Moving and Storage Company. It is currently there in storage with the bill paid in advance for six months."

"Any more?"

"I had Morton enquire about a rental at that address and he was told that Miss Phillips had to return home because of illness of her father. That's all we could get. Morton got that information from the landlord after expressing first a desire to live there and second asking why the previous tenant moved out. Put it so that the landlord had to show him her letter to prevent a possible tenant from thinking that there was something odious about the premises."

"Then what?"

"That's all. Morton considered the place—apparently—for several days after putting down a twenty-buck deposit. Gave it up and forfeited the deposit on the grounds that his wife wanted a four room place."

"Um. Gone without a trace?"

"Seems so. Excepting that she went into 7111 Bridge, and we've not seen her since."

"How long did you watch?"

"Constantly for ten days. Not a sign or a trace of her there."

"But—"

"Yeah," replied Stacey's unhappy voice. "We cased that joint too. I've had at least seven operatives hit that front door, on every sort of pretext from stolen nylon hosiery to roofing salesmen, and from governmental surveys on this and that to gents who insist that they look at the electric wiring, the plumbing, and the foundation. The joint is owned and tenanted by an elderly gentleman who has retired. His wife lives there too. One servant, a doddering old fogy who must have been the owner's father's gentleman's gentleman."

"What's his name?"

"Hoagland."

"How about the car in the garage?"

Paul could almost hear Stacey shrug. "So far, there is nothing suspicious about it from a legal stand point," he said. "You'd have one hell of a time proving anything. So a woman—none too well acquainted with you—resigns from her position on a perfectly logical grounds, moves from her apartment on similar grounds, and deposits her car in a strange place and disappears."

"But that last is the important thing. She disappeared."

"Yeah? Where does her father live? Maybe she did go there?"

"You're the detective," said Paul. "Chase it down."

"This will cost like hell," warned Stacey.

Paul laughed. "What I've got will pay for plenty from now on," he said.

"I'll re-open the case, then."

"You shouldn't have closed it."

Stacey groaned. "How did I know you were that anxious?"

"I was."

"Okay. But I wanted your approval before I broke this thing wide open."

"Will it?"

"Sure. The first time I go to 7111 Bridge and ask about that automobile in the garage, which is registered under the name of Nora Phillips, someone is either going to get nasty, call the police, or start asking me embarrassing questions that might lead to Paul Grayson."

"Stacey the guy I found dead on Proxima I is another dead ringer for myself. That makes two characters killed off that resemble me. It looks like a plot to me."

"How was the deceased rendered that way?"

"He was hit by a meteorite."

"Act of God, I calls that," muttered Stacey. "You wouldn't go so far as to suggest that God is on your side?"

"When a meteorite hits a man and a spacecraft in the same shower, both of which are prowling on a planet where they had no business and shouldn't have had any curiosity, it begins to look as though celestial mechanics, formerly run by the Act of God, might have been given a little aid and aim by the machiavellian hand of man or men unknown."

"How could you aim a—"

"Haul it to the right spot and drop it from a good height from a spacecraft. That's for the big one that wrecked the ship. Carry a boatload of little ones and drop 'em on the head of the character you desire to erase. Not one of them penetrated to the depths I'd have expected, now that it comes to mind."

"Okay, Paul. I'm on the trail again. I'll send a man to collect your corpse and we'll attempt to identify it. Maybe that will give us a lead."

"Check," said Paul, and he turned away from the telephone with a heavy heart.

He recalled the lissome warmth of her body pressed eagerly against him; could a woman offer herself falsely with that much ardor?

Paul's clenched fist came down upon the palm of his other hand in a loud, determined smack! By all that was holy, Paul intended to find out. He answered his question honestly: Yes. There are women who could play any act, do literally anything humanly possible to obtain their wants. On the other hand, Nora might have run afoul of whatever interest it was that apparently stood in his way towards linking Sol and NeoSol by Z-wave.

Had he been uninterested in her as a person, he could have shrugged it off with but a minimum of hurt and wonder. But Paul made up his mind to find out about her, to take either one of two courses as far as Nora Phillips went. If Nora were in league with those who stood against him, he wanted the dubious pleasure of showing her that she could have been better off by following a more naturally honest plan.

And if Nora Phillips were in trouble because she was seen in Paul's company, he wanted the extreme pleasure of belting the living hell out of her abductors personally, while she watched wide eyed, and then escorting her gallantly to some place where pain and strife could be relegated to the background.

To do either, Paul must not stop working towards his goal. With determined step, Paul headed for the offices of the Terran Physical Society with his personal recorder, upon which the semi-conversation from the Z-wave was impressed.

This time it would be Grayson's Theory. And it would be presented to the T.P.S. without the possibility of Haedaecker's interference or scorn.

Charles Thorndyke was a man well worthy of the scientific honors he owned. Unlike Haedaecker, he did not flaunt them at every hand, he used them only when it was necessary.

And unlike Chadwick Haedaecker, Thorndyke was the kind of man who would have rejected his own pet theory instantly upon the first glimmer of proof that he was in error.

He listened to Paul's tale with growing interest and then he listened to the recording.

"This is a big thing," he told Paul after Grayson was finished.

"It is my greatest hope realized."

"We have a lengthy paper on extra-solar gravitational phenomena to be presented next Tuesday. I am going to cancel that for your presentation." Thorndyke looked at the ceiling.

"The chance of voice communication with NeoSol is as great an advancement as the discovery of the telegraph," he said. "It must not be delayed one moment!"

"I've always believed that," said Paul.

"Why didn't you speak up before?"

"Doctor Haedaecker has always vetoed any such suggestion."

"Why, for the Love of Heaven?"

"He said that everything had been tried."

"Balderdash!" exploded Thorndyke. "Negative evidence is never conclusive!"

"I could not argue with him."

Thorndyke smiled. He nodded. Being armed with a hope and a firm belief is poor weapon against a man as deeply entrenched as Haedaecker, whose minor pronouncements made news and whose hand could write an appropriation for a million dollars to pursue some experiment.

"Once this is presented, you will no longer be a small voice crying out in a veritable wilderness. You will probably end up with a job to do as big as Haedaecker's. I can't understand him."

"Nor can I."

"You're certain that you presented your idea correctly?"

"So far as I know. I've been talking about this thing for years, ever since I got the idea."

Thorndyke laughed. "I know what happened," he said. "Your initial idea was but half formed and therefore incorrect. But as you improved upon it, your own arguments became trite to yourself and even less convincing to Haedaecker, who was convinced against your idea. He'll have to change his line next Tuesday."

Paul left in a fine state of mind. He was ahead of the game for the first time in his life and he enjoyed the feeling.

The question or who or what wanted to stop him was something that he could never find out until the other side made another move. As for Nora Phillips, following her trail was a job for an experienced man like Stacey. The third item was Haedaecker.

Paul did not agree with Thorndyke. Haedaecker was not merely misled in this thing. Haedaecker had good reasons why he wanted the Z-wave experiment hushed up. Haedaecker's Theory had been the making of the man himself. Once that theory was broken down and shown incorrect, Haedaecker would no longer be the great mind that he had been. Haedaecker liked power and adulation and naturally was disinclined to let it go lightly.

Paul expected trouble with the physicist.

And Paul would have preferred to circumvent trouble, to go around it, to avoid it. But Paul was experienced enough to know that the act of avoiding trouble more often made the trouble pile up until it reached terrifying proportions.

So instead of staying strictly away from Haedaecker's office, Paul strode boldly in. Forewarning the enemy of your intentions is said to be bad. But now and then, telling the enemy what you are going to do—and then daring him to try and stop you—will make him back up, because it tends to convince him that you are equipped to do as you want to do, regardless of opposition.

Chadwick Haedaecker greeted Paul cordially. "Everything go all right?" he asked.

Paul nodded. "The reports on the radio signal have been turned in, complete with recordings and my own comments."

"Good." Haedaecker turned to a map on the wall. He consulted a list beside the map. Then he turned with a smile. "That was the first," he said. "The next signal doesn't come in for almost six months. Then, my young friend, you will be the busiest man in space for the next two years, hopping hither and thither to check in the network. I'm glad that everything went as expected."

"Everything did."

"Good. This first one was the one that proves we're right. Now that we've got one checked in, we can take the rest with less wonder and concern." Haedaecker looked at Paul sharply. "But this isn't all you came to tell me about."

"No," said Paul quietly. "It is not. Doctor Haedaecker, I am not one to fly a false flag. I dislike the idea of thrusting a man's ideas back down his throat abruptly and in public."

"Just what are you driving at?" demanded Haedaecker. "Upon Proxima Centauri I, I definitely proved the error of Haedaecker's Theory. I received a Z-wave—"

"Ridiculous!"

"I did," stated Paul flatly. "And so I am telling you because I feel that you should have some opportunity to protect yourself."

"I need no protection."

"You have always defended your theory viciously. You have never permitted the merest possibility that you could be wrong. I have proof, now."

"Impossible."

"I have," said Paul. "And I intend to show it. So, if you care to make any statements which will change your previous attitude, do so."

Haedaecker looked at Paul queerly. "Just what would you recommend?" he asked.

Paul smiled. "If I were you," he said. "I would accept the defeat of your theory graciously."

"Indeed."

Paul made an exasperated noise. "I'm only trying to save your embarrassment—"

"You insolent young puppy! You—trying to help me!"

Paul took a deep breath. This was not going well at all. But on the other hand, Paul knew that he was no longer a small voice, to be throttled by the mere gesture from Haedaecker. Paul was in full control of the situation whether Haedaecker realized it or not. Furthermore, the years-long awe of Haedaecker and his iron-handed rule had not left their ineradicable mark. Unlike the child, ruled by stern parents, who defers to their orders long after maturity because of habit, Paul's former deference was gone. Perhaps the only difference was that parents seldom lose their command of respect because the maturing offspring learns as the years go past that their seemingly arbitrary rules were actually born of wisdom that the child could not understand. Whereas Haedaecker was a god with feet of low-grade clay. When the mighty fall, they fall far and hard.

"I was trying to save you embarrassment," snapped Paul.

"Once the truth is known, that you refused to permit any experiment because it might shake the foundations of Haedaecker's Theory, your entire policy will be destroyed."

"So what would you have me do?"

"Why not sponsor this idea?" suggested Paul. "Be the first to proclaim, happily, that Haedaeckers Theory was in error and that you now join in the hope of connecting Sol and NeoSol by real communications."

Haedaecker shook his head coldly. "I'll sponsor no such ridiculous thing," he said. "Because it can not be! You—"

"But I have proof!"

Haedaecker stood up. "You have not!"

"I have!" thundered Paul. "And I intend to show it!"

Haedaecker sat down again and placed the fingertips of each hand against the other, making a sort of cage. "Now I'll warn you," he told Paul. "Your proof is false, whatever it is. And if you should make the mistake of making a public spectacle of your efforts to disparage a well-founded law of physics, I shall take measures to ensure that you never make such an idiotic error again."

"Why don't you fire me?" taunted Paul.

"As soon as you publicly violate my rules, I shall."

"Then come to the T.S.P. next Tuesday," snapped Paul, "and watch me break both your rules and your theory with one fell swoop!"

Haedaecker shrugged. "I'll be there to watch you make a fool of yourself," he said.

Paul turned on one heel and left.

CHAPTER EIGHT

STACEY'S VOICE WAS as dry as ever. "Busy, Paul?"

"Just polishing up my talk," he said. "I'm due to lecture in an hour.

"Well, don't be nervous."

"I'd be less nervous if I knew what was going on."

"This might help. First, your corpse was none other than a three-time loser named Clarke and a pot full of aliases, none of which are worth mentioning. As dead as a mackerel."

"What are we going to do about him?"

"It's been done."

"How?"

"Don't ask."

"But isn't this disposing of evidence?"

"Sure. But if any crime has been committed, he did it, or attempted to. He is no loss to the community."

"But that is against the law."

"So is kissing a woman who is of no relation to you in public in this state," chuckled Stacey. "You'll only get involved in a lot of official curiosity if you disclose the death. That will get you a grilling and a mess of suspicion to fight against, while the birds who set him on you will be forewarned. They'll be free to plot further while you are busy defending an innocent stand. Besides," he added with another chuckle, "there is nothing like making them chew a fingernail, wondering just where their plans went a-foul.

Let them scurry around instead of you. If I guess right, they are not quite certain whether the man now talking to me is Paul Grayson, bona fide, or their little masquerader.

"But why, for the Love of Heaven?"

"Look, mes infante innocente, this is twice that you've met a character made up to resemble you. This means an intended masquerade. I don't know why. But I'll bet a hat that there is a motive to it all."

The last was so obvious that Paul saw no reason to comment. Stacey continued, "One more item before I go away and leave you to your test tubes. Nora Phillips."

"Yes," came Paul's eager reply.

"Posing as a man making a survey, I, me, myself twiggled on the doorbell at 7111 Bridge Avenue this afternoon after canvassing the entire neighborhood up to that point to make it look good."

"Go on."

"Nora Phillips is their niece. The elderly gentleman said so. She parked her car there for the time being since her pappy, brother to his wife, is desperately ill on NeoSol."

"So?"

"She'll be back, but they did not know when."

"Get her address?"

"Couldn't get too curious. No."

"Damn."

"Why?"

"Somehow, Nora is tied up in this. On my side."

"Okay. I'm going to follow one other lead. Take it easy, Paul, and give the physicists hell."

"I'll try."

"I will begin at the beginning," smiled Paul, wishing he had the air of a professional lecturer and the literary ability of an author, "space was first conquered by rocket propulsion. Eventually a base was established on Luna and the space stations set up. Operating in space, the physicists discovered the super-velocity drive, which like electricity, was used long before people began to understand it.

"The rocket is a clumsy device and ill-adapted to anything but limited, professional use. But the superdrive made space travel practical for the ordinary man. Space was truly conquered then, and today men live on Venus and on Mars. Precariously and uncomfortably, but they live there. Men have spread throughout the solar system, working in mines and medicinal farms and jungles. Their tenure of employment is dictated by the rigors of life on these inimical planets of Sol.

"With the superdrive, explorers chased through the nearer galaxy, seeking a planet suitable for colonization. While most stars have been found to have planets, there was not one found that filled the bill until they located NeoSol and Neoterra, both of which resemble Sol and the earth to a fine degree.

"Radio linked the colonies of Sol, and after NeoSol was colonized, radio linked its spread-out colonists.

"Forty years ago, Carrington discovered the Z-wave, an outgrowth of the superdrive. Then the instantaneous Z-wave replaced the slow radio transmissions that required teletype and code communications, and voice to voice contacts prevailed throughout the solar system, and throughout the system of NeoSol.

"But the Z-wave did not cross the gulf of interstellar space, and years of experimentation followed, all of which failed. Then, twenty years ago, Chadwick Haedaecker suggested the theory now known as Haedaeckers Theory, which tended to show that the Z-wave propagated because of the fields of force generated in the central cores of stars. Since that date, only desultory attempts have been made to test the Z-wave in deep space. Experimentation had stopped, for all practical purposes. About the only people who have given the matter much thought are students of theory, and a couple of hardy souls like myself, who—I have been accused and of which I must admit—hoped to become rich and famous by making some extraordinary discovery.

"I will now advance the idea that I hope will be eventually known as Grayson's Principle.

"The basis of Grayson's Principle is that the Z-wave will not propagate between points that have not previously been linked by electromagnetic waves!"

This caused a storm in the auditorium. A showing of frantic hands flowered above the sea of faces and the hall broke into a growling murmur of muttering voices, discussing pro and con.

The chairman came forward and spoke to Paul: "Shall I call order, or would you prefer to have a mid-lecture discussion?"

Paul smiled nervously. "I was prepared for this," he said.

"The rest of this will run better if we get this one point settled. It will be too long from now to the end of my lecture to make these men hold their questions."

"Good!" smiled Thorndyke. He rapped for order. "Gentlemen," he said, speaking over the incomplete attention, "Mister Grayson has just made a rather shocking statement, which is cause for controversy. He has suggested himself that a mid-lecture period of questions will hasten our understanding of his theory."

There was a burst of applause and the flowering of hands went up again.

"Edwin Johnson," said the first man naming himself. "Granting that it takes light one hundred and forty years to cross between here and NeoSol, I suggest that the entire galaxy has been coupled by electromagnetic waves for two thousand million years."

"I said 'linked'," explained Paul easily. "This question is one that stumped me for a long time and was possibly the one thing that prevented the advancement of the principle long before. But the detectors we employ to detect those frequencies we term 'light' are not similar to those we use for the longer frequencies of radio, even though both are electromagnetic waves. Light will not travel along a conductor, although it is true that the longer waves will be transmitted through a waveguide made of dielectric that is transparent to them. Ergo, it is the means we use to handle these frequencies that establish the 'linkage' rather than the medium or the wave itself."

"I am Fred Hughes," said the second. "Do you mean to state that the Z-wave has never been known to operate between points not previously linked by radio?"

"That is right."

"You've investigated everything?"

"Mine is negative evidence, I admit. This is why it is hard to establish as truth. But remember, the solar system was linked by radio long before the Z-wave was discovered."

"How about spacecraft?"

"Once the Z-wave linkage is established by its forerunner of radio, it is complete and can not be broken."

"A spacecraft employs radio until it reaches the superdrive point. Then—?"

"I have had no opportunity to check this point as yet. I believe it has to do with the Doppler effect. Remember that the selectivity of the radio used in space is such that a Doppler shift will not detune it grossly. Obviously, superdrive will completely ruin such tuning."

"But this has been tried?"

"Yes. It was once hoped that we could link to NeoSol that way. The connection failed as soon as the ship entered superdrive."

"But interplanetary ships employ Z-wave."

"I have had no opportunity to check this on an interstellar scale. I shall at the earliest opportunity. It is my belief that the radio beacons between earth and Venus, for instance, are maintained at both ends by receiver and transmitter, the receiver being used to control the transmitter and keep the beam properly centered and to check its presence. This contact made in both directions along the spacelanes, maintains the operation of the Z-wave on the ship, running at higher than the speed of light. The radio is, of course, useless. But the Z-wave, propagating at some figure we cannot measure yet, suffers no Doppler effect."

"I am Grant Lewdan," said the third. "Has the Z-wave ever been tried in the depths of interstellar space?"

"Yes."

"Did it work?"

"Up to a certain point."

"Then why didn't they pursue it?"

"This answer demands that we all understand the psychology of the human being and the mechanics of the scientific method. I will answer this first by analog."

"Presume for the moment that radio cannot propagate across a space that communication has not crossed previously. Then consider Marconi on his first attempt to send radio waves across a hundred feet of vacant lot. What is the method used in testing an unknown method of communication? The transmitter is started, and the operator either calls or signals by waving his hands, that the transmitter is now working. As soon as the hand signal is seen the receiver is checked, found to be working. Remember, this radio works because of the previous linkage by communication in accordance with our hypothesis. Success is noted.

"Then the distance is increased by many miles from mountain top to mountain top and a blinker system is employed to carry the experimental information back and forth. Again the transmitter is started and the blinker used to inform the other party that he is to watch for the radio's response. Again, it works, since communications have been established. For the third time, the radio equipment is separated by the antipodes of the earth and a telephone or telegraph connection is established. Again the transmitter is started and the signal is sent; again there is success. Now, gentlemen, the inference is that radio will work to a distance encompassing the entire earth.

"Now postulate a spacecraft taking this same equipment to the Moon. Lacking radio, no means of communication are practical. Let us say Venus instead, gentlemen, since a magnesium flare might be used from Luna. So, on Venus, there is no means of communication other than radio, which depends first upon the establishment of other means of communication ere it will work.

"A failure is noted."

"Now," smiled Paul, "this is what happened in deep space. I would like to read an excerpt from the Communications Expedition Number Three:

" '...Two spacecraft were dispatched from Pluto and proceeded outward for approximately one light hour as established by the timing wave from Pluto. The Z-wave was tested and found available...' Here follows a couple of columns of figures regarding strength and so on. '...At one hundred light hours, the same test—was made and found successful...' At this point, gentlemen, remember that they used the timing wave from Pluto to establish their distance, which established radio communications.

"Now, remember the techniques employed in such tactics. It is not necessary for the spacecraft to wait a hundred hours for the arrival of the wave. The wave is sent forth a hundred hours before the ship gets there so that no waiting time will be necessary. In fact, they tried it at one thousand light hours, since that was the distance previously established by the timing wave from Pluto. Again it worked successfully. The timing wave had been started about twelve hundred hours before, and as usual it was so-coded that at any point along the line, the ship could stop listen in, and mark the time. It was sort of, like a rope with a series of knots in it.

"Having made this approximation, the ships went into deep space, about three light years distant from Sol where they were not closer than three light years from any star. At this distance, the radio signal from Pluto had not arrived, and they had no idea of waiting for three years for it since they did not conceive of Grayson's Principal. But they communicated with one another.

"One light hour, waiting for the timing wave, and it was shown successful. I read again:

" 'At ten light hours, there was no success. Our technical officer then spent many hours checking his equipment while the navigating officer used the scooter to run back and forth with Spacecraft BurAst 7,331 to ascertain whether the Z wave gear was in operation. The arrival of the timing wave distracted his attention for a period of about five minutes during which he established the separation between the two ships. Upon returning to the Z-wave equipment and completing his many investigations as to sensitivity and function, he was satisfied that it was in operating shape. At this point it was tried again, and twenty minutes of two-way conversation ensued, proving that the Z-wave was operative at a distance of at least one hundred and seven point three eight light hours, as established by the timing wave. Second Technical Sergeant Frankford Brown was reprimanded for removing the Z-wave gear from the rack and panel and placing it on the test-bench and thus wasting many hours.

" 'The equipment was again tried at one thousand light hours, but no success was found even though ten or twelve hours ensued during the listening test. Because our supplies were now running low, the test was abandoned at this distance and...' Here, gentlemen, follows an account of at least a hundred hours of testing constantly with the two ships at varying distances. Success came sometimes, complete failure at others. There is a complete set of spacial maps, but these show no contours of signal strength nor correlation.

"Only a man who believed that the Z-wave followed radio communications would establish such a correlation."

"And how was this correlation located?" asked Lewdan.

"Because I noted that when failure came, it was noted at distances. 'Approximately ten light hours...fifteen light hours...three light hours.' But when success came, it came at, "Seven, point nine-eight, or fourteen, point four-two light hours. In other words, gentlemen, they knew their separation only when success came and they could measure the distance accurately by the radio timing wave."

During this time, the hands were dropping as the answer to one question answered the questions of others. At the end, there were no more hands upraised. Thorndyke then said: "We are now ready to continue with this lecture."

Paul took a gulp of water and started off again:

"I have one other item to bring forth. I have been working with the galactic survey—" and Paul went on for many minutes, explaining in detail what they had been doing and why. He finished up with his determination to test the Z-wave in accordance with his own theory. Then he said: "I have here a recording made over the Z-wave receiver I took with me to Proxima Centauri I. As you know, the interstellar beacon was erected on the top of the Z-wave Central Building. No visual connection seems necessary, but we all know that dielectric or permeabilic coupling serves in many places far better than a conducting link; it is my idea that similar factors to permeability and capacity will be found in the Z-wave. However Z-wave Central is *all* supplied from *one* power line. Here is a physical connection.

"Upon my arrival at the Proxima Station, this Z-wave recorder was started with the radio. You will hear, in the recording, which was made through a microphone to pick up the room-sounds as well as the Z-wave broadcast, the arrival of the radio signal from Terra, the timing signals, a few of my own comments made, I must admit, in the stress of enthusiasm, and finally, the terran side of an interplanetary Z-wave conversation between a woman and her man. While I deplore any public airing of the personal affairs of any man and woman, this is of the utmost importance to Civilization, while the subject of her conversation is such that she can have only pride in having it made into history. For," he added softly, "hers is the voice of true, honest affection, faith and trust in her mate, and such is well worthy of a monument in the halls of history!"

There was a round of good-natured applause at this moment. And then the recording rang out:

"...but it won't be long, my dear...of course, it seems so... Do that, by all means... In a month, you say? ...I'm very happy about that..." the signal faded and in the background the audience could hear the measured cadence of the radio timing signals, with a few of Paul's own personal comments of exultation. Then the Z-wave signal came in again, "...Terry said so... How do I know...? By all means, my dear..."

Paul turned the recording off amid the thunderous roar of applause.

CHAPTER NINE

WITH A SMILE of self-confidence, Paul faced the cheering auditorium and gloried in the praise. It—this moment—was payment in plenty for years of struggle and of being a third-rate voice crying against the stone wall of authority.

He took their cries of praise with a deferent attitude, but remained on the podium, which indicated that he had more to tell. They subsided after minutes of wild applause, and Paul continued:

"Across the galaxy between here and NeoSol," he said, waving a hand which caused a wall curtain to rise, showing a planar map of the star region between the two inhabited systems, crisscrossed with red and blue lines, "the galactic survey has a veritable network of radio beacon signals. From star to star they go, directly and in cross triangulation, in collateral paths and in long sweeps. The red lines show what distance these radio signals have progressed as of three days ago; the length of the continuing blue lines show the distance between the stars yet to travel ere contact is made. Such is the separation of stars in our galaxy that the next three years will see greater numbers of final contacts made. I shall be a busy man, for I will be making these final, contacts one by one until the entire pathway—tortuous as it will be at first—is open to NeoSol.

"Gentlemen, they drove the Golden Spike in 1869, coupling America's East and West by railroad. Three years, two hours, and forty-five minutes from this very instant, we shall drive the Golden Key home in the Z-wave link between Mother Earth and her distant daughter Neoterra!"

Again came the thunder of applause.

"Thank you," said Paul. "Are there any more questions?"

"One," called a voice from the rear.

"Yes?"

"This recording of the Z-wave was made from Z-wave Central?"

"Yes!"

"Just for the purpose of circumventing any such odium of doubt, is there any method by which you can definitely determine the time of origin of this recorded transmission?"

"Not at the present. It can be established by the radio beacon records that I was on Proxima I at that time—what I hope to do is to have the unknown woman come forward and identify herself and the time she used the Z-wave."

"Then other than that there is no way of proving that this recording might have been made on terra a month before you left?"

"I—"

But Thorndyke interrupted. "Gentlemen," he said, "no man in his right mind would attempt a fraud upon this body. I have no doubt. I firmly believe that Paul Grayson has presented evidence that he has collected in true scientific honesty!"

This brought another round of cheering. And in the midst of it all, the questioner came walking down the aisle toward the platform. Out of the shadows he came, and Paul tensed for the imminent battle of wits, for the questioner was none other than Chadwick Haedaecker.

"Where did you get that recording?" he shouted over the cheers of the crowd.

"On Proxima."

"On the Z-wave?"

"Yes."

"Doctor Thorndyke, may I have the stage for a moment?" Thorndyke nodded, wondering what this was all about. Paul stepped aside as Haedaecker took the podium. "Gentlemen," said Haedaecker, "for some number of months, my young friend here has been avidly attempting to force me into trying experiments made years before. He has a personal, ingrained belief that Haedaecker's Theory is at fault. You have heard his alleged recording—"

"Alleged!" stormed Paul.

Haedaecker held up a hand. Then he pointed out to the audience. "Doctor Haddon, could this message have passed through the Z-wave Central?"

A hush fell on the auditorium. Haddon rose and cleared his throat.

"According to my records, Z-wave Central was inoperative for a fourteen day period immediately following Paul Grayson's departure for Proxima Centauri I. Certain repairs were needed, and the Z-wave equipment was shut down for that period. All Z-wave messages terminating on Terra were shunted through the Auxiliary Tandem Z-wave Station at Oahu, Hawaii. The Proxima Beam was shut down, too, since the radio signal emanating from it would not reach Proxima for four years, and that which Paul Grayson was to measure had been emitted four years ago. It was not deemed reasonable to maintain the beam—"

Paul gulped. "This is preposterous," he roared.

Haedaecker merely smiled. "So is the truth," he said sourly.

Thorndyke said: "Then Doctor Haedaecker, it is patently impossible for the energy relation to have caused the transmission of the Z-wave such as Paul Grayson suggests?"

"Impossible."

Thorndyke faced Paul. "Then why was this farce perpetrated?"

"This was no farce," Paul almost shouted. "Haedaecker has always discouraged anything at all that would cause him to retract his own precious theory. He will lie, cheat, and steal—"

Thorndyke turned to Haedaecker. "Can this be true?"

Haedaecker smiled genially. "Grayson is young and dreamily hopeful," he said blandly. "Grayson has all of the hope and faith for mankind that a Saviour, a Saint, or a complete idiot might have. He believes firmly that if enough people want something to obtain, by sheer effort, will-power, and determination, they can make it so."

"But why was this done?"

"Grayson hoped to stir up enough hope to have a research group assigned to crack this impossible problem."

"It is not impossible!" Now Paul was shouting.

Haedaecker shook his head. "You have no evidence whatever. You are now where you have always been. You base your argument on a hope and a prayer but have nothing concrete to show for it." Haedaecker faced the auditorium with a raised hand. "I am a physicist," he thundered. "And I have been reviled by my former employee, Grayson, for attempting to suppress any ideas that would show Haedaecker's Theory might be in error. This is a cruel attack. Unwarranted and unkind. Like my fellows, I firmly believe that theory always must be bent to follow fact; that when any theory is confronted by experimental evidence to the contrary, it is the theory that must be changed, because the fact remains indisputable! Let but one man show me the error in Haedaecker's Theory, and it will be relegated to the discard by no one quicker than Haedaecker, myself! God Knows, gentlemen, I despair of offering a theory that stands against the innermost wishes of mankind!"

Thorndyke turned to Grayson. "Where did this recording come from?"

"I made it on Proxima!"

"Possibly," said Haedaecker scathingly, "but by what method?"

"It was made honestly!" shouted Paul.

"Honestly," sneered Haedaecker. "With both Z-wave Central off the air, and the radio beacon inoperative; both important factors in your pet idea were not running at the time you claim that this recording was made!"

Paul shook his head angrily. "If the Z-wave Central and the beacon were turned off," he stormed bitterly, "then how did I receive this on my Z-wave Receiver?"

Haedaecker's voice was wholly scornful "A well-planned script," he said, "written and acted by an accomplished actress, recorded by Grayson—doubtless. Mister Grayson your plea that this unknown woman on your record come forward for honor and identification might be accomplished. Which of your many girl friends did this?" snapped Haedaecker with his sudden verbal attack.

"No one—" Paul stopped as the familiar voice on his recording went through his brain as it had so often since he heard it on Proxima I: ...but it won't be long, my dear... Of course, it seems so... Do that, by all means...' And as the well-remembered voice seemed to speak aloud, Paul recalled another voice, the voice of a most attractive woman, replying to his suggestion that he call her: 'Do that, by all means.'

Then Paul knew. Not only the voice, but the mannerism. 'Do that...'

Not truly a command, but far more than mere acquiescence. That was Nora Phillips' way, her voice, her mannerism.

A cold sweat broke out on Paul Grayson's forehead. Two men had died because of this. Why? True, both were criminals, but what possible attraction could Paul's grand dream of interstellar communications have for a thief, a felon, and a murderer?

Two men had died, and then as Haedaecker's technicians cut off the hoped-for sources of signals from Z-wave Central, Nora Phillips had come forward to supply Paul with the necessary evidence to success.

Why? Certainly she could not hope that his unsupported story would stand up against the certain statement that Z-wave Central was down and out. Besides, there was not time for a spacecraft to get to Proxima I between the time that Z-wave Central went off the air and the time that Paul recorded the signal. Had Nora Phillips been on Proxima?

Someone had!

Someone had been there, lying in wait for Paul Grayson—for what inexplicable reason Paul could not begin to name. And someone else had been there, too, lying in wait for the interference. Someone had irrevocably removed the criminal lying in wait for

Paul, and then had blithely furnished Paul with the signal he had been waiting four long years to hear.

The answer was hidden behind the heavy mahogany door at 7111 Bridge Street, despite the placid appearance of a man retired from business, his elderly wife, and doddering manservant. For Nora Phillips had disappeared behind that door.

"What have you to say for yourself, young man?" demanded Thorndyke.

Paul blinked at the chairman. He was completely stunned, absolutely beaten, shocked to the core. He shook his head. "I swear—" he began.

He was interrupted by the shout of "Fraud!" from the rear of the auditorium. Instantly the place was in a violent uproar, those who had applauded the loudest were now shouting for Paul's head.

"Fraud!"

"Throw him out!"

"Liar!"

The stairways at either end of the stage filled with hoarsely shouting men who came up slowly but with determined step, gaining confidence as they advanced.

"Throw him out!" screamed a voice.

"Out!"

"Away!"

Thorndyke hammered on the pulpit with his gavel. He might as well have snapped his fingers at the hurricane. The rap of authority was lost in the disorderly cry of an angry mob. Men of learning, wisdom, education, their civilized veneer hurled away by disappointment, anger, and the smell of fraud, came forward with animal hatred, intellectually naked.

Paul looked wildly around the stage as the foremost of the mob came to the top of the steps. This was the time for escape, whether he was right or wrong, honest or the fraud and liar they called him. No time for argument, only flight.

He faded back against the curtain. They came forward at him, warily awaiting some move of his. Had Paul moved fast, they would have leaped like predators; so long as he oozed back with no overt move, they prowled instead of jumping. Perhaps the only remaining vestige of their lifetime of training was their desire to wait until he struck at them first, that they wanted Paul to strike the blow that would invite them to strike back. This was a mob, lynching mad.

Paul looked over their heads to the fire exit. It was the only avenue of escape, but blocked by twenty madmen. He pressed back against the curtain, wondering if he would get out of this alive.

Then the howling died like the turning off of an overloaded sound amplifier.

For out between the curtains stepped a burly policeman. His nightstick was firm in his right hand, the thong wrapped tight around his wrist. The business end of the heavy stick rested in his left palm. His revolver hung in the holster, its safety strap unsnapped.

He was the very essence of authority: big, uniformed, immobile.

The advance upon Paul stopped. Paul breathed a prayer of thanks.

"You're Paul Grayson?" he asked.

"I am."

The policeman's voice was flat, hard, and dry. "Did you know there was a dead man aboard your spacecraft?"

Paul blanched. Stacey had said—

"Uh-huh. Y'do. Paul Grayson, I arrest you for implications in the murder of John Stacey. Better come quietly. And remember that anything you say may be used as evidence against you!"

Stacey!

The world took a quick spin about Paul's head. Stacey!

There was sudden motion and the quick, lashed Snap! of handcuffs while Paul's tired mind was still racing in the dream-world of complete disbelief. He went woodenly with the police-man.

Behind him, he heard Haedaecker say, "And now it is murder, to boot!"

CHAPTER TEN

THERE IS SOMETHING about a pair of handcuffs far above and beyond the mere chaining of wrist to wrist. Mobility is not decreased, and the flailing of hands against an enemy is not greatly impaired. But the idea of being manacled presents a condition in psychology of complete defeat.

In completely bewildered defeat, Paul Grayson looked down at the chromium handcuffs with an air of blankness. John Stacey—Z-wave—Nora Phillips—

The policeman led Paul Grayson from the hall amid a complete quietness. Only when they were beyond the curtain and heading towards the stage door did the buzz of outraged conversation start, almost covering the pounding of Thorndyke's gavel.

Then the outer door closed behind them and the noise was cut off. Something in Paul's inner mind felt grateful that the car awaiting was a standard model of police car instead of the traditional patrol wagon. There is something even more damning in being carted away in the paddy-wagon.

The completely stunning abruptness; the positive cliff of success from which he had fallen into the chasm of absolute futility shocked Paul into a feeling of unreality. He felt like an outsider, watching a complete stranger being led in docility towards a police car by a uniformed policeman, obviously the perpetrator of some outrageous, illegal, immoral, unethical act. He could not identify this illicit individual with himself. It was a horrible dream—

And in this dreamlike state, Paul took note of a series of completely *non-sequitur details* which his mind recorded in minute detail. He noted a woman in an outlandish hat; a man in tuxedo with a wrinkle across the facade of his boiled shirt. The sidewalk was rough under his feet. The street was asphalt instead of concrete. Mars and Venus were in quadrature—it must be quite early because Venus sets not too many hours after Sol. There was a light blanked out in an electric sign advertising some obscure brand of cigarettes—Merr cool—and Paul wondered quickly whether the missing space represented 'y' or 'i' or 'o' because he did not smoke that brand. A convertible coupe roared past with a redhead's hair blowing back, there was a dent in the left-front hubcap. The police squad car was Number 17. A woman that Paul instantly catalogued as the Boston-Type Dowager sniffed and turned away. A girl giggled as her boyfriend led her towards a cocktail lounge. The handcuffs jangled and caused more attention than the presence of the policeman. Down the street a theatre marquee flashed, advertising a stage production called 'The Bright Young Man!' As it caught Paul's eye, the box office closed and the theatre marquee went dark—

Then having noted more of his urban surroundings during thirteen seconds spent in crossing a sidewalk than he had in several years of living there, Paul found himself installed in the front seat of the police car between two burly officers. Paul was not a small man but he felt like a midget between them.

There was no noticeable grinding of gears nor jerkiness as the car swooped away from the curb, and the siren wailed to clear the street before them. Expertly the driver maneuvered through a red light and turned against traffic, swerving in and among the hesitant cars like a fencer.

Then they were beyond the busy thoroughfare and racing down a quiet street, their own siren creating a shrill that could be heard for blocks. Even inside of the car it was loud; outside it must have been terrific.

The radio broke into life: "Attention! Attention! All cars—Attention!"

The driver and the other policeman stiffened slightly. The driver turned another corner onto a traffic street. Three or four blocks along, the bright blue lights of the police station called like a lighthouse, marking the Journey's End.

"Attention! Attention!" said the radio. "All cars be on the lookout for Police Squad Car Seventeen. Stolen—"

The policeman not driving was fumbling in a pocket; found a jangling set of keys and fumbled with them uncertainly. Then Grayson's manacles fell away as the squad car drove up in front of the police station.

"Lively, Grayson," snapped the driver as the car came to a quiet halt.

Still in a complete daze, Paul obeyed stiffly. He followed the driver out of the squad car from the driver's side, squeezing under the steering wheel and forced by the pressure of the other policeman behind him. He was unceremoniously hauled into a waiting sedan, pushed again from behind, and then before he could get his balance the car lurched forward and away.

"That'll kill 'em," chuckled the policeman that had rescued him from the stage.

"Dump their rig and the drunken cops right in front of the station," chuckled the driver of the police car. Both were shucking their blue uniforms. And the driver of the large sedan was not driving like a maniac. He kept to sane speeds, but used side streets.

"Stolen—?" murmured Grayson. Paul was still dazed. Something was going on but he did not know what. He had been ridiculed, charged with murder, arrested, and—but he had not really been arrested for these were not officers of the law. "Wha—what—?" he blurted.

Both of the erstwhile officers laughed. One of them hauled a small flask from his hip pocket and handed it to Paul. "You've had a rough time," he said. "Take a bracer."

Paul took a big swallow; it was good whiskey that burned just right on the way down. The glow in Paul's stomach took some of the troubled puzzlement; some of the daze from him, but the dizziness and the feeling of unreality remained.

"What's it all about?" asked Paul uncertainly.

"You'll find out later."

"Why not now?"

"And spill before the boss tells his tale?" laughed one of the men. "Just pull yourself together, Grayson. Be happy that we got you out of a bad spot."

"I am, but I don't understand."

"You will soon enough. Take it easy."

Paul relaxed. It was obvious that they would tell him nothing. Some of the daze left, but it left Paul with mixed emotions. Convinced of his own innocence of any crime; equally convinced of his correctness regarding Haedaecker's Theory but completely bewildered as to the latest mix-up with Z-wave Central; angry about Stacey—Paul Grayson was convinced that the right way to handle false charges was and is to face them firmly and display the fact that you have nothing to fear. He had always felt that the very display of self-confidence and obvious indignation over the accusations would carry some weight in his favor. He had read of cases in the newspapers where the murderer was found with the smoking gun in his pocket and the blood on his hands but still protested complete innocence in a baby-faced, wide-eyed manner, but Paul felt that such protestation could carry no weight because the lawbreaker could not be convincing with the truth in his mind working against him. Like everybody, Paul felt that he was different; this was a different case. They would believe him.

So Paul disliked the idea of running. Running away was itself an indication of guilt. He had never been able to define the proper line between the desire for privacy and the necessity of keeping something under cover. Like many other idealists, Paul felt that any man whose life was blameless should not object to scrutiny.

But in this particular case, even while Paul was objecting to the idea of running; preferring to face the music with his convincing innocence, Paul was also aware that one man facing the anger of a mob can do very little to make them listen. He shrugged as a more pleasant thought came to him. He could easily show proof that his escape was not the flight caused by guilt but the honest fear of bodily harm from a mob incited to lynch-heat by the machinations of a personal enemy.

Paul sat up, a bit relieved. He looked out of the window and recognized the street; they were about half way between the middle of the city and the spaceport.

Maybe now he might be able to collect some more information. Still the idealist, Paul could not understand why any man would work violently against a common blessing that could cause no harm. Paul believed that the possibility of opening communications with Neoterra was such a blessing.

But merely starting with a hope and an idea to help Mankind—and make himself famous—Paul had triggered off some inexplicable train of events which included murder, theft, falsification of evidence, impersonation—

Impersonation!

Not only once, but twice—*thrice!* Twice had Paul been impersonated for some reason or another. Now there had been the impersonation of policemen. Twice this impersonation could have been directed only at Paul's discomfort. Now—

He looked at the two men that sat on either side of him.

Friends—or enemies? Had they helped him or had they captured him for themselves? And in either case, what were they going to do with him, after they had taken him—where?

The car turned a sharp corner, slowed in front of a large house, and turned into the driveway.

The address was 7111 Bridge Street!

The elderly gentleman eyed Paul quietly. Stacey had described the man as a doddering old fogy, if this were really Hoagland, or really the same man that Stacey met. But somewhere Stacey's unusually-sharp evaluation of people must have fallen flat, for Hoagland was only one-third of Stacey's description. He was neither doddering nor a fogy. He was old in Grayson's eyes.

He looked sixty-odd. He might have been older, for his type of man tends to retain the appearance of youth. There was a bit of spring to his walk and a set to his jaw; a sharpness to his eyes and a complete self-confidence about Hoagland. He was far from bald, but the hair was white-silver. He wore it carelessly but not unkempt; it was a sort of pride, Paul guessed, to half-mistreat a feature prized and lost to other men.

"Please sit down and relax," he said. His voice was hard and low-pitched and not a trace of cracking-with-age. Instead, it crackled with virility. "You might as well take it easy and save your strength. You're not going anywhere."

"What is this all about?"

"We'll get to that shortly. I have not had this privilege before; I am Charles Hoagland, Mister Grayson. I gather that my boys were timely."

"It was—" Paul started, but stopped lamely. The puzzlement welled up in him again and confusion filled him; confusion that contrasted sharply with this man who seemed to know all of the answers.

"I am glad. A troublesome mob is a dangerous thing. You might have been harmed."

Paul nodded his head quietly.

"Mister Grayson, you are a busy little man."

Grayson stiffened. He did not like the appellation even though he knew that his size was sufficient to give him tolerance at being called little; he did not have to prove otherwise.

"Just what do you want with me?" demanded Paul.

"Mister Grayson, either you are a genius or an idealistic fumbler. We hope to find out which."

"When you find out, will you let me know?" snapped Paul sarcastically.

"Be only too happy to," smiled Hoagland. "So we'll start now. Just how solid are your theories about the Z-wave?"

Paul shrugged. "How solid is any theory about anything?"

"Let's not argue."

"I am not arguing. I am stating a fact."

"You are stating an argument; you have just answered a direct question with a hypothetical proposition."

Paul grunted. "May I ask you a direct question?"

"Ask. I may even answer, depending upon the nature of the question."

"Then, just how solid is your knowledge of science—any science?

"Sketchy. Some men hire carpenters, some hire accountants, I hire scientists."

"Then let me explain my first reply. Any scientific theory undergoes several transformations before it is an accepted fact. For instance, some phenomenon is caught or observed by some experimenter. To explain the phenomenon, the scientist suggests an hypothesis. To further the art, the hypothesis is expanded so that other experiments can be performed. These have the dubious character of predictions; if such-and-such is the explanation, then if we do this-and-so, then something-that will take place. Physical laws and limitations are set up, and while one group works according to these laws, another group will try to ascertain whether or not the same effect can he produced because of some other proposition. Frequently the original observation produces erroneous evidence, and then the conditions are changed to meet the experimental evidence as such progress is made. Eventually the original hypothesis will become a theory.

"In shorter words," continued Paul thoughtfully, "an hypothesis is a suggestion untested. A theory is an hypothesis which is undergoing test and for which some basis of truth is evident. A fact is a theory for which there is considerably more favorable evidence than unfavorable evidence, and a law is a fact against which no one has ever come up with any evidence to dispute it."

Hoagland smiled tolerantly. "And what is Grayson's Principle, and why is this called a 'principle?' "

"Haedaecker's Theory is that the Z-wave will not cross interstellar space because of the lack of solar activity. Grayson's Principle is that the Z-wave can be made to cross interstellar space under one certain condition, and that this condition is a prime limitation even in intra-solar communications. The 'principle' terminology," smiled Paul, "is like so many other names. Pedantically it is a principle because it is a prime factor. On the other hand, the name has a sort of ring to it when spoken aloud. I have an idea that 'Lorenz' is put before the 'Fitzgerald' because of the auditory ring; ending a name with a sibilant makes the possessive case difficult. 'Planck's Constant' rings better to the ear than 'Planck's Factor' and 'Avogadro's Law' is easier to manipulate than 'Avogadro's Principle.' These are not selected deliberately, they are chosen inadvertently by lecturers who tend to emphasize a phrase by its sound—even the unskilled lecturer will do this; a pure scientist with no grandiose ideas will automatically select a name that presents no lingual tongue-tripping."

Hoagland smiled. "Ah, how we progress behind the scenes; from 'Fission-reaction' to 'A-Bomb' because of headline news-print space. Semantics was a fine, definitive term until Korzybski got the word involved with dialectics. Possibly Korzybski decided that 'semantics' rang better to the ear than 'Dialectics.' But let's get back to Grayson's Principle. Take it from there. Mister Grayson."

"The main idea is—"

"I know the main idea. That was your hypothesis, unsupported by evidence. What I am interested in is whether Grayson's Principle has what it takes to become Grayson's Theory."

"I—You mean, was I successful?"

"At last you have arrived at the salient point. I mean exactly that."

"I don't quite know."

"You received a Z-wave message on Proxima?"

"Yes."

"Then—?"

Paul grunted. "Everybody knows more about this than I do. I received a message. I was then informed that it was impossible for me to have received a message because Z-wave Central was not running."

"How do you account for this message?"

"I can't. Maybe," and here Paul looked Hoagland in the eye, "maybe Miss Nora Phillips can explain."

"Who?"

"Nora Phillips," said Paul sharply. "Or have you never met her?"

"Should I have met her?"

"Look, Hoagland," said Paul evenly, "I don't know what this is all about. You've got the chips and the cards and the dice. Your playfellows accused me of complications in the murder of John Stacey, ergo you must have heard of him. And Stacey's only connection with you is because he was engaged by me to find out what kind of game Nora Phillips was playing with me. Since you know the connection all along the line, you are also aware of the fact that Nora Phillips entered this house, and that Stacey came here seeking her, having informed me of the first fact. So since we're all aware of some of the facts, let's not play any more games than necessary to save face, huh?"

"You talk rather boldly for a man in your position."

"Hell's Eternal Bells, should I grovel in fear? You and whatever other factions are shoving me around obviously want me alive for some obscure reason, otherwise I'd have been eliminated instead of impersonated. So long as I am alive I can continue to hope for the future."

"Oh, we have no intention of eliminating you."

"Then what's this mad game all about?"

"We have no intentions of forearming you, either."

Paul shrugged. "It will be useless for you to deny that all this mess has nothing to do with the Z-wave and Neoterra."

Hoagland eyed Paul humorously. "My young friend, you have the makings of wisdom. I am glad to hear you realize that your only cry to importance is your firm belief in the error of Haedaecker's Theory."

"Maybe you won't mind explaining one small item."

"Maybe."

"If—for some reason—I am in your way because of the Z-wave, why was a man impersonating me, who could only impersonate me for a limited time?"

"Occasionally," said Hoagland loftily, "some broad highway to somewhere must be blocked for a limited time only."

"So I got a crack on the skull that wouldn't last. Eventually a man impersonating me would head for Proxima I to do something there—God knows what—while the real Paul Grayson was free to complain to everybody that he was really not on Proxima I doing his job?"

"Someone slipped. Supposing," Hoagland suggested, "that you were held incommunicado while your double went to Proxima I and performed your job, complete with the automatic motion picture cameras you installed for—ah—posterity and Haedaecker's greatness. Your double returns and hands in his—your—report. Later the man leaves for parts unknown and you are released, complete with the conviction that yelling to the Authorities about your imprisonment would be at variance with the report, the pictures, and the job's completion. Everything is done as your ultimate superior wants it done, and then you go to him complaining that you were held prisoner. Or—would you, Grayson?"

"Well, I—"

Hoagland laughed heartily. "You might if you were the simple, honest soul. But Paul Grayson has been making plans to test the Z-wave on Proxima I for a long time and couldn't afford to have someone asking questions as to why Paul Grayson got himself into a cockeyed mess."

"But what would it accomplish?"

"Stall you for some time."

In the back of Paul's mind there was a picture of a very attractive woman offering up eager lips and the warmth of a vibrant body beneath sheer silk—setting up the clay target. He had to know, he did not want to merely guess the answer, he—but Nora Phillips had turned up just as Haedaecker was getting nasty. Had she turned up to stall Haedaecker? Hoagland wanted the Z-wave business stalled for some reason. Nora's actions appeared to be that of someone bent upon aiding Grayson. Even—in the long run—her falsification of the Z-wave reception on Proxima I was one step in getting mankind interested in the problem of communicating with Neoterra.

"So you erased him? When he failed, I mean?"

Hoagland looked unhappy. "Unfortunate but necessary. However, Joel Walsh was a type of character that Mankind can well do without."

Grayson grunted angrily. "Why not bump him first?"

"Until he proved completely useless, he had a place," said Hoagland coldly. "There's just enough bad in the best of us, to quote an old cliché."

"I suppose when a player has enough pawns he can afford to sacrifice."

"Only useless pawns."

Paul looked sourly cynical. "And I am the White Knight?"

Hoagland smiled affably. "And you balance very badly while sliding down that poker. Again your humility signifies the beginning of great wisdom. I'd hardly call you a Bishop."

Paul snorted through his nose. "If we want to make some more puns," he said flatly, "I'll admit that I've been rooked. But who is the queen in this mad game, Nora Phillips?"

"Hardly."

"You mean you'll not tell me the objective. Okay, Hoagland, we'll play one more gambit. I suppose the capture of the White Knight is worth the sacrifice of two pawns."

Hoagland smiled self-confidently. "I call it the capture of a Rook as well as the White Knight for—did you say *two* pawns?"

Grayson eyed Hoagland distastefully. "Who was the guy on Proxima?"

"Proxima?"

Paul sat back in his chair with the first feeling of returning self-confidence that he had enjoyed since the moment of his downfall in the lecture hall. "Hoagland," he said, "you've made me very happy."

"How?" snapped the other.

"I've always had the conviction that God was a swell Fellow who, like the rest of us, was still seeking the completely Holy Truth. But happy, understand, in knowing that He did not really know everything because when He did there was no more future, for Him, for us, for anybody. Equally less-than-perfect is the Devil, who does not know everything either. Hoagland, you're just a minor devil."

"What do you mean?"

"There was a guy on Proxima about to impersonate me—or maybe impersonate the impersonation you provided. I can see one faction bumping off parties of the second part. But Hoagland, old devil, if you don't know about the mess on Proxima, you don't know that instead of one conflicting faction against you, you've got two!

"Because the guy you did not know about was polished off by another gang that you do not know about! How do you like them apples?"

Hoagland blew out a breath that sounded like the sigh of Autumn.

CHAPTER ELEVEN

CONSIDERING THAT the time elapsed between Paul's first contact with Nora Phillips and his meeting with Hoagland was less than one month, during which Paul lived in an incomprehensible maelstrom, the following ten months were sheer boredom. For Paul was removed from 7111 Bridge Street and taken aboard a spacecraft bound for Neoterra, one hundred and forty light years by distance and three hundred and eighteen days by the fastest spaceliner going. Ten months plus, spent in a shell of metal, completely self-contained. There were no viewports for a ship exceeding the speed of light was enclosed in its own warp of space and one could not see out. There was a broad port-dome for the landing and take-off pilot, but looking out through that dome of glass into the awesome nothingness of supervelocity made men a little bit crazy. Some went stark mad.

Time was measured by ship's clocks and ship's calendars, timed in divide-down networks from the master micro-timer that measured the flight-time in microseconds from the moment of superdrive until the end of the flight.

Paul had a lot of time to think, but nothing to do. Eventually Paul knew that thinking supplied nothing but additional complications introduced by his own mind. By the time the trip was half over, the network of fact and fiction revolving around Nora Phillips was so involved that any single additional fact would have destroyed the whole picture. Nora was either angel or she-devil.

It was the latter reasoning that stopped Paul from brooding over the problem. Paul wanted neither saint nor she-devil. One was untouchable and the other undesirable. Paul wanted an uninhibited loveliness, with the indefinably correct admixture of bawdiness and propriety, of Madonna and Magdalene, of soul and sex—*sana mens in sana corpore,* as Julius Caesar would have put it.

The fact that the Galactic Network was progressing week by week only gratified Paul, even though he knew that someone else was racing madly back and forth across the star-trails checking the signals in one after the other. All Grayson needed was the initial radio contact, the Z-wave contact could progress from there.

To while away the time Paul called upon his memory to fill in the spaces between the stellar radio stations between Sol and NeoSol. He did this with the aid of the pilot's star maps which were made available to him. It was a flat map instead of the three-dimensional space-model necessary for true distances, but it served as well as a Mercator Projection of the earth, which is a spherical body and far from flat.

In the space model, the first link was to Proxima, a sort of test link started some time before the rest. There were four other links that led from Sol to nearby stars, spread out in space-angles from one another. From these, each had three or four lines out and still away from Sol, some crossing the near gap and some crossing back between the other first-step stations until a complete pyramidal cross-connection of solid triangulation was obtained.

Then across the longer reaches of space, long-term links were running between longer-distance stations. These would complete other space-triangulations across the galaxy, year by year until the final radio beam from Sol to NeoSol landed, one hundred and forty years from the start.

Each completed link between star and star would improve the surveying of the galaxy and bring NeoSol's dimensional error down and down through the banks of figures best stated by exponents of ten. Astronomers work in light years, man works in miles. An error of a 'light month' in one-forty light years is not much error, but an error of 2,000 million miles is still a long way for man to correct for.

So Paul made a planar chart of the galaxy between Sol and NeoSol, and from memory and calculations he filled in, week by week, the completed links.

The first linkage had been computed and started so that a small group of men (of which Paul was one) could race from star to star checking-in the arrival of the radio beam. It took ten days to go from Sol to Proxima, the rest of the network had been started so that—at the best of astronomical calculations—the whole pattern would end up, one after the other, spread apart long enough to enable the group of beam-checkers to go from station to station.

The map would not be fixed. Stars move with respect to one another, and this factor would be part of the measurements. On a star map or planetarium, this motion was impossible to show from one year to the next, these were 'fixed stars.' But for data fed into the Elecalc to determine the time of drive, the angle, and the velocity, the finest measurement of distance was none too good.

But even some grasp of the true immensity of space, with its tiny pinpricks of solid matter scattered sparsely in a vastness of sheer, black nothing, was lost on the travelers between Sol and NeoSol. For as far as they were concerned the journey was not much longer than the famous voyage of Columbus. Miles meant nothing; there were too many of them. Time was the essence, and ten long months passed between take-off and the ultimate recovery of their own time and space, where the cheerful stars winked out of a coal-black sky.

The dispersion was not too bad. NeoSol was a light-week away, at about a forty-five degree angle from their course and position. The small-copy of the Elecalc went to work in the course computing room and once more the ship took to the silent, black vastness of super velocity until the second drop into reality. They were a half-million miles from Neoterra on the second hop, and there was no room to use supervelocity now, so the next few hours were spent in matching the galactic drift of NeoSol, and finally Neoterra. But after ten months of living in an electric-lighted capsule of metal, a half day of jockeying before landing was pleasant.

But as the ship started to drop down toward the planet, Paul realized with a shock that it was not Neoterra. As space-trained as Paul was, even he could not tell one star or one sun from another until something more featureless is offered for comparison. The planet was definitely not Neoterra, and this Paul knew only because it obviously bore no atmosphere. All he could be sure of was that this star was close to Neoterra as stellar distances went, but which star he had no way of knowing. He knew that the star was not NeoSol because none of the planets of NeoSol were without atmosphere.

Such an absolutely minimum of negative evidence could only tell Paul where he was not; He was not on a planet of Sol nor NeoSol.

As the ship came close to the surface of this planet, Paul noted the radio-relay station below them, and here his recollection bore fruit. This planet was of a star about five light years from NeoSol.

He thought carefully. The star from Sol bore no more than a catalog number, being of insufficient size to warrant notice by the ancients who gave the stars their names. Someone had dubbed the planet Harrigan's Horror in dubious honor of Lew Harrigan, who had been the engineer who put up the relay station and had lived in pressure-buildings for several months.

Harrigan himself would be coming to Harrigan's Horror in about two months to check in the arrival of the beam from Neoterra, just as Paul had gone to Proxima ten months before. Just what Hoagland's crew of cutthroats intended to do on

Harrigan's Horror, Paul could not determine from the myriad of unpleasant possibilities he could conjure up.

But he knew—and he was not wrong—that they would tell him very soon.

Below them, a half-mile or so from the relay station, a small spacecraft stood with its nose in the air. The big spacecraft landed near the small one, and Paul was handed a space suit.

"Get in," said Evans. Evans had been one of the pseudo-policemen back on Terra.

"What's next?" asked Paul.

"Get in—you'll find out."

"Why not let me in on it."

"You'll learn. Get in it or we'll be glad to take you out across this airless planet without a suit."

"That wouldn't do you much good."

"No?"

The man's attitude convinced Paul that this was the termination of any idea of keeping him alive. Up to now they had been saving him. Obviously for this. Paul's faith in the idea that kidnapers do not kill people after keeping them alive for almost a year began to wane. For some reason it had been necessary to keep Paul alive this long, but now—

But Paul had no intention of dying by going out across Harrigan's Horror in his city clothing.

Paul looked across the face of Harrigan's Horror, and blinked. The huge emblazoned registry number was half-hidden around the side of the space ship, but Paul knew every rivet in her. That ship was Paul Grayson's BurAst P.G.1.

A glimmer of hope came. He got into the space suit and was led across to the smaller ship by Evans. A pilot in the BurAst ship let them in through the airlock and swung his helmet back over his head and greeted Evans glumly.

"Thought you'd never get here," he said.

"When did you take off?"

"Hour after you did."

"Been here long?"

"Hundred and seven hours Sol."

Paul looked around. Everything was in place, everything in order. "What goes on?" he asked.

Evans turned to him. "I don't mind telling you. Hoagland has no intention of letting you or anybody else start this Z-wave business between here and home."

"Then why this stuff? Why this set-up?"

"You've stirred up enough interest to make some men curious. Now you'll stop it."

Paul scowled at Evans. "Look," he said testily, "this Z-wave communications is not going to die with me. Killing one man isn't going to stop curiosity one bit."

Evans laughed. "You've stolen a spacecraft belonging to the Bureau of Astrogation, the one filled with Z-wave gear. A fugitive from justice, you've come to this station, which will be the next radio beacon checked in which is also close enough to Neoterra's Z-wave Central for you to make connection and get whatever contact you need for your Z-wave line across space.

"Now, Grayson, Item One: Your ship is a bit roughed-up because of a hard landing, so you can't take off. You've been very busy laying a line from the station to your ship so you can tap into the radio beacon, and so you've used up quite a bit of your air. Since you have not the keys to this station, you cannot get in there, and besides you'll find that your space suit is inclined to be dangerously leaky. In shorter words you're trapped on this ship for want of air, and you'll find that whatever you think you can think of, several others have thought of it first and done something about it.

"Item Two: Harrigan will not be checking this station upon beam-arrival. Like the rest it is automatic, and it will register. Harrigan is going to be very busy elsewhere. In other words, you'll find that your one chance for salvation is to establish Z-wave communications back to Neoterra so you can call for help.

"Item Three: regardless of what you do about it, you will be found here about four months from now, the victim of asphyxiation, caused by being trapped here. You will have done a major effort toward making your Z-wave gadget work. Having failed in the moment of desperation, the two worlds will hear about it, and men will then discount your wild theories."

93

"And if I should succeed?"

"You won't. We're better chess-players than that."

"In other words, Harrigan is a friend of yours."

"That's part of it."

"And I suppose when I'm found there will be all sorts of records and data and frantic experimentation to show that I tried and failed?"

"You get closer and closer all the time."

"But you can't stop progress."

"Maybe we don't want progress completely stopped. Only stalled for some time."

"But what reason can you give—"

"We're not stating any reasons, Grayson. We have our reasons and to us they're good ones."

"But—"

"Stow it. Grayson. And—have a good time!"

Paul got a good view of the picture after they left. His masquerader might have returned from Proxima I with honest data about the beam, but Paul Grayson might as well have been found in a wrecked landing on Terra with evidence that indicated complete failure in the Z-wave. There—or here—what difference?

So in the next few hours Paul ransacked his spacecraft in complete futility. He was trapped on Harrigan's Horror. Had Paul been ten times as proficient as he was with tools and calculations, the BurAst P.G.1 still would have remained where it stood snuggled down in the heat-eroded ground of Harrigan's Horror. His spacesuit—the one they left him—was nothing to wear while wandering around on the sunside of a close-in planet. He doubted whether he could cross the distance between the BurAst P.G.1 and the relay station, even had he the air to spare.

Of course he had quite a bit of air, both bottled and revitalized from the greenery in the hold. But the greenery was none too healthy and the bottled goods were almost gone. His compressor could have been made to work and Paul could have made it to the station, but for what? To stand there and die? Or to die along the route in a leaky suit? Breaking into a fort was no more problem than breaching a relay station from the ground. They had been built to last for years against wind, erosion, burglars, pirates, and/or the pressures of the inner air against airless planets such as this.

But Paul's problem was not merely escape. He might have tried to make the relay station if this place offered any hope. Even then, Paul might have been able as a last-ditch measure, to break into the relay station somehow.

Assuming that he could break into the station, that would let the air out. The only way one could break into such a station without letting the air out would be through the airlock, and breaking into that sort of bank-vault construction was no easier than cracking the wall without letting the air out.

The nearest radio receiving set was five light years away at NeoSol, and if he could beam the radio call, it would take five years—

He looked at the Z-wave equipment and thought. Could it—?

Whatever the rest of the universe thought about Paul Grayson and his idea about the Z-wave, Paul still had faith. Furthermore he knew as much about Z-wave gear as any other man alive, up to and including Haedaecker himself. Evans said that the Z-wave wouldn't work; how bad could they foul Z-wave equipment? Could they foul the junk so bad that Paul wouldn't be able to make repair? Or would they—

Paul tried the radio. Naturally it was silent. But it was not dead. It gave a rattle of cosmic static.

Four thundering blasts came in across the ultra-short wave band, four of the beacon's outgoing transmitters un-modulated, directed at other stations across space to the nearer stars. He tried listening along the frequencies of the local oscillators of the receiving sets set to collect any incoming beacons but he realized that they would not be turned on yet; there was point in keeping the transmitters on, but there was no use in turning on a receiver four or five years before the signal got there. He hit another transmitter and as he listened to the un-modulated signal, it began to pip in a timing-signal sequence that some technician would use five to fifteen—or more—years from now when it arrived at some other star-station.

They had not fouled the radio. But that was like letting a prisoner on Antarctica keep his hearing aid. Not worth a damn for helping him escape.

Paul then tried the Z-wave. It was not dead, so far as Paul could tell. It did not crackle with cosmic static, but there was a faint hiss. Paul wondered about the connection to the station across the plain. They must have some sort of connection otherwise the flanged-up evidence would not ring true.

Paul began to tune the Z-wave receiver, just partly in hope and partly for lack of something to do.

"Damn!" he swore.

"Grayson! Grayson! That you?"

Paul blinked. Hearing things—?

"Grayson! Paul Grayson! Is that you?"

Paul grabbed the microphone like a drowning man clutching a straw. "Hello! Hello Neoterra. This is Paul Grayson marooned on Harrigan's Horror with a low air supply. I'm about two miles from the radio beac—"

"Grayson! Forget it. I know where you are. This isn't Neoterra. This is your old friend Evans waiting around in space until you stop trying things. For all we know, you might be able to figure a way out. Take it easy, pal. Such energy takes a lot of air— and you haven't much left..."

CHAPTER TWELVE

NINE DAYS HAD PASSED according to the Solar clock on Paul's instrument panel. Nine days with the air slowly becoming stale. It was beginning to smell a bit, now. Paul did not notice it particularly, but someone just in from a planetary atmosphere would say that the air reeked to high heaven. His senses were beginning to numb. This was not a fast death, but slow and sordid. Paul yawned constantly, and took deep heaving gulps of air only to try again.

Paul fought sleep. He fought it because he knew that he might drift off to sleep never to awaken. But he had no recourse. Most of his time he spent a-sprawl on the cot in the instrument room because he had too little energy to be up and around and when he fought himself to get erect, there was nothing to do but to curse at the inert machinery. He had tried everything. He had considered everything, even up to and including the start of a diary in the hope that someday someone might find it.

But it was a fruitless task. Sort of like putting a daily account on the bottom of a cave in the hope that someone, someday, might investigate the cave and find out what happened.

He did not know the periodicity of Harrigan's Horror. But the sun—still a catalog number—was running lower along the horizon. The beacon had been placed near enough to the South Pole of rotation so that it could always look at the distant stars to and from which the radio beacons ran. This was a nice job of latitude selection regarding the plane of the planet's ecliptic and rotation for the Galactic Survey beams.

But Paul was dully uninterested in facts. He slept more than he knew and was awake much less than he believed. His dreams were vivid enough to make him believe that he was awake, excepting those that dealt with Nora Phillips and John Stacey, neither of whom could have been there.

He was asleep, dreaming fitfully, when the spacecraft dropped down in a landing that would have made the air on any normal planet scream. It came down at nearly five gravities, its deceleration calculated to a fine degree of precision so that the zero-velocity moment of its computation coincided with the instant of contact. The drivers ceased and the ship settled into the gritty ground of Harrigan's Horror.

He did not hear the swift manipulation of the airlock from the outside controls.

"Grayson!" came the cry. "Paul Grayson!"

Paul looked up dazedly, sitting up. He was weak, and dizzy. But Paul pulled himself erect with the determination that he would not let them see how badly off he was. The very deliberate attempt showed them—showed them a man whose cheeks were hollow, whose lips were a bit blue, eyes glazed and whose mind was dull.

He believed that he greeted them blithely, but what came from his mouth was a dry croak. Then he went to sleep again, sitting up on the cot, complete with a five-day beard, and a shot-to-hell nervous system.

But they wasted no time. Bundling him into a spacesuit, they let the air out of the BurAst P.G.1 with a blast and hurried him to their own ship. Then they took off at six gravities, a force that bent them all into their cushions. It did not touch Paul. He was dead to the world in the first pleasant, honest, comfortable sleep he had since the air began to go foul.

And once again there were a couple of days of timelessness. It was very pleasant to have someone massage your muscles, to be steamed to the boiled-lobster point and then quick-frozen in a cold shower, followed by the ministrations of three dozen professional wrestlers. Gallons of cold water and miles of fresh air, a daily shave with a hot towel and a facial massage, good food and boiling tea, a pipe of aromatic tobacco, forty-eight hours of deep sleep…

And Paul, dressed in clean shirt and slacks and once more back to normal, was facing an elderly gentleman that looked like Santa Claus.

"I'll come to the point," said the elderly gentleman. "I am Franklin Huston. I am one of a group of men whose desire is completely political. This time it is also a bit personal. Perhaps you are one of the few men we can talk to who knows something about Nora Phillips."

"I have met Nora Phillips."

"We know."

"I'd like to meet Miss Phillips again."

"That all depends."

"On what?"

Huston spread his hands. "Possibly upon whether she is still alive."

"Alive!" roared Paul.

"Yes, alive."

Paul shook his head. "If they killed Stacey, they would not stop at—"

There was a moment of silence. "Stacey was killed?"

Paul looked up. "Almost a year ago. Of course, it is barely possible that the news would be here by now. We took off very shortly afterwards in a fast ship, and the official news might be still on the way."

Huston hit his palm with his other fist. "We need something faster than ten months communication-time!" he cried. "Hell! We're no better off than the Pilgrims, hoping for some news from England. Grayson, what happened?"

Grayson started to explain, but half way through he stopped thoughtfully. "I've missed a point," he said. "I don't know that Stacey was killed. After all, the men that arrested me weren't officers. Just henchmen of that guy, Hoagland."

"Quite! Now, while there is a school that seems to apply logic to human motives, or tries to, there is another school that claims that the way people do things are entirely dependent upon their point of view and no one can catalog human nature. Grayson. I've known Hoagland a long time and spent most of that time fighting him one way or another. He is as cold-blooded about murder as a snake. But he is a sort of 'string-saver' as well. Anyone who has a bare chance of chipping in something toward the furthering of Hoagland's plans he will keep alive—and it is no great problem to keep them sequestered off somewhere away from contact until he needs 'em.

"For instance, Hoagland would be disinclined to kill Nora Phillips because in some way she might be useful to him—if only as a hostage. John Stacey is another item; Stacey might be kept alive for some reason. This is a big-time game, Grayson."

Paul grunted unhappily. "A year ago I was a man hopeful of trying out an idea. I've spent the last year being harassed, threatened, kidnapped, and shoved around. It looks like a big game to me but I don't know what the rules are or what the prize is to the winning side."

"You don't?"

"It revolves around me. I can see any number of reasons why people would go to bat for a system that will lead to communications across the galaxy. But for the life of me I can't see why anybody would prefer isolation."

"Paul, as a student, how did your history compare with your math?"

"None too well."

"Why did the Puritans leave England in the first place?"

"Something about their religion."

"The books call it religious freedom. The fact is more likely that they did not like the way things were being run in England. Well, forget that and tell me why the American Revolution was fought?"

"Because of taxation."

"Balderdash. That was just an excuse. I've heard that roar about 'Taxation without representation' every Fourth of July since I was a kid. Sure it was that, but why? Why? Well, because it took months for anything to cross the ocean, letter, information, data, anything. A representative would always be some months behind the demands of his job, and his people would be months behind him. The upshot was that people were being ruled—note that I said ruled—from a distance in time and space.

"Neoterra is being ruled by Terra, remote in time and space. At this moment, Grayson, Neoterra can go in one of two ways. I should say Neoterra and the whole galaxy. This is the crossroads, the fork, the place where one single decision or act will dictate for the future the entire history of mankind among the stars.

"One way is to have each stellar system set up its own autonomous government, an entity in itself, until at long last we have a million stars with its own set of rules and regulations and customs. Then someday someone may discover some means of cutting down the flight-time between the stars, and then we shall have a fine millennium of galactic wars for this reason or that, until the galaxy is settled down to some form of integrated government.

"The second course, Grayson, is to start this thing off with a solidarity. Let mankind spread through the galaxy, but let each new stellar system recognize that it must be a part of the whole, and not a world in itself with no outside interference.

"Remember, strife between men ended with the community, strife between communities ended with the state; while strife between states ended with the country. Finally strife between countries ended with the unification of Terra. But in this unification there is plenty of self-government. Eventually strife between worlds must end with the galactic government—unless we can bypass the colonization, growing into autonomy, and then formenting strife—and this faction on Neoterra hopes that this time mankind will get off on the right foot.

"And the way to do it is to let people know on Neoterra what happened on Terra yesterday and not next year!"

"The Z-wave—"

Huston smiled. "Serene in your own little Terra, you do not even know of the wrangle we are now going through. Of course it takes ten months for a fast ship, and the news is so remote and far away. The President of Neoterra will be elected in a year. We have already two vigorous candidates, one of which is speaking vigorously for autonomy and freedom from Terran intervention. The other is for continued harmony. Promise the people something positive and they will vote for you. But we have nothing to promise—save the interstellar link of the Z-wave. A damned poor offering."

"I'd say it was damned good."

Huston eyed Paul sharply. "How do you know?"

Paul opened his mouth and then closed it again. "I don't know," he said at last. "I think—"

"Not good enough. Not by far."

"But I've been circumvented and frustrated and I—"

Huston slammed a fist down on the desk. "Grayson, we found you and slid you out from under Hoagland's watchful eye for one reason only. You stand as a symbol to the people of Neoterra. You are a possible symbol of communications. With Paul Grayson free to work on the interstellar Z-wave, the political campaign will get a transfusion of new blood."

"When do I start?"

Huston nodded. "Now. But not here. We will have no damned nonsense. The fate of this political campaign rests upon your work."

"I see that."

"Four months flight time from Neoterra there is an equilateral trinary—"

"Latham's Triplets. One of the network beacons is on Latham Alpha IV."

"You will go to Latham Beta III where we have an extra-terran botanical research outfit. You can set up a laboratory there and go to work."

"But why not go back to Harrigan's Horror and pick up the radio beacon when it gets there? We can save a lot of time."

"Grayson, you are a symbol. You may be a tin God with feet of clay for all we know. So far all you've done is to create a ruckus, hollering against Haedaecker's Theory which you have not substantiated by any shred of evidence. Faith is a wonderful thing—I wish I had more of it than I have—but hardly a bulwark against the slings and arrows of life. So we'll not dicker with a proposition that may go wrong."

"But if I am to work—"

Huston smiled serenely. "I've often wondered why they call it 'Political Science' when the main idea is to get your point across whether it is true or not. We'll have no part of any experiments that may deal in failure. You'll go and work on Latham Beta III where reports of progress can be made without having a lot of curious people around to watch the answers."

Paul scowled. "And it isn't going to take more than a week following the initial announcement of success before someone is going to try it from Harrigan's Horror to Neoterra, or from Proxima I to Terra itself. Then what—?"

Huston put the forefingers of his hands tip to tip. "Well, you see, it is not quite as easy as you first imagined. It takes quite a bit of specialized equipment, and therefore the simple test will not work. You'd be glad to make a demonstration, but you are far too busy making a set-up that will ultimately bring a voice-to-ear communication between Terra and Neoterra, which is of course, the final touch. Why bother going through a lot of piddling little demonstrations to prove what you already know?"

"And in the meantime?"

"In the meantime, Grayson, you're going to have to work like the very devil to keep your research even with the reports we are making about your progress."

Paul eyed Huston coldly. "I suppose that was the main idea behind that flanged-up conversation I caught on Proxima I?"

"Yes."

"Nora Phillips has been very helpful, hasn't she?"

"You recognized her voices?"

"Yes."

Huston looked at Paul sympathetically. "I hope for your sake—as well as hers—that she is alive."

Paul grunted. "I've been a sucker."

Huston laughed at him. "And you'll be a sucker again, Paul. Forget it, for the moment. We're all suckers. It makes life interesting that way. You get going and see what you can do. Remember, I'll not hamper any progress. But we will most certainly see to it that any negative reports are multiplied by Minus One before they are made public."

"So—"

"Get what you need for experimentation and see that you make an ostentatious show of it. Drop a few hints about the Galactic Network and make a long-range prediction that within a year or two people can pick up a telephone and talk to friends on Terra."

Paul eyed Huston. "That won't be hard. I'm convinced—"

"Just be properly vague and unspecific. If you've got to talk at length, take a verbal swing at Haedaecker. Leave the political angle out of it; this is strictly science and you're a scientist and not a politician. Besides you've spent so much time a-space that you've lost voting residence anyway. This is at least a free chance for you to work, Grayson."

"I'm not too pleased at the basic conditions," said Paul, "but I am pleased at any chance to do something about the Z-wave."

"Then make the best of it."

CHAPTER THIRTEEN

LATHAM'S TRIPLETS, Alpha, Beta, and Gamma, were at the corners of an equilateral triangle about a quarter of a light year on a side. Beta III was a small planet possessed of a somewhat odorous atmosphere that was unpleasant but not deadly by any means, Beta III was not capable of supporting human life—if by 'supporting' is meant that the planet shall be called upon to accept, foster, and maintain in growing population a colony from Terra without outside assistance. A dearth of light metals on Beta III meant that man got insufficient salt to maintain the chemical balance established over a few million of Terran years. There was an abundance of heavy metals there which eventually caused an upset of the digestive tract. There was also something—or lack of something—in the makeup of the planet and its edible flora and fauna that tended to lower the birth-expectancy rate among couples who lived there. Paul did not care to ask which side of the fence Huston was on; one cultural faction wanted this something—or lack of something—isolated because knowing what it was would permit its eradication and thus cause a rise in the birth rate. The other faction wanted this something isolated for reasons best explained by Margaret Sanger.

But for Paul's purpose, Latham's Triplets was an ideal laboratory and proving ground.

Huston's offer was valid enough; he backed it with a half dozen young technicians to do whatever Paul wanted, and included a group of three small but very fast spacecraft for making tests in space itself.

While the galactic survey had picked Latham Alpha IV because of its ecliptic tilt, and Latham Beta III was semi populated by a few hundred botanical researchers, none of the other planets of the system were being used. Paul selected Gamma II as the third relay station and his group set up both radio beacons and Z-wave equipment on each planet, one of them being not far from the Survey Station on Alpha IV.

Setting both Z-wave gear and radio beacons in operation complete with their timing gear, it was Paul's hope to show that the arrival of the radio beacon wave was coincident with the establishment of Z-wave contact. Then because this short distance did compare to true interstellar separation, Paul would have a talking point to make the big attempt across some real distance when one of the Beacon Stations checked in.

He considered for some time the possibility of sneaking in to one of the already-closed contacts, of which there were many, with many more being completed every week. The thing that stopped him was that the success at the Proxima I to Terra original contact had established the fact that the Galactic Network was functional, and now every station along the line that had contact already made was more than likely to be visited regularly by various technicians for one checking job or another. He would never know just how much time he would have unmolested.

While he had few qualms about working on the stuff, Paul still felt a vague fear at the idea of getting involved with the Bureau of Astrogation, for he was undoubtedly a wanted man on Terra, even if Neoterra did not seem to care. With his crew checking each of his own stations, Paul took off in his spacecraft at a speed just below the speed of light. A microwave beam went spearheading into space, and the velocity of Paul's ship created a Doppler shift that permitted him to receive the microwave frequency as one of the extremely long waves of low-frequency radio. Hour after hour he raced into space, checking both the radio and the Z-wave, raced ahead of the long finger of energy, then slowed until it caught up with him.

Suddenly the idea struck Paul. If he could not safely remain in the vicinity of a radio beacon station that had been checked-in, why couldn't he tap one end of the radio beam while one of his men coupled onto, not at, but near the other end?

Paul flopped ends with his ship and raced back to Beta III.

Twelve days later Paul was floating free a couple of million miles above a planet known only as 'The Ninth Planet of General Star Catalog Number 311' or in bureaucratic lingo: G.S.C. 311 was the star, and the planet was IX. As nearly as he could recall the lineup of the Galactic Survey network, G.S.C. 311 IX had checked-in some weeks ago with another star with a catalog number some five and a fraction light years distant.

The beacon signal from the planet below him roared in like thunder. It overrode the 'zero' position of the volume control enough to drive the loudspeaker into a blubber of noise.

Somewhere five light years distant, Toby Morrow, one of his men, should be waiting. He might have a bit of trouble finding the beacon with his spacecraft receiver at that distance. Noise was bothersome stuff, and the nature of the signal after crossing light years of space was not often high enough to come in strong and clear on anything but the specialized Survey Stations, where the input coils were immersed in liquid air to cut the random thermal agitation of the electrons in the wire.

Paul watched the clock and promptly at 0600 hours he snapped on the Z-wave transmitter and receiver, clutched the microphone and tried to think of something heroic to say. He gave up trying to be heroic after a few seconds, and merely said: "Toby! Toby Morrow! Can you hear me?"

The Z-wave receiver was silent.

Paul tried again and again, calling until his throat was dry, wishing ruefully that he had made a record to play into the transmitter. He pondered on the uncertainty angle; he could not be sure that Toby was observing the same set of conditions as he was, since they were separated in time and space; very well separated by five light years, in a universe that would not permit gross matter to exceed the speed of light, but forced such high-velocity matter into a completely-enclosed bubble of its own type of space.

It had been demonstrated that matter increases in mass as its velocity rises, and the formula claims that the mass becomes infinite as the velocity of light is reached. But space itself is warped by mass, and as the velocity rises toward the speed of light the mass increases until space is warped completely around it, creating a special transitory space of its own. Tests had been made with timed supervelocity missiles running toward an uninhabited, useless planet. The missile in its own warp of space had passed through the planet without making any fuss or mark on either the planet or the missile. Then men had tried it. Obviously matter occupies space, but specially warped space did no more exist for real space than otherwise.

Only the law of equal and opposite reaction brought the ship back to real space once the drive was cut. The potential energy caused by the warping of space released once the power was withdrawn, and like a spring tightly wound and then released, the whole condition returned to its original state of inert stability.

Paul had no way of knowing whether Toby had hit a snag somewhere along the line. Again he thought of the short-term experiments that had been made and smiled unhappily. He would have liked to check Toby, whether his watch was properly set; if his receiver was turned on. But once checked, what was to prevent Toby from falling ill, his watch from running down, the blowup of some bit of vital equipment, the failure of something basic like a power supply filter condenser, or even to prevent Toby from turning off the Z-wave receiver just because the slight speaker hiss annoyed the man, running continuously for better than a week.

All Paul could do was to keep on calling. His first attempt had been steady for a half-hour. He waited for a half hour and then called again:

"Toby! Toby Morrow. Can you hear me?" Paul went into a ramble of talk, just to keep the circuit alive. He recited poetry, discussed physics, and finally he broke into song:

"Round and round and round on the deuterons,
Round and round the magnet swings 'em
Round and round and round go the deuterons,
Look at those neutrons pouring out there!"

Then the Z-wave chattered into life. Paul jumped with excitement and reached for the volume control to bring the roar of voice down to a recognizable level.

"That's a lousy program we've got."

"Well, turn it off."

"Better we should shut the station off!"

"Hey! This is Paul Grayson—"

"We know who it is," came the sharp reply. At the same instant a powerful light flashed into the viewport, and Paul looked to see a spacer bearing down on him. As he watched, there was a flash of orange flame at the nose.

He did not see the shell. But whether it was one of the standard solid rounds used to check whether a planet or meteor were contra-terrene, or whether it was loaded with high explosives, a four inch projectile is nothing to be hit with in space.

His hand reached for the high drive. Paul could outrun any projectile that way, once his ship got started.

But another spacecraft passed at his side close enough to count the rivets, and as it passed him it began strewing space with a myriad of baseball sized chunks of solid matter. To start the high drive now would be death in a matter of seconds. The first few would be pushed aside, the next batch would ricochet from his hull. The batch he met just before he reached the high-space velocity would come through like a shotgun blast shattering a brick of cheese.

"Turn off the Z-wave!" came the command. "Turn it off or the next shot will drill dead center."

Paul hesitated.

Another flare came from the oncoming ship and the shell drilled deep into Paul's spacecraft, among the machinery and stores. Bulkhead doors clanged shut, the whistle of air rose and then fell as some compartment or other down in the bowels of the ship blasted its air out through a jagged hole in the hull.

"Next one will be through your department!"

Paul shrugged unhappily and snapped the toggle switch on the Z-wave transmitter. The other ship came alongside, threw out magnetic grapples, and then they came aboard in space suits through the airlock. They waved him aside and took over the controls of his ship.

Stolidly and silently they drove him toward G.S.C. 311; IX, landed high on a crude spaceport and escorted him to a new building where he faced a hard-looking man who chewed a cold cigar and eyed him with a great amount of pleasure.

"Well look who's here!" he gibed.

"What of it?" snapped Paul.

"Lucky us. To think that of all the stars in the galaxy Paul Grayson would fasten his eye on us! My friend, you have no idea what a shock that Z-wave gave us. We broke three necks getting out there before you could do some harm."

"So you've caught me. But catching me isn't going to stop progress."

"How vitally correct you are."

"You—"

"Pardon me. I am called Westlake. I am what is known as a henchman, hireling, or employee of people who prefer to see the Z-wave communications stalled."

"'How long can you prevent it?"

"Long enough," said Westlake. "After that it can start with a big bang. It would be helpful."

"You aren't going to get away with this, you know."

"Who—me? I'll bet I do. Just wait and see. I do admit that Z-wave communications would be helpful. For instance, if we had Z-wave contact with Neoterra I could find out what happened between the last information I got—which came from Terra—and your subsequent arrival here. Last dope I had was your capture and transmittal to Neoterra where some plan was being cooked up for you. Now, confound it, we've got a few months to wait between my telling the folks back home that I've collected you and what do they want me to do about it.

"Another angle, Grayson, is that if we had Z-wave networks, I could be sure that our friends on the other end of the line were as quick as we were. If we knew that—"

Westlake paused and then laughed. "Hell, if we had Z-wave networks running, I wouldn't have been the happiest guy in the galaxy to catch you."

"You're one of Hoagland's gang."

"That's as good a guess as any."

"Then suppose you tell me where Stacey and Nora Phillips are?"

"Oh, I don't mind. They came with the first line of information about you. In fact, I'll have you meet them. They'll let you in on a lot of things about this place—which will save me a lot of time. Burroughs! Burroughs! Burroughs, see that Grayson gets to talk to John Stacey and Nora Phillips in the closed conference room."

"Right!"

Stacey came first. He looked, nodded, and said: "I was wondering when you'd show up."

"I'm here. But about you?"

"So very simple. The rooker rooked, the seeker sucked in. It's a long time ago, Paul but do you remember when I called you just before you went to lecture?"

"Yes. You'd been to the house on 7111 Bridge Street."

"I left the upright coffin labeled Telephone Booth and walked right between two large determined characters who insisted that I continue walking in their direction. I gathered from their conversation that someone responsible for their movements was irked at one Paul Grayson, and anger at Grayson included anybody else who had been seen talking to him for the past eight years. I was then bundled aboard a spacecraft and brought here. When did you miss me?"

"That's all you know?"

"The Oberspinnenfuhrer is not exactly loquacious. Nor am I an honored guest to be greeted with shouts and glee. These spiders close their trap doors when I am around."

"Oh, then you didn't know that a couple of burly policemen arrested me for your murder."

"They did?" blinked Stacey. "What did they use for corpus delectable?"

"They didn't have to. They were probably the same pair of large determined gents that corralled you. This time they were dressed in clothing that belonged to a couple of real cops."

"And from there where?"

"I was hauled off to Harrigan's Horror."

"Where in the name of—?"

"Planet near to NeoSol, next Survey link station from Neoterra. I was to be used as a decoy or something." Paul went on to explain. "The one thing that did occur to me along the trip to NeoSol was that if these guys would lie about their status, there was no reason to expect the truth about you. Nora now—?"

"She was here when I arrived under lock and key. She is quite a dish of tea, old man."

The door opened again to let Nora Phillips come in. Paul had been right in his appraisal of the woman. Imperfections in her dress or makeup did not lessen her appeal. She had been more than a year and a half without a hairdresser, her clothing was rough-woven crude and cheap. Not a trace of cosmetic was on her face. The light in her eye was dulled, and her litheness had become apathetic. Month after month of hopeless waiting had taken the ambition out of her.

But she was Nora Phillips nonetheless. Paul went to her and put his arms around her. She looked up at him quietly and then put her head down on his shoulder. She did not cry. She did not have to cry.

She relaxed against him and let him hold her; letting Paul give her some of his strength. It was a futile thing. Paul felt that he had no real comfort to offer. In fact he was in just as bad a position as she was.

His hand stroked her head, and she moved slightly, wriggling close to him.

Stacey coughed slightly. "I hate to bust this up," he said softly. "And maybe I shouldn't, because you may not get another chance.

But now—after a year and a half—maybe we all could learn something about what the hell is going on. At least tell me."

Paul tightened his grip on Nora for a moment, holding her close. Raising her face, he kissed her gently before he moved to sit across the conference table from John Stacey.

"Don't you know anything about it?"

"I did mention a slight reticence; a certain lack of volubility on the part of mine host. This," said Stacey pointedly, "is the first time I've seen Nora Phillips close enough to let someone else touch her."

"Careful," said Paul. "This place is wired for sound, no doubt."

"We're not telling anything that the Management does not know," said Stacey. "And if we are, they'll not interrupt. Go on, Nora. Give. Remember, I'm the detective. In the novels I'm the guy who knows all the answers, forms the decisions, finds the clues, and solves the case. Just furnish me with one answer, one clue, one decision, and one solution and we'll have Professor Moriarty in jail by morning."

Nora frowned at Stacey. "You take this lightly."

"I shall—as soon as I can get some—bedeck me out in sackcloth."

Paul, who knew Stacey's manner, shook his head at Nora. He pressed her hand a moment and then said, "Nora, some people get mad at the milkman and then take out their mad at everybody else they meet for a week. The other extreme is Stacey, who has the viewpoint that he and we are still alive."

"I'm that way," nodded Stacey. "No one ever got anywhere by yelling about the bum deal they got. It's the guy who puts his head down and shoves—and the bird that gets mad at the universe because some bum stepped on his foot in the subway is the guy who loses a lot of friends."

"I'm—"

"Forget it and tell us," suggested Stacey.

"This is a political battle," said Nora. Then she went on to explain, as Huston had explained to Paul. When she finished, Paul smiled knowingly.

"What?" she asked him.

"Hoagland's gang bumped off the guy that clipped me because he flopped. But on Proxima there was another guy made up to resemble me—and he was clipped by someone else."

Paul looked at Nora. "Probably the same guy that so conveniently provided a recording of your voice to convince me that I'd solved the problem of Z-wave transmission," he said sharply.

Nora shrugged. "That was Ed Link," she said simply. "What happened?"

"Someone dropped what looked like a meteor shower on the bird."

"That sounds like Link's idea of handling it," she said.

"But the deceased?" asked Stacey. "Upon whose side was he aligned?"

"Not on Hoagland's."

"Certainly not on Huston's."

"Nora—tell me—why did you make that false recording?"

Nora looked at Paul, and then pulled him to her and hugged his head against her cheek for a moment. "Paul, as a scientist you couldn't understand the man on the street. We wanted something to show Neoterra. You don't understand this. But Paul, what would have happened if you had gotten away with it?"

"But I did not."

"Just pretend. Set up a hypothesis for a minute. Suppose that you had been able to convince the Terran Physical Society that you had received Z-waves from Terra while you were on Proxima I."

"I'd have been the man of the hour. I'd have been handed a large appropriation and a project of my own to pursue this—but Nora, it will work. Why did you feel that you had to falsify?"

"Paul, you are the only man in the known universe that does not think Haedaecker's Theory is valid. Please go on—please?"

"So I'd have been able to pursue my work unhampered, and—"

"Now suppose that you were unable to make the Z-wave contact again?" suggested Nora. "Remember, the recording was the only contact but the Z-wave—regardless of your belief—does not really work."

Paul shrugged. "Lacking a repeat, I'd have begun to study the connection a bit more," he said.

"So the upshot would have been—*Hope*—for those who wanted communications between Terra and Neoterra."

Stacey looked wistful. "Quoting some great poet that I don't remember other than that it was not Edgar Guest or John Paul Jones:

"Of all sad words of tongue or pen
The saddest are these: It might have been!"

"So what do we do now?"

Paul looked at Stacey. "This is G.S.C. 113; IX. Hoagland's gang have Z-wave equipment here, probably trying to see whether or not I am right. So the thing to do is to get free long enough to use the Z-wave equipment for a call for help."

Nora shook her head. Paul looked at Stacey. Stacey looked at Nora and said, "I don't know anything about it." Paul looked at Nora.

"Don't you believe either?"

Nora clung to him, hugged him to her, cradled his head against her soft breasts and caressed his cheek. "Paul—Paul—Paul; I do so desperately *want* to believe—I want you to be—everything—I want you—"

Paul relaxed in her arms for a moment then moved away from her; holding her by the shoulders and looking her straight in the face, he said, "But—?"

Nora buried her face in his shoulder. A sob wrenched her and she clutched at him frantically.

Then she looked up with tears welling on the brim of her eyes tried to speak but choked and buried her head in his shoulder once more.

Paul put his hand under her chin, lifted it from his shoulder and with his other hand dashed the tears from Nora's eyes.

"Tell me," he said gently.

"Paul—Paul—oh Paul, I love you and this hurts—but for all of your faith, you have not one shred of evidence."

CHAPTER FOURTEEN

LIKE MOST HUMAN BEINGS, Paul could comprehend the actions of someone of his own type. But he could not understand the mental machinations of people who had other motives and other interests in life. Nor could he seem to make other people understand that his continued interest in the Z-wave was only just and sensible. After all, he had never had an opportunity to try it.

To Paul it was just that simple. Just let him try it. He had so much faith in it that he could not foresee his next reaction if failure came. Paul did not consider failure as a possibility, but if he did fail, he would automatically begin insisting upon a chance to continue, insisting that something had gone awry, or that there were factors that must be studied.

This sort of attitude was acceptable to Paul, yet he could not comprehend the contemplated action of the political factions he was involved with.

For instance, one faction was going to falsify evidence in order to swing an election. This seemed dishonest to Paul. He wondered just how they could justify their act. The other faction was keeping him prisoner so that he could not furnish any evidence at all.

But eventually one side or the other was going to find that its evidence was in error. Then what? Supposing because he had been kidnapped by this particular gang and thus gave some concrete evidence of negative result, Hoagland and Westlake and the rest were elected—after which the Z-wave contact proved good? Or, if Huston and his crowd got elected on the strength of the Z-wave contact, and then because Paul was captive and unable to make it work, there was no Z-wave communication with Terra.

How could they justify their claims in the face of the emptiness of their prophecies?

Paul could not understand the political mind and the thinking of the man on the street. He could not even apply such thinking to his own case. The fact that for eons, politicians have been making promises that were unfulfilled after election did not register with Grayson.

The thing to do, of course, was to escape. Then he could work and bring out the truth—which to Paul was single-valued and positive—and thus do away with all of the half-truths, lies, and fingers-crossed statements.

But how? He had to admit that he was not ill-treated. He believed that both sides were willing to have Z-wave contact with Terra, for commercial reasons, but he knew that only one side wanted communications now. Ergo the opposing side which were his captors would treat him well in the hope of having him work for them once the election was over.

Paul shrugged. Whatever the cause, he would not cut off his nose to spite his face. His was no interest in political fray. He wanted to work with the Z-wave.

In fact Westlake and Hoagland had one facet that looked reasonably good. Their party was for autonomy, and if Paul worked for them, he would be forever free of any legal attachment to Terra. And doubtless Haedaecker and the whole Bureau of Astrogation were out gunning for Paul Grayson if for no other reason than the stolen BurAst P.G.1. Were Huston and his coalition government to get in, Haedaecker could swing a large club over the various integrated wings of government and make Paul's life precarious.

So Paul was on the fence so far as his work was concerned. In fact, at the present moment Paul did not think highly of either political ambition, since their high ambition was tarred with a wide, full brush of downright thuggery.

Escape, of course, was an easy word to say. It was true that Paul's incarceration was nothing like being cooped up in a jail cell. His door was closed but not locked; he had plenty of time and opportunity to see and talk to both Nora and John Stacey, and to make friends with other political prisoners. Across the broad plain was a spaceport and some spacecraft that came and went, but going there and taking off presented the problem of getting away with it. He was somewhat reminded of the signs reputed to be placed around the penal grounds on Antarctica. There were maps of the South Polar Region of Terra, with latitude, longitude, and the distance in miles from the penitentiary to the nearest shred of civilization carefully and accurately marked. Listed below the maps was a roster of average temperatures for the district at any time of the year, and the whole thing was a great deterrent to walking out of the place and trying to cross a few thousand miles of very cold nothing in order to get to one of Civilization's Southern outposts—where the escapee's name would be posted long before he could arrive.

The only way a man could escape was to have some means of communication so that friends could come to his aid. Paul's only method of contact was the Z-wave.

They did let Paul tinker, and they even let him work, but they would not let him near Z-wave equipment that was connected with the radio beacon. Toby Morrow helped Paul with calculations and theory, being the only one among the prisoners who had done any work with Grayson.

Morrow, of course, had been picked up by Westlake's crew on the planet at the other end of this leg of the Galactic Survey Link, along about the same time that Paul had been grabbed near G.S.C. 311; IX. It was apparent without saying anything about it that Westlake's gang had been working with the Z-wave in the hope of establishing the validity of Paul's statements.

But so far, they had not been able to make contact apparently, and Paul had not been able to, either.

So as the days passed into weeks, Paul once more reconstructed his map of the Galactic Survey and connected this star with that, and the other with the fourth. It was beginning to fill in, now.

Paul viewed it with interest, occasionally wondering who was checking the beacons in his place.

But it was filling in, and it reminded him somewhat of that game played with dots, in which each player takes a turn connecting two dots with a line, the idea being to complete squares yourself while preventing your opponent from completing any. Usually the first several moves are drawn here and there with no particular pattern. Then as the game progresses, more and more lines connect more and more dots until it is impossible to draw a line between two dots that does not also connect two other, previously drawn lines.

The galactic map is far from a square, otherwise all of the lines would have terminated at the same time.

Even so, there were whole lengths of solid line, zigzag across space between the nearer stars that would make a solid connection between stations thirty-to-fifty light years apart. And every week saw another connection made, and each connection completed the connection between isolated groups. It took on a maze-like appearance; Paul thought that if it were stretched out and the collateral paths were added, the thing would have reached between Terra and Neoterra and halfway back.

So Paul added to his map as the weeks went on until there were only a few open stretches between Sol and NeoSol. He thought ruefully that it was a damned shame that the whole Galactic Network would be completely closed before he got a chance to try the Z-wave. Instead of starting with one contact and working his way across, the first interstellar contact via Z-wave might well be a complete attempt between the two planets, one hundred and forty light years apart.

It was a curious proposition; Civilization had been geared to a constantly accelerating life up to the time that Mother Earth and her daughter colony obtained—and found that they were irrevocably separated in time and space by about ten months and one hundred forty light years. Fast, pre-guided spacecraft could hiss through the distance as message couriers in about eight months, but the power needed for such ships reduced the payload. But letters were the best means of communication, for a businessman would be out of touch for at least twenty months if he went himself.

So Mankind struggled along as best it could, hoping that someday someone would be able to lick the problem.

Even Paul's group was able to witness the regular arrival and departure of couriers and men who came on official business. When one of the faster ships brought Hoagland himself, none of the prisoners gave any special attention to his arrival.

Hoagland told to Westlake, "That was a sharp job, Westlake."

"I thought so."

"But your report forgot to mention one item. You did state that Grayson was trying to tap the radio beacon from a couple of million miles out, and that you caught him and his partner on the other end of the beam. But you forgot to mention whether your own experiments were successful."

Westlake laughed. "Only in catching Grayson and Morrow. That was coincidence of the upper brackets."

Hoagland smiled. "That it was," he said. "But have you gotten any evidence?"

"None. We'd been trying Grayson's idea for months without success. When the Z-wave broke into life we thought it was working until we located the source and went out to pick him up. The boys at the other end heard the same thing, did likewise, and then came scurrying back home to let me know about it. So we collected Grayson and Morrow in two fell swoops."

Hoagland nodded again, and then said: "Westlake, how good a gambler are you?"

"I like to play safe," said Westlake.

"How safe?"

"Plenty."

"Then you won't like this. But I'm going to make one gamble, and one bet on a certain thing."

"Yes—and which is which?"

"Without a doubt Grayson got the equipment he was using from Huston and Huston's crowd of coalitionists. They set him up on some planet with a laboratory under their direction, and are probably running the Neoterran Press ragged with glowing reports of Grayson's howling success—carefully guarding their statements with cautious warnings that The Public must not expect Z-wave communications with Terra overnight, but someday-soon-et-cetera, and so forth."

Westlake laughed. " 'The police anticipate an early apprehension of the criminals,' sort of thing."

"Exactly."

"Furthermore I will be a bad prophet if I am incorrect in assuming that when Huston started Grayson on his job, Huston gave orders that Grayson was not to do anything that would gain him any notice whatsoever. On the idea that the first mention of failure would puncture Huston's political propaganda."

"All reasoning based upon the 'what would I do?' theory. Good and sound I calls it."

"Right. Now, here is the certainty. If Grayson is the kind of idealist that I think he is, Grayson will at the first opportunity make some check of the Z-wave—in fact, he has tried to set it up already. He will try again if he is permitted."

"That's your certainty."

"Now for the gamble. I've read all of Haedaecker's Theory and find it solid. I've read Grayson's line of reasoning and find it logical."

"Then which is right?"

"Haedaecker based his reasoning on fact. Grayson set out to poke holes in it and—like so many idealists—he proceeded to leap upon any facet that supported his theory against Haedaecker, while discounting anything that mitigated against him.

"So," smiled Hoagland affably, "the thing to do is to permit Mister Grayson's escape in a ship loaded with Z-wave gear. Let him take his friends, Phillips, Stacey, and Morrow."

Westlake nodded slowly. "I get it. Grayson will not make his next attempt in secret. He'll try it and we'll have observers to watch—and report his failure."

"Right."

Not much later, Hoagland's ship took off for Neoterra. Another ship took off for Terra with messages. Out across the broad plain, Paul could see from his window that the only ship remaining on the rough spaceport was his own spacecraft; the one furnished by Huston. Morrow's little job had been taken off somewhere. Paul shook his held unhappily. Someone was willing to pour a lot of money into this business. Spacecraft were expensive, yet they were being bandied about and traded like horses in a rustler's camp.

While all Paul needed was entry to that one spacecraft over there, plus about ten minutes of free time...

Grayson paced his room until dark, muttering and grunting un-happily. Time and again he returned to the window to look long-ingly at his spacecraft, and time and again he wondered whether it would be possible to steal out across that mile or so of sheer flat plain and get into the ship without being seen. In broad daylight it would be impossible. But the encampment was somewhat south of the Polar region where the big beacon station was situated, and the planet was progressing along in its year so that very soon the beacon station would be entering the half-year of night. The encampment had been in perpetual daylight, a 'Land of the Midnight Sun' latitude. But now there was a short night beginning, which would lengthen as the year progressed.

It was dark...dark...

Paul looked out of his room. The corridor was dark. Deliberately, Paul stood there with the door open, waiting. He had gone out before, but had not gone far before someone came sauntering by to engage him in conversation. Pleasant conversation that carefully avoided mention of the fact that this talk was between jailer and prisoner and that one was keeping an eye on the other.

Paul sauntered down toward Toby Morrow's room. The door was open and Toby was fiddling with something at the top inner corner of the jamb.

"What gives?" asked Grayson.

Toby jumped like a startled doe, settled down as he saw Paul, and then took a deep breath. "Don't scare a man that way," he complained. He took another deep breath. "I've just discovered the burglar alarm," he chuckled. "And fixed it!"

"From here?"

Morrow waved at the open door. "Been open for an hour. Nobody came. Thought you were it, Paul."

Grayson smiled. "I doubt that you did much, Toby. Something's blown out somewhere. I got out without fixing my door and no one came for me, either."

Morrow nodded thoughtfully. "Most alarms are designed so that any tinkering with them will result in sending the alarm," he muttered. "Closed-circuit propositions. I'd just located the contactor on my door and was jamming it shut. That would take care of my door but not yours. Now let's see what could be wrong—"

Paul grunted. "Let's not waste time in figuring out what's wrong with the enemy's burglar alarm," he said. "This is no time to be overly helpful. You go collect John Stacey and I'll find Nora Phillips and we'll meet down in the front hallway."

"What gives?"

"Sitting here like a fool doesn't make me happy. I want action. Why don't we try to get away, Toby? What can we lose?"

"Nothing but some breath. Okay, it's a deal."

Paul went down the stairs cautiously, along the corridor below until he came to Nora's room, and then without rapping he opened the door and stole in, closing the door behind him.

"Paul!" she cried. "What—?"

"Collect yourself," grinned Paul. "We're leaving." He did not think until much later that he had not bothered to knock, nor had he apologized for bursting in this way. It had come as a natural way, a normal thing. Modesty, propriety, and convention were only words and totally useless commodities when escape from imprisonment looked possible. And it was also much later before Paul realized that Nora must have agreed with him, for she wasted no time. In the darkened room there was a wild flurry of arms, legs, and clothing, a nightgown dropped carelessly on the floor and trampled as Nora slid a dress over her head and at the same time tried to fumble her feet into her shoes.

There was the whisk of a hand smoothing cloth over skin, and then a quick step. Nora bumped into Paul, and clutched at him. He put his arms around her and held her for a moment, enjoying the warm softness of her against him.

Then he turned away and led her to the door.

They met Stacey and Morrow in the downstairs hall. "Okay?" he asked in a hoarse whisper.

"Looks so," said Morrow.

"I don't like it," said Stacey.

"Why?"

"Looks too easy."

"Don't be so everlastingly suspicious," said Nora.

"Oh, I'm not the type to admire the denture of a gift horse," responded Stacey. "Not until later. So let's get going."

Paul opened the door. "This is it!" he snapped. "Run for it!"

"Wait a minute," objected Stacey. "Not straight. Head left, you two. We'll go right. Cut a large circle and don't run. Just walk as fast as you can and be as quiet as you can. It's as dark as the Devil's hip pocket out there, but sooner or later someone will realize that all is not well with the Boys at Home. Now!"

"Now!"

They separated. Blind-black outside compared to the lights in the hallways of the house, Paul and Nora picked their way carefully until their eyes became adjusted to the dark. Then they could see the dim lights of the buildings across the plain. They left their former home and swung wide, angling away from the line between the house and the ship. Paul paused once, listening, and heard a faint crackle from some distance—either Morrow or Stacey had stumbled over something.

They were halfway there before any hue-and-cry was raised. Each pair had gone out in a diamond-shaped course until house and spaceship were almost a ninety-degree angle apart.

Paul wondered; they were far from the house it was true, but they were almost as far from the spacecraft now as they had been when standing on the front steps of the house. His mathematical mind made a quick computation and he smiled, audibly chuckling.

"What?" said Nora in a low voice.

"I was just thinking that we are now point seven zero seven of the original distance from the spaceship."

Nora laughed gently. "Some man," she said. "Has no time to kiss me in my room, but has time to play trigonometry here."

Paul patted her gently. "Trig is something I can do without putting all I've got into it. No—"

From a distance there came the faint ringing of a bell.

"Nice man," said Nora. "I forgive you—until later."

Lights went on across the plain, men stormed out of the big building and leaped into a command-car parked on the road in front of it. The command car roared into life and started across the plain toward the dormitory.

"Now!" said Paul. "Down!"

They hit the dirt side by side as the headlights swung around. Then the beams of light were gone and Nora and Paul were upright once more and running.

Noise meant nothing in face of the roar from the jeep's engine; the car was careening across the plain madly, and Paul knew that no one aboard the car would be able to keep a sharp lookout for any running figures. About all they could do was to hang onto the racketing jeep.

The spacecraft loomed larger before them. The roar of the jeep died as the car reached the dormitory, and Paul looked back over his shoulder to watch the men pile out of the car and head into the building on a dead run.

"Faster!" he breathed.

The ship was a hundred yards away—and Paul could see Stacey and Morrow running in from the other side—when there was the roar of the engine again. The headlights swung around to catch them, but this time they did not care. It was run for it; no time to play cat and mouse. The engine whined high. Paul put on more speed, running away from Nora.

"Paul—"

"Come on," he snapped over his shoulder. "Don't talk—run!"

He raced away from her, outdistanced her; the jeep's roar coming louder and louder.

Paul reached the spacelock and fumbled with the outside controls.

Ponderously the lock opened, swinging aside just as Stacey and Morrow came panting up.

"In!" snapped Paul. Then he turned, caught Nora's hand, and hurled her headlong through the opening. He leaped in after her, tripped over her sprawling ankle, caught the flipper switch to the door as he fell, and scrambled to his feet as the spacelock door started to close.

The roar of the engine still came through the closing slit; a shot pinged against the steel hull. Paul forgot about the spacelock and headed up the runway to the control room.

He hit the control panel with both hands; flipped the warm-up switch and the low-drive at the same time. It would be a ragged take-off, with the ship rising as the driving generators warmed up instead of taking off with a hot drive. He waited with one hand on the high drive switch, waited and waited and waited. Another shot pinged against the hull, one glanced from the view-dome but it was at such an angle that it merely nicked the ultra-hard glass but did not crack it. It sang off high into the air.

Stacey and Morrow came into the control room, panting, and half-carrying Nora between them.

"What are we waiting for?" snapped Stacey.

"Getting up steam."

"What is this, a Stanley Steamer?"

"Just takes as long," grunted Paul. Then the low drive took hold. The ship lifted uncertainly, awkwardly, quaveringly, and slowly. Not the quick rush-upwards of the well-prepared ship. But as the seconds passed the ship steadied, the controls got less mushy, and the drive became more certain. A light flashed in through the port, their erstwhile jailers had aimed a spotlight on the ship, and with the light there came the pattering of gunshot. A flat bark came from below and Paul braced himself for the impact that did not come. A miss!

Then he snapped the high drive and the floor leaped upward under them. Chair cushions flattened, and then filled out again as the hydraulic compensators went to work. Behind them the planet diminished in size visibly, and then, at once, the viewport just became black and featureless outside.

Paul leaned back in the pilot's chair. "Wow!" he yelped.

"Made it!" said Stacey.

Paul got up and went over to Nora. "I wasn't running away from you," he said plaintively. "It takes time to get the door open—"

"I forgive you," said Nora with a smile.

Back below them, Westlake said: "You're sure you missed?"

"I'm a master gunner," said the other. "It takes a good gunner to miss a ship that big when it is that close. I missed all right."

Westlake smiled. "We sure made that look good. But God what a job of timing! I thought we were going to have to blowout a tire to keep from catching them!"

CHAPTER FIFTEEN

ONCE IN SPACE and safely away—Paul gloated that the former captors were without spacecraft now—he stopped the flight of the ship and spent a couple of hours making some course-calculations. The return to Latham's Triplets was jerky because he was uncertain of the distance and so they made it in five approximations, ending up finally with only a few hours to go for landing.

Paul's first interest was his laboratory set-up. There had been plenty of time for the three-way hookup to be established, and for all he knew the boys he had set to checking it might have completed the connection, proved in the Z-wave, and gone home to Neoterra with the glad news in their hands.

He entered the laboratory on Latham Beta III, and his face fell. Dust covered the equipment, the pilot lamps were out, and obviously nothing had been done for weeks, if not months. It was untenanted and untended.

Paul went to the supervisor of the botanical set up.

"I don't know, he said with a certain disinterest. "Your boys fooled around for a couple of weeks after you left and then decided that you'd gone for good. They might have sent word back to Neoterra, but it seemed a better idea to pick up and go home. So they did."

Paul went back to the laboratory. Nora said, "Paul, let's go to Neoterra."

"Why?"

"I want Huston to know I'm all right."

Paul looked at her blankly. "They might have left the radio beacons on," he mumbled.

"What?"

He told her again.

"But we'd best get to Neoterra."

Paul shook his head. "Nora, Latham's Triplets is one of the best places to test this Z-wave in the system. I've got to stay and check it."

Nora shook her head. "Paul—"

Paul looked at her. "Nora," he said soberly, "we're at cross purposes again. Two things are important in my life. One of them is Nora and one of them is my work. My girl and my work do not agree—or let's say that my girl does not agree with my work. Until I get a chance to prove my work, there will always be this conflict. Since it takes such a short time to prove my work, why not wait?"

Nora looked up at him. "I'll wait," she said simply.

"Will you marry me—now?"

Nora smiled. "Yes. If you don't mind a wife with literally nothing to wear. Everything I own is on me right now, but won't we have to go to Neoterra?"

"Here we go again," growled Paul.

Nora laughed and kissed him. "Do you want to wait three months for the radio beams to cross Latham's Triplets?" she asked him.

"I—wait a minute!"

"What, Paul?"

"It is barely possible that—" his voice trailed away as he eyed a dusty calendar on one of the desks. He went to it and began flipping pages. "It's barely possible that my gang did not turn off the radio beacons for a couple of weeks after I got caught by Westlake," muttered Paul. "Just barely possible—"

He went to the beacon receiver and turned it on. Impatiently he waited for it to warm up.

It came to life and Paul tuned carefully through the band where he expected the beacons to come through. There was silence. He ran the dial far to one side, and then to the other. At one point he picked up some 'side splash' from the big interstellar beacon on Latham Alpha IV, leakage from the tight beam.

He sat up stiffly.

"Nora, will you wait a week?"

"Week?"

"I've caught some of the radiation leakage from the big transmitter. We can use that."

"And if you fail?"

"I won't fail."

"Then if you succeed?"

"Nora, if I succeed, I'll ask you to wait another three months. Because if I succeed, I'll want to wait until the Galactic Survey link between Latham Alpha IV and Old Baldy comes in. Then—"

"How are you going to check between here and Alpha IV?"

"Stacey and Morrow and you and I—" he said. His voice trailed away for a moment, and then he forgot what he was going to say because he was busy with the instrument panel.

Albert Donatti had been editor of the Neoterra *News* through three changes of policy. The *News,* claiming to be politically neutral, was definitely neutral on the coalition side, presenting the autonomy party in less than favorable light, while tending to gloss over any missteps taken by the coalitionists.

Like the other newspapers, the Neoterra News subscribed to the NeoSol Wire Service, and so Al Donatti got the same news that the other subscribers did.

Al had been sitting at his desk all morning trying to think up something bright and brilliant to say about Huston and his plans, or something bright and derogatory to say about Hoagland's gang. Even Donatti had become tired of making the same veiled remarks regarding the possibility of furnishing Terran and Solarian news before it was ten months old, but he knew that the one way to hold the home tie was to keep on offering hope.

The virtual disappearance (for Hoagland was not inclined to give out his plans) of Paul Grayson had put a crimp in the schedule, for they never knew when they said one thing whether the other side would be able to come up with incontrovertible truth to the contrary. With a few less facets to play upon, the editorializing of Huston and the Z-wave was almost reduced to the constant harping on a single subject—which is tiring even to the most ardent enthusiast. Even a faithful believer wants some shred of proof.

So the coalition party was in the same state as a prizefighter who has trained too fine; who has reached the pinnacle of physical perfection some time before the fray. The additional newscopy that would have been furnished by Paul Grayson's presence among the coalition group had been diminished. That additional space would have kept the campaign rising upward.

It had been a long dry stretch, even for an imaginative editor with a bill of goods to sell. Manufacturing news is one of the hardest things in the world after the process has gone on for month after month. Donatti was reaching the end of the string, and there were still months to go.

Donatti groaned, and then looked up to see a copy boy approaching, waving a reel of recording tape in one hand.

"Yes—?"

"Z-wave! Z-wave!" said the copy boy breathlessly.

"So what—?" grunted Donatti, taking the reel and slipping it into his playback.

It started: "NeoSol Wire Service. Neovenus, Four August. Archeologists today discovered the traces of a crude civilization dating at least seven thous—"

Donatti groaned. That would make page eighteen, sandwiched between an ad and the local theatre column.

"—and years old. No trace of this civilization remains today. Crude pottery and some stone arrowheads—"

"Crude pottery and stone arrowheads," snapped Donatti. "So what? What's this Z-wave business?"

"—were found among buried sub-humanoid bones. It has been an elementary principle among archeologists that proper burial of the dead is an indication of intell—"

"Hell!" exploded Donatti. "Z-wave! So this thing came Z-wave from Neovenus. They all do!"

"—igence. The arrowheads bear a remarkable resemblance to prehistoric arrowheads found on Terra. However no connection between the stellar planets can be assumed, since arrowheads are a natural bit of design among primitive peoples and—"

Here there came another voice! Superimposed upon the dry voice of the commentator for NeoSol Wire, the whole was almost impossible to decode and separate:

"—like the lever as the basic simple machine which would be *"Stacey, Morrow! Can you hear me? I'm on the air."* "Yes, discovered as soon as the first man discovered how to use a *by all that's holy, we hear you! Or at least I do! Morrow? This* stick of wood as a means of prying a large boulder aside from *is Stacey on Latham Alpha IV, can you hear us on Latham* the opening of a likely cave, the similar use of a lever some *Gamma VI?"* "This is Toby Morrow, fellers. Both of your *sta*—where else in the galaxy would not mean that some cultural lions are coming in like a ton of bricks:" *Nora, now will you* connection had ever existed between the distant cultures. How— *believe me?" "Paul. I do want to believe you, but isn't this a* ever it is of basic interest to know that there was a civilized *rather short distance as interstellar distances go? Three light* culture in the galaxy other than Solarium Humankind. Doubt—*months is not anywhere near as far as several light years.* less as the galaxy is explored, other cultures and civilizations *"But this is just the beginning! Can I bring you the rest?"* will be discovered. It is more than likely that other civiliza—*"Do that, my dear and you will have forever proven your* —tions will be found which are still thriving. In fact it is not *place." "With you'!" "With me'! No, Paul, I mean with the* unlikely that our technical perfection may be overshadowed *worlds of science and men. You should know your place with* by some greater culture whose history of development may *me."* *"Should I?" "You should, Paul." "Where?" "You wouldn't* extend back earlier than the history of Mankind. *want me to say this over the air?" "Not hardly."*

Donatti listened to the unmistakable sounds of ardent osculation with a saccharine expression on his face. Then the fatuous look died to be replaced by sudden excitement. With one hand he stopped the playback and with the other he grabbed the telephone.

"Get me Huston!" he roared.

"What do you need a telephone for?" asked the operator. The connection was made in a hurry.

"Huston! The Z-wave is in!"

"In?"

"It's in, dammit and I've got proof!"

"Proof?"

"Don't stand there gabbing. Get over here!"

"You're sure?"

Donatti laughed. "I've just heard Nora kissing Grayson via Z-wave!"

"You've—what—?"

"You heard me—"

The phone clicked.

Donatti reached for the intercom. "Stop everything!" he roared. "Break down the first page and set up for bright red ink! Seven-slug banner: Z-WAVE! across the top in red. Get that started and we'll write the story on the lino. Morgan! Get over here and do something about it! You can run a lino; don't bother to script it first, go down and set it up! Timmy! Bust out a picture of Grayson and Nora Phillips if you can. Jones? Start a Page Three blast against Haedaecker and his dammed 'Haedaecker's

Theory.' Jason? Make a repro of this tape. Lewiston! Bust into the soap opera just before the grand climax with a 'special announcement.' Brief and not too informative, details later, you know. Forhan, see if you can get a statement—as if we need one, but it'll do no harm—from Senator Beaumont. Morganser, do the same with Representative Horace. We'll print 'em side by side. Carol, go out to Dirty Joe', and bring me back a gallon of black coffee."

The *News* office was ticking like a time bomb about to go off when Huston came in. His first words were: "Did anybody have the brains to try calling 'em back?"

"Ah—I doubt it."

"Dammit, do it! You try calling 'em back!"

"And you?"

Huston scowled. "They're out there on Latham's Triplets, all alone and unprotected. Y'know what happens next?"

"I can imagine."

"Well, this is what amounts to war. I'm collecting what I can to go out there and see that they're protected!"

"Good luck," said Donatti. "Y'wanna hear the record before you take off?"

"I can wait that long. Yes!"

The superimposed recording was just ending when one of the office boys brought back two papers. One of them was Donatti's, with "Z-WAVE!" in a bright red headline across the top.

The other was as red, as large, and as vigorous. It said, merely: "LIES"

"This is still a dirty fight," said Huston sourly. He scanned the opposition paper with a sneer: "Prepared recording, false evidence, untruth, political maneuvering, smear technique, untruth, false hope, clever machine politics. Oh hell, Donatti. Y'know the only way to shut these bastards up?"

"I can guess."

"Well, that's what I'm going to do!"

Huston left Donatti's office on the dead run.

Hoagland faced his underlings across the desk, his eyes glittering. "So I played a hunch and was wrong. It's not gone yet. All we have to do is play it close."

"But what can we do?"

"Outguess 'em!"

"How?"

"You're not very bright, are you?" sneered Hoagland. "Good thing Jeffers is running the paper. You know, don't you, Jeffers?"

"Sure. All I have to do is to reproduce a recording of Grayson's first false attempt on Proxima I."

"Right. And then?"

"Then the only thing that will convince the great public is to have the President of Terra himself make a talk over the Z-wave between Terra and here. And don't think that Huston won't try."

"Of course he'll try. Even if he were far ahead, he'd try, because he is no idiot. But if he doesn't?"

"Then the failure itself can be used."

"Correct," said Hoagland. "So you stay tight at your desk and get ready to blast 'em out of their pants when President Bennington doesn't come through." Hoagland turned to a tall, slender, elderly man with a bit of a squint that came, extraordinarily, out of sharp eyes. "Astronomers!" he snorted.

Doctor Hargreave shrugged. "That's why the Galactic Survey was started," he said quietly. "Because we did not know the precisely accurate distances between the stars. Don't blame me. Your election date was set by law a long time ago. Don't blame me if the Galactic Network is completed before Election Day. We had only physical observation to go on. It's not my fault."

Hoagland nodded unhappily. "I know," he admitted unhappily. "But if the Galactic Network is completed before Election Day it will be my failure!"

CHAPTER SIXTEEN

FOR FOUR SOLID MONTHS, Al Donatti tried to reply by Z-wave and failed. This was because Grayson was busy following the radio beacon between Latham Alpha and the next Galactic Survey station along the network. Because of daily contact and a certain amount of quavering faith, no one dared to retune the Z-wave dials.

Paul and Nora followed the beacon in almost to the station. Then, because Paul did not know that he had already established contact across a myriad of relay connections all the way back to Neoterra, he waited in space until he could pick up the beacon beyond the next link.

Two light weeks out beyond the radio link, Paul was still conversing with Stacey and Morrow.

"Now?"

Nora nodded. "You've done it," she said.

"We're in."

Here was no grand celebration over a quick success. Here was the culmination of gradual acceptance, a sort of growing-in of knowledge, gradual and complete. It was hard to define the line between promise and fulfillment. Only by personally setting a date and using it as the time-mark could the time of proof be set. But this was it.

"Paul."

"Yes?"

"I'm glad—for you."

"And you?"

Nora nodded happily. "Pretty soon, Paul?"

"Any day in the week."

Nora pouted. "Paul, I want some clothing. I feel seedy."

"You look good to me."

Nora laughed. "I'll look better in some new clothes."

Paul eyed her carefully, boldly. There had been clothing on Latham Beta III for Nora, lend-lease from a few of the botanical worker's wives that were reasonably similar in size. The dress that Nora had worn during the escape from Westlake's little college had been the best fitted among the clothing, and Nora wore it now. She knew that even though it was a bit overworked, she looked better in it than in any of the clothing she had borrowed.

Nora returned Paul's appraisal of her with a flaunt of her hip. "So?"

"So!" he said.

Paul turned toward the control panel and made some computations and some settings on the dials.

Nora pouted.

"Why the cloud-up-and-rain?" he asked.

Nora chuckled. "Trigonometry," she said.

"First things first," Paul replied. The floor surged upward, causing Nora to lose her balance. Paul caught her neatly.

"We're on our way," he said.

Nora looked up in his eyes. Silently. There was no point in saying anything. The Z-wave, proved-in months ago on Neoterra, newly proved to Paul and Nora, was a sort of landmark that did not require any further amplification. That was finished and done.

There had been restraint. Now it seemed childish like a youngster who saves the fanciest chocolate for the last and best. This was the last and best and both of them knew it.

Her lips were softer, warmer. More eager. In all of their previous lovemaking there had been a strident vigor and an avid clutching for one another, a sort of regret that fulfillment was yet to come, but not yet here. Now this frantic reaching seemed gone. Paul knew the free relaxation of Nora's softness against him, he felt the sweet lassitude soften her. His hands caressed her and Nora moved to relish the caress.

"Paul—I love you."

"I know—you don't mind if I know?"

"I want you to know—"

Eleven days later they landed on Latham Alpha IV.

Stacey greeted them with, "So now what, children?"

"NeoSol."

Stacey eyed them with envy. "Somewhere along in this mad pattern I recall vaguely that I have a wife named Gloria and a daughter, both of whom think I am deceased. Looking at you two makes me want to howl at the moon—if I could find a moon to howl at on this misbegotten planet. You can head for Neoterra, but does anybody mind if I head for home and fireside? I want to walk in and be a great shock to my wife."

"You—"

"Shut up," snapped Stacey. "Or I'll tell Nora about you."

"Please do anyway."

"Stacey, you stay out of this."

"Bribe me, chum. I'm not incorruptible."

Nora smiled. "Maybe I can offer something—"

"Possibly."

"Like a sum of money or a—"

"Nah!"

"Personal gift—"

"What kind?"

"Such as a good book?"

"Nah."

"He's hard to please," complained Nora.

"I'm not hard to please. Just keep making offers. You'll hit on something."

"I'll tell Gloria," suggested Paul.

Stacey cleared his throat. "Gloria is a very smart woman," he said. "She would believe you only if she had seventeen confirming witnesses—or the odd look on my face. So—gawd! What was that?"

The ground trembled and the air racketed to the blast of explosion. A flash of white flame filled the sky.

Had the blast been atomic the shock wave would have flattened the Latham Alpha IV station. It was that close. But it was just common high explosive of the chemical type that shattered at them, and cracked a couple of windows in the Relay Station not far away.

"Bombs!" shouted Stacey.

Paul raced to the control panel and set the drive; he wanted to get a long way from there and he did not care which way. Just away...

Hoagland's crew had gotten off first. This followed a certain kind of reasoning that shows less troublesome planning to destroy than to protect. His crews had driven their ships as fast and as hard as ships and men could stand the gaff. The flight had dropped down out of supervelocity one by one, a quarter of a light year from Latham Alpha, coming into real space in a volume spherically as large as the outer limits of the Solar System.

Here the earlier arrivals had waited for the followers, since no two ships could drive at precisely the same speed across a galactic distance. They had closed down into formation as they came out of superspeed, each arrival taking its place in the space pattern.

Finally Hoagland counted noses and found them all in place. Then—

"Latham Alpha IV. The Galactic Relay Station!"

The ships went into superdrive briefly to return a few hundred thousand miles above the ice cap where the relay station stood, waiting the last few hours of its term of years for the arrival of the last link in the Galactic Network. Hoagland's flight lined down on a long curve, one ship after the other, each pilot aiming for the station.

It had been the first bomb, a clean miss, that had alerted Paul Grayson's little group.

"Get that ship!" roared Hoagland.

The leading ship, having bombed and missed, curled upward after its bombing dive, circled around and got on the tail of Grayson's spacecraft. The second ship made a closer miss, circled the course and laid its nose behind the first.

A burst of orange flame licked across the nose of Hoagland's Number One craft and the shell glanced from Grayson's flank, sending a ringing crash through Paul's ship. All three of them looked behind to see ship after ship line up to race after them.

Paul reached for the high drive. It was almost warm enough to use—

Huston's flight had taken off a few hours later. There had been a lot of preparation: Data regarding dates, flight velocities, and some calculations as to the completion of the Network. Then a courier ship had been prepared—prepared like no ship had ever been prepared before.

Unmanned, but timed to perfection, courier ships crossed space between Sol and NeoSol in half the time of passenger flights. They carried tons of official mail; ordinary commercial mail was not permitted here.

In Huston's special courier the tons of official mail had been whittled down to one piece, four pages of micro-typewritten tissue paper and the remaining load had been filled up with additional power pack. The timing had been calculated to perfection and the timing circuits had been carefully checked by the Standards Technicians. Then the drive had been set and the ship had taken off for Terra in a flight calculated to make space-crossing history.

Only then did Huston's flight form and leap into space from Neoterra. Driving as hard and as fast as men and machinery would permit, Huston's crew came down out of supervelocity four months later, a couple of light months South Galactic from Latham Beta. Like Hoagland, Huston waited in space until the stragglers came through.

Unlike Hoagland, Huston had to wait because he was going to defend, not make a destructive attack. Once the flight had formed, they circled Latham Beta and headed for Alpha in superdive. They came in to one side of Alpha IV, and circled the planet less than a hundred miles up, coming around the planet in time to watch the first line of Hoagland's ship start the bombing run.

"You know the score!" snapped Huston. "That relay station *must* remain intact until the Network Beam gets here! Protect it!"

Huston's flight spread out a bit and streaked across the ice cap, hitting Hoagland's bombing curve in the middle, ship after ship. Orange flames licked the noses of Huston's craft and the shells screamed across the ice cap to flash in and around Hoagland's flight. The careening ships and the flight of screaming shells destroyed the flight perfection of the bombing pilots.

The ice cap blazed with dots of flame and pillars of smoke as the bombs landed in a shotgun pattern around, but never quite on, the relay station. Huston's men spotted the hare-and-hounds game forming at the upward swing of the bombing run and the ships roared for counter-attack.

Like twin corkscrews, both flights spiraled up after Grayson's fleeing ship.

"Grayson!" roared Huston. "Grayson!"

"Yeah—?"

It was Z-wave now, because all of the ships were close-locked in combat. Not the galactic separation that made original contact necessary.

"Grayson, this is Huston. How long before the beacon beam arrives?"

"Hours.'"

Huston groaned. "'We've got to defend that station for hours or defeat Hoagland completely!"

Huston's flight split into two, one of them spiraled down to race in a large circle high around the relay station, the rest of them remaining in the locked spiral of the flight.

Grayson snapped the high drive and his ship flashed into super-drive and away.

Hoagland's flight gave up the chase and looped up and over and down towards the station again. Huston's half-flight cut the corner of the curve and passed through Hoagland's ships, the space-rifles barking. It was a maneuver similar to "Crossing the Tee" in naval warfare.

One shell drilled in through the fore port of Hoagland's ninth ship and the velocity of the ship carried the racketing bit of metal back through the guts of the ship where it glanced viciously from wall to wall. Lights went dark and then the ship lost drive as the round hit some of the vital wiring. Inert, the ship continued on its course freely, curving down towards Alpha IV to land with a blossom of flame as the driving-chambers blew their atomic load.

Space flashed bright as one of Huston's craft rammed its enemy. A flare of molten metal splashed wide and bits of solid, jagged hull sprinkled space with deadly missiles that caused the following ships to veer wide. A third ship exploded violently as one of Huston's shells drilled the drive chamber.

One of Huston's ships ran into one of the jags of hull and went inert. The pilot fought it while the crew struggled with the ruined wiring. Arcs and flares filled the ship as the air dropped in pressure within the ship, then the electrical arcs went out as vacuum came.

Struggling against no-gravity, the crew floated in the ship, hurling tools to direct themselves, tossing cables across the hull-spaces. A dim light came on as the ship dropped toward the ice cap, then the drive returned part way. The pilot fought the ship down to a racketing, sliding crash that hurled up a fountain of chipped ice and strewed the furrow with fragments of ship.

Those of the crew who survived the crash leaped from the ship through jagged holes in the hull and raced for the relay station. All of them remembered one main tenet of warfare: Eventually, no matter how outrageous or how efficient grow the mechanized weapons of warfare, it is the man with the bared knife that subdues his enemy on the contested ground!

Revolvers shattered the locked door of the station and the men took shelter inside. They might be sitting ducks for a bombing run. If their pilots could stop Hoagland's bombing runs, Hoagland's men would eventually have to land and make for the station on foot. Then they would be ready!

The downward circle of Hoagland's flight circled the entire planet, crossed below the antipodal ice cap and came roaring across the planet just above the stratosphere. Huston was waiting for them and the two flights plowed into one another head on. Now both flights were facing each other and the space-rifles vomited their rain of solid shells.

Had this been a battle between trained and well-armed space forces, it would have been sheer carnage. But the space rifles were not radar-trained nor electronically fired. These were ships of commerce locked in combat as deadly as man against man, but lacking the finer techniques of modern mass killing. Ship after ship trained on one another and raced towards one another on dead course.

The space rifle spitted as fast as the perspiring gun-layers could serve the breech. It was *Blam! Blam! Blam!* with the pilot holding the course dead true, nose toward nose across the ice cap, each pilot trying to make the other pilot swing aside first, daring and trying to keep his own nerves from screaming while he looked death right in the eye and spat. Untrained by experience and lack of enemy-courtesy, there was no commonly accepted rule regarding the final tilt from the collision course. Some went left, some went right, some went up. Some dodged down and hit the planet with a racketing crash and a shower of ice—amid the vomit of flame as the drive chamber let go. Some veered into one another's course and the stratosphere flashed high and wide with flame and terror.

Others missed cleanly, circling left and right; others coursed up and over, with one pilot tightening the curve to the plate-buckling strain-point to circle the course and end up with his nose and the space rifle looking down the drive chamber of the enemy.

One of Hoagland's pilots circled up, loosing a bomb as it rose. Huston's pilot ran into the bomb and the sky roared white and hot.

Then both flights were through one another and circling high above the ice cap for another run. They met ten thousand miles in space, wide spread and raced at one another in a mad dogfight.

On the ground below, survivors leaped from cracked ships and raced to safety. Pitifully few survived. Aligned man against man and group against group—for they were spread out across a twenty mile area—they fought with revolvers and stalked one another across the hummocks of ice and laid in wait in defiles and passes, converging on the station.

Holes poked in the ultra-hard glass dome near the edge of the station wall sprouted revolver barrels. The relay station became a blockhouse protected by Huston's survivors. The first crash had been a blessing instead of a defeat, for Huston's men defended the station against Hoagland's surviving crews. Huston's survivors made their way to the station, leaving their dead and the dead of their enemy on the ice behind them, and bit by bit the numbers embattled in the relay station grew.

For anyone of Hoagland's men, once within the station, could stop this battle merely by firing a single revolver shot through one of the vitals of the radio beacon receiver. Or hitting it with any hard instrument. Or just by flipping the "ON-OFF" toggle switch that controlled the entire station.

Both flights, diminished now, hit one another in a mad pass high above the planet. Space filled with bits of jagged metal and the silent shells that would someday end up as satellites to some distant sun—to possibly confuse some space miner that found a piece of nickel-steel completely machined and fitted with copper expansion-bands in an orbit around an unpopulated stellar system.

Numbers being equal, Huston's men had one small advantage. They wanted to hit Hoagland's crew. Hoagland's gang had two objectives. They wanted to destroy the station, and so part of their efforts were directed towards the station itself while only the rest were directed at Huston's flight.

The flights passed through one another leaving space strewn with ruin; and circled down on opposite sides of a great circle to cross the ice cap face to face again only a few miles above the relay station perched precisely on the polar axis. The wind whistled and the odd-smelling atmosphere took on another odor as the battle raged briefly above the relay station. The ice was dotted again with divots of flaming hell thrown high by missed bombs and water ran from the hot craters in starred rivulets to freeze later in a curiously beautiful pattern.

Again diminished, the flights whirled, stalking and sparring like swordsmen, cautious, angry, hating.

And while the embattled fleets of spacecraft circled one another, Paul Grayson was far in space, coming out of superdrive, confident that he had outrun or at least disappeared from instant contact with the enemy. Alpha IV was far, far behind. Latham's Triplets were only stars in a neat equilateral triangle below. Very bright stars, but none the less true stars showing no disc to the naked eye.

"Now what?" asked Stacey. "That was damned close, Little Friend."

"Do we go back?" asked Nora.

"I'd rather not," said Stacey. "I prefer to die in bed at the age of one hundred and seventeen after a long, pleasant, active, and interesting life."

"Huston is down there, too, you know," said Paul thoughtfully.

"So what?"

"He apparently came with quite a gang."

Stacey grunted. "Let's wait until we're sure that the unpleasantness has subsided. Someone will be yelling 'Veni Vidi Vici' and I want to be sure that the guy yelling 'Vici' is on my side."

Grayson shook his head thoughtfully. "Huston got here," he said.

"So?"

"Hoagland and his gang must have—" Grayson's voice trailed away as Paul went into another reverie of thought.

"Paul, this is what is commonly referred-to as patently obvious."

Paul snapped out of it again.

140

"Y'know," he said slowly, "neither Hoagland nor Huston would be a-roaring down here with fire in their eyes if they did not know we'd succeeded."

Nora blinked. "They must have overheard us," she said.

Paul spread his hands. "Why not? The link was solid between Latham's Triplets and Neoterra. We might have interfered with their Z-wave."

"That's fine reasoning. But now take the next step and where are we?"

"Huston wanted to know how long before the beam came in," said Paul. "Then he groaned and said that they'd have to defend the station for hours."

"After which," said Stacey, "we left somewhat precipitously, if not graciously. I don't blame us, but of course, we are sort of biased by our own feelings."

"But why?" asked Nora.

"I've been away from the Galactic Survey for a long time," said Paul thoughtfully. "It's more than possible that Latham's Triplets is the station that completes the link. There is always some question as to where the final beam would cross because we were not sure what the precise stellar separation was. In fact," he said with a smile, "this determination of stellar distances was the reason for originating the Galactic Survey. Now, if Latham Alpha turned out to be the final link, coming a bit early, and Haedaecker's Theory was wrong, the link between Sol and NeoSol could be complete by Z-wave once the radio contact checked in. Huston might have some plan—" again Paul trailed off as he began to think about the subject deeply.

"And," prompted Nora.

"The final link should be heading towards Alpha IV quite close by now," said Paul. "We'll tap it before it lands."

CHAPTER SEVENTEEN

THE COURIER SPACECRAFT DROPPED down out of supervelocity and emitted an overwhelming blast of radio signal. One half of the output tube operating life went into Eternity in one half minute of intense power.

Minutes later space stations picked up the radio blast and had radiogoniometers pointing the angle; which, when correlated with other space stations, bracketed the courier spacecraft nicely. A telemeter beam fingered out and caught the radio-controlled circuits of the courier and the courier turned obediently and started to blast towards Terra.

It landed in a screaming arc and came to rest, smoking both outside and inside, for the driving circuits had been running at overload for nearly four months. Technicians at Great Lakes Spaceport trundled the courier along a runway and dunked the whole thing into Lake Michigan where they watched the clouds of steam boil up and then subside as the hull cooled. They waited, and then they breached the message hull, which was a separable nose.

Accustomed to finding tons of mail, they were shocked to find only one officially sealed envelope addressed to the President of Terra.

They put it on a mail speedster that arched high into the stratosphere and into black space itself in a vast segment of ellipse to drop into the hands of the Capitol's techs within a matter of minutes. Here the official envelope by-passed any number of official channels...

President Bennington heard the diffident rap on his bedroom door and grunted unhappily. Then he came awake and realized that nothing less than an official Affair of State would cause his Aide to rap on his door.

Bennington snapped the light on near his bed and went to the door in his pajamas. "What's up, Phil?" he asked as he opened the door.

Phillip Vanderveer smiled apologetically. "I don't know," he said honestly. "But when a courier spacecraft comes from Neoterra with only one piece of mail labeled 'Private, Important,' and addressed to you, it must be both private and important."

Bennington smiled. "Cigarette?" he asked.

"Here, sir."

"Come in," said Bennington, accepting the smoke.

"But—er—"

"M'Lady is sawing wood. This may be important enough for fast action, Phil. Come on in and for—"

Bennington opened the envelope with a thumb and spread out the pages. He looked and then found a magnifying glass and went to work on the micro-typewritten pages.

"Phil," he said slowly, "forget about this until three days from now. Then see to it that Chadwick Haedaecker is summoned here for a—" Bennington went on to peruse a calendar and then a clock, "—an official session!"

The following day Phillip Vanderveer reported that Haedaecker was out on some tour of the Galactic Network and was not expected back for some time. That was too bad, but not a bar to the future actions of President Bennington.

He spent the next two days closeted with his aides writing a flowery speech of fancy phrases that would do the trick. He decided finally to make his speech from America's White House, and went with the First Lady to Terra to that shrine where Free Men were first welded into a Strong State, because there in America the seeming incompatibility between Freedom and Empire had been favorably resolved.

Bennington prowled the mansion, looked at the shrined artifacts, and was he, himself, impressed once again. Somewhere in the middle of the road there was the right path between the extremes of anarchy and tyranny. To be really free, every man must be released from any governing, which would make him a unit weak enough to be assailed by any grouped force. To *rule* men meant they had too little to say about their own lives.

Bennington slept in a bed once slept in by Andrew Jackson.

It was midnight of the third day. The shrined White House was a blaze of lights. Newsmen and radio technicians trod the revered halls and strung their wires.

The connection to Z-wave Central had been made, first. The other lines to the rest of the world were ready. The lines to Z-wave Central were ready to bring the message to the planets of Sol—and all that remained was the final connection that would bring President Bennington's address to the worlds of NeoSol.

Bennington sat at his desk with a fountain pen altering the long speech. He was not entirely satisfied with it. It contained flowing passages calculated to jog the emotions, words carefully selected because of their syllables to cause a ringing cadence which would cause an emotional reaction. It was flowery and forceful. It was long; starting on a slow measure and rising to a proper climax, completely a mathematico-musico-psychologico compilation intended to sway emotions and minds in the right direction. He stood up from time to time and delivered portions of it. Playbacks returned both his voice and his appearance to him, and Bennington worked on slight faults of either until his delivery was perfect.

Outside of his room, bustling technicians checked their circuits and Washington itself was alive with the tenseness of waiting.

Tired—and with hours to wait yet—Bennington laid down on a couch to relax. His slumber was fitful, dozing interrupted by vivid dreams, by slight noises, by quick flashes of intense thought by his mind, which was not convinced of the necessity for relaxation. Finally he drifted off deep, completely relaxed for the first time in three days.

They counted—afterwards—that President Bennington had only a total of nine hours sleep in seventy-two.

Then a bell rang. A siren wailed. A blast of salute-cannon shook the city, and the radio across Terra blasted into life. People across the worlds of Sol awoke; they had been sleeping lightly, awaiting The Moment and now it was here!

Radio sets left running burst into life, waking people everywhere among the planets of Sol at the same instant.

The Galactic Z-wave had come to life!

Light-years across the galaxy towards NeoSol, Paul Grayson talked into a microphone. And on the planets that were Sol's Children, a thousand million loudspeakers thundered forth his voice!

"President Bennington! President Bennington!"

Bennington awoke from his fitful nap with a start. The door to his room opened. Phillip Vanderveer stood there looking in. He approached.

Marian Bennington smiled quietly. "This is it!"

Bennington looked at her queerly. His wife. Somehow strangely unimpressed by the solemnity of it all; peculiarly self-serene among all of the importance of the moment. His wife,

144

greeting him with a slightly amused expression. Greatness, of moment or of person seemed a bit remote. Bennington gulped at her and smiled.

"Take it easy Hal," she said. She kissed him gently as he leaned towards the microphone.

"President Bennington speaking."

"This is Paul Grayson riding the Latham Alpha IV beam towards the station. Thank God you're ready!"

"What—?"

"We're fifteen light minutes out from Contact. Huston is fighting to keep the Station alive; Hoagland is trying to kill it!"

"Fighting?"

"Space battle!"

"Dammit man—Oh God, it's four or six months flight time there, isn't it?"

"Yes," said Paul. "Just stick around. We'll win!'"

"Grayson, you've got to win!"

The ice cap was dotted with craters. Tiny spots of black among the sea of glittering white were men struggling in the icy cold to reach the fight for the final link between Mother Earth and her distant Daughter. In the sky above, Isolationist and Coalitionist fought with nerve and iron to separate versus maintain the original solidarity of the galaxy.

Paul, riding the front of the incoming radio beacon beam, had no idea of how the fight was going.

But of Huston's hundred ships and one hundred and seventeen of Hoagland's only nine were left with Huston and seven left with Hoagland. The collected survivors in the relay station numbered thirty souls—determined souls of the same determination of the men who stood at Concord Bridge.

The plain around the station was a mess of bomb craters; desperation measures but all misses. The glass dome itself was holed with a half-gross of shells fired into the station, and three of the big parabolic antenna-reflectors were drilled with four-inch holes but still electrically functional. Master fighters now because they were survivors, Nine and Seven faced one another cautiously. They raced in, faced one another harshly, like frigates sailing in to receive a heavy broadside, clashed, and came on through as Five and Three.

Huston's crew circled in a mad melee, five of them in overwhelming odds now. They herded the Three high, caught them in an englobement, and made a flaming kill a hundred miles above the planet, then raced forward as Hoagland started to flee for his life, his campaign defeated.

With the ice cap dotted with death and wreckage, Huston's command ship left the other four to guard the Upper Sky while he scouted the surface, using his power ruthlessly to cow Hoagland's separated survivors into abject surrender.

Then, in complete victory, Huston raced his command ship in a vast circle around the damaged but still running Relay Station. It would go deadly hard with anyone who tried to interfere at this instant.

Huston's engineer snapped in the Z-wave.

"Grayson! Grayson! Are you—are you?"

The Z-wave receiver in Paul's ship brought this call.

He snapped the toggle and said: "Huston? I'm riding the radio beam down to Alpha IV."

"Bennington?"

"I've got him on the Z-wave!"

"Let me—connect me—"

Paul reached for a cable with a double-ended plug and shoved both ends home in his patch-panel.

"Mister President, here is Mr. Huston!"

"Bennington! Bennington! You're ready?"

On Terra, President Bennington nodded and said: "Any time."

Huston said, "Good. Thank God. Grayson, can we—?"

Paul considered. "Can you get in touch with the Latham Alpha IV Station direct?"

"Take some doing, but—"

"President Bennington, the Galactic Link is almost complete. It's Z-wave via radio contact from Terra to me. It's Z-wave from me to Huston; and from Alpha IV to Neoterra it is again Z-wave via radio contact. As soon as Huston taps the radio beam from Alpha IV, we can get you through to—"

A flash of fire-white-hot and vicious-blinded Huston and his crew. It killed all the men on Alpha IV friend and foe alike. The sound—

The sound was a flat and completely-gone silence. The contact had been destroyed before the link could convey any sound.

Down from the black sky a single ship had driven at velocities too high for the radar to catch. It had come at near-light velocity from somewhere, had passed Alpha IV at a tangential altitude of a thousand miles—and had loosened something.

The "Something" had been unbelievable tons of lithium hydride, neatly tamped and packed around a fissionable detonator.

The super bomb drilled into the planetary crust a full quadrant South—at the Equator of Alpha IV—and exploded. Slowly and majestically, Alpha IV expanded. The crust separated along the fault-lines to expose the planetary magma. Ice met molten lava in a riot of exploding steam; mountain range fell into the sea, livid streamers of tortured matter flared forth, and the surface heaved, bubbled, and collapsed and the smoke and dust and soil of Alpha rose into the atmosphere to mingle with the clouds of vaporized metal and superheated steam that roiled and blasted away from the planet into space.

Latham Alpha IV contracted into a boiling mass of energy, distributed and re-distributed and re-re-distributed throughout the planetary mass.

Gone was the ice cap. Forever lost were the men who battled face to face and gun to gun to keep the Relay Station running. Then Latham Alpha began to expand. Slowly and majestically it grew, as the volatile material became gaseous with the energy hurled into it. The flaming-white glow died into a furious orange-red as the localized areas of energy spread out and the whole of the planet began to radiate dully.

Across space, heading into a boiling planetary surface that had no receiver to collect it, came the Galactic Radio Beam. It entered the roiling planet and died, and what missed the planet either splashed aside from the space-stressed energy or went on and on and on through space unchecked and unheeded.

Huston's spacecraft, hurled upwards by the force of flaming gases, bounced around viciously until Huston's pilot snapped the high drive briefly, first on and then off.

"Grayson?"

"Huston! What has happened?"

"Super-atomic."

"God!"

"But the Relay—The Network?" Paul thought a moment.

"I've still got Bennington," he said. "And—" here Grayson's voice paused for a moment.

Grayson's ship had been at One Light velocity, following the Beam towards Alpha IV. Now as he sat at the console of his ship's drive, he reached for a switch that swerved the ship aside in its course by just a few milliseconds of arc.

Seconds later he passed the boiling ruin of Alpha IV by a half--million miles, still following the head of the Galactic Survey Beam.

As Paul passed the planetary ruin, he snapped another switch, picked up the microphone and cried:

"Al Donatti! Al Donatti!"

And down from Neoterra came the reply. "Grayson? You've got Bennington?"

"On the other end!"

Back in the White House, President Bennington sat before the broad desk, looking at the microphone with an odd expression on his face. Somehow flowery speeches and fancy, well-calculated words seemed a bit pale and unconvincing in the face of men who lived and died for a Grand Principle.

He looked up at the wall.

He saw a bronze plaque.

"President Bennington! Speak up!"

Bennington started. It was Madison—was it Madison or Jackson?—who said that an American could tell the President to Go To Hell, and all the President could do was to argue with him—or go fishing?

Bennington tore his carefully prepared speech down the middle. He stood up and looked at the bronze plaque, and began to read it:

"Fourscore and seven years ago—"

Across space to Latham's Triplets went the Z-wave, connected at long last by the original Radio Linkage. Across from Grayson's spacecraft it went to the completed Z-wave link to Neoterra, to come bursting forth from a thousand million loudspeakers across the worlds of NeoSol.

NeoTerra heard it, and NeoVenus listened. The isolated colonists on NeoGanymede cheered and the folks on far NeoPluto nodded their heads knowingly.

"—engaged in a great civil war to determine whether that nation or any other nation so conceived and so dedicated can long endure—"

"Grayson!" came the whispering of the radio—a mundane instrument of no great interest to anyone. "Grayson—we've caught him."

"Who?"

"Your pal Haedaecker. He bombed Alpha IV!"

"But—?"

"We'll twist his arm, Grayson. Maybe he'll explain the guy who tried to shoot you to bits on Proxima I. Maybe a lot of other things. Anyway, he's the joker in this deck."

Stacey eyed Paul with a glitter. "D'ye mind if I start going home to my wife?"

Paul snapped off the communications panel entirely. "They've made it," he said. "It'll be complete from now on. And we'll crisscross this galaxy with radio beacons from star to star and bit by bit until the Z-wave contact is complete between Mother Sol and any of her Colonies."

"Let's take Stacey home," suggested Nora.

Paul turned to the panel and set some switches, adjusted some dials, and threw in the main switch. The floor surged below them and Paul put his eye to the spotting telescope as his ship began to move.

Paul yawned as the minutes passed and the ship gained speed towards Sol, aimed by his watchful eye. Time passed, and Paul, finally released from all of the trouble and worry, began to hum. Eventually he began to sing, in that off-key voice:

"Round and round and round go the deuterons!
Round and round and round the magnet swings 'em!

Round and round and round go the deuterons—"
Nora interrupted Paul with the final line of The Cyclotronist's Nightmare:
"Aw, let's turn the damned thing off and go to bed!"

THE END

FROM DEEP WITHIN EARTH'S BOWELS THEY CAME...

It seemed impossible. Gold from Fort Knox being stolen? Priceless bars of gold were missing from what was one of the best protected, most impregnable structures on Earth. Or was it?

Then one day bars of gold starting disappearing from within one of the Fort's most secure underground chambers, setting off a panic that soon rippled through the entire United States government. How was it even possible? It wasn't until a scaly green arm reached out and dragged a guard into one of the Fort's deepest gold vaults that the truth was guessed: we were being invaded! Invaded by a race of creatures from deep inside the Earth…

CAST OF CHARACTERS

JOE GRANGE
Millions of dollars in gold had been stolen from Fort Knox. It was up to him to find out who or "what" was behind it.

HARRIET FULLER
This good-natured WAC was incredibly beautiful. Looks can sometimes change, though.

THE BAJII OF URPADU
He had to keep the nobles from the underground cities placated at all times, lest he give them reason to cut out his heart.

THE MAGICIAN OF HOLGG
He had sent his agents to the upworld on a secret mission. All he wanted them to do was steal the gold out of Fort Knox!

COLONEL FULLBRIGHT
As an intelligence officer for the Army, it was hard for him to believe that a soldier was abducted by a green-armed monster!

GEORGE MURDOCK
He appeared to be just a military guard who was in the wrong place at the wrong time—but yet something else seemed amiss.

NELLAFELLO
As Royal Chest Surgeon he had plans of gaining the Bajii's favor. All he had to do was offer the bloody heart of Joe Grange!

THE THING FROM UNDERNEATH

By
MILTON LESSER

ARMCHAIR FICTION
PO Box 4369, Medford, Oregon 97504

CHAPTER ONE

CORPORAL Joe Grange was assigned to Fort Knox the day after the first bar of gold disappeared.

On the bus with Joe were two F. B. I. agents, a Colonel of Army C. I. D. and a grim-faced Under-Secretary of the Treasury, all bound for the fortress from which, miraculously, a bar of gold worth forty thousand dollars had disappeared. Joe didn't miss any of the excitement: he was a sleepy-eyed, slow-speaking, deep south-looking, freckle-faced young man who, on appearances at least, was never taken very seriously. That was the general idea, for Joe was a member of Army Counter-Intelligence. As such, and even though he held the rank of corporal, Joe could out-rank every other investigator on the scent of the missing gold—when rank was necessary. Until it was, though, Joe remained simply Corporal Joe Grange, attached as a photographer to Headquarters Fort Knox Public Information Office. Nobody, not even the Fort Knox Commander, knew that Joe was a Counter-Intelligence agent.

The Public Information Office was crawling with civilian reporters when Joe got there. The theft of a bar of gold from Fort Knox, naturally, was big news. It was the story of the year and somehow it had leaked out almost immediately.

Missing: one bar of gold.

Thief: Unknown.

Method of theft: unknown.

Time of theft: unknown.

Likelihood of apprehension: nil.

This was the report that reluctantly left the hands of the Public Information Officer, a Major Spoonley. It was the report that had all the reporters buzzing when Joe got there and the report that sent them scurrying around the Fort looking for answers on their own.

Lieutenant Anders, Chief of the Photography Section, told Joe, "Corporal, you sure checked in at a hell of a time. I tell you what, if there's nothing doing over at the dark room, why don't you take the rest of the afternoon off? The Spoon is in no mood to have pictures taken—which sure as hell isn't like The Spoon, but what the hell, gold bars don't get stolen every day."

The Spoon was Major Spoonley. Joe nodded, tossed a stiff salute at his immediate superior, and returned to his barracks. Headquarters Detachment was special troops mostly, and Joe got into a poker game with members of the Fort Knox band for a few minutes, playing long enough to establish the fact with the enlisted men that he was a slow-talking, slow-thinking, slow-acting photographer. During the game the topic of the gold theft came up. It seemed to amuse the daylights out of Fort Knox's musically talented soldiers. The Fort, they pointed out, was absolutely impregnable—not that it had been attacked. The Fort, they added, had a staff security system that would leave J. Edgar Hoover gasping. Every worker who came within proximity of the gold was searched daily. There was no way in and no way out, except under the scrutiny of guards, who themselves were watched by watchers who watched one another.

In short, the gold could not have been stolen.

A second gold bar was missing on the day Corporal Joe Grange arrived.

And two on the next day.

And three on the day after.

Reporters were herded off the base. Visitors' passes were suspended. All personnel leaves were cancelled. No one off the base was allowed on and no one on the base was permitted off.

And four gold bars disappeared the very day this order became effective.

Eleven gold bars, worth forty thousand dollars each. That was almost half a million dollars in pure gold, a sum which—naturally—the U. S. Treasury would hardly miss. But it meant that Fort Knox was not impregnable. It meant that, theoretically, the gold reserve of the U. S. A. might be drained off several bars at a time by some unknown thief, stealing in some unheard of way, from a facility that was absolutely burglarproof.

On the day of the first really big theft, Joe met Harriet. She was Harriet Fuller and she was a Wac P. F. C. and she typed and mimeographed the Fort guard roster that daily augmented the M. P. guard patrols with sentries from Headquarters Detachment. With The Spoon's blessings, Joe was taking pictures around the Fort for a magazine spread on the robberies. It was either Joe, or a civilian photographer, so the civilian photographer remained in Lexington, enjoying the fruits of his expense account, while Joe did the work.

"Smile," Joe told Harriet, sighting her through the camera's finder. She said cheese and added, "What's it for?" and Joe told her about the civilian magazine and she said she thought he was new here and Joe admitted he was.

"You won't believe it," Harriet said, "but Knox is usually a kind of sleepy post where nothing ever happens."

"I guess you're right, I won't believe it," Joe drawled, and smiled. Harriet was easy to smile at. She had a breath-taking figure, although you had to guess at much of it thanks to the camouflage of the Wac uniform. She had the healthy, scrubbed good-looking face and the blonde hair of the Dutch you find around Reading, Pennsylvania. She didn't look too bright, but she didn't look stupid either.

"That's all you do," she asked, "take pictures?"

"Well, it's enough for me," drawled Joe, as if any little thing was enough. Then, abruptly, he added, "Lunch?"

"All right, corporal."

At which, they exchanged names. Lunch in the PX cafeteria was pleasant enough. They talked about each other and about the gold theft, and Harriet knew as little as anyone. Over coffee Joe said, drawling and innocent:

"You know, you could do me a favor."

"I'll be glad to, Joe."

"I know I just got here, so it will be a while before I pull guard duty, but—"

"Corporal of the guard, you call that guard duty? It'll be a lead-pipe cinch."

"Anyhow," said Joe, "you won't believe this, but I'm eager."

"For guard, you mean? I'll tell you a secret, Joe: I've already been bribed by a few guys."

"Is that so?"

"Sure. They're just like you, curious. Since it's impossible to steal anything from Fort Knox, but since gold has been stolen, they want to go prowling around and see what's what."

"That's the general idea," said Joe, delighted that it hadn't been his idea alone. "Me, too."

Harriet studied his face a moment, then nodded. "Naturally, this is on the Q. T.," she told him. "I could get myself in a sling for even thinking of it."

"Naturally," said Joe.

CHAPTER TWO

The Corporal of the Guard's small office was located a dozen strides down the corridor from one of the big vault doors that led to the underground vaults housing the gold. Actually, there were two Corporals of the Guard, one from the MP's and one from Headquarters Detachment. Tonight Joe was the Headquarters man, complete with white helmet, white carbine sling, white cartridge belt and leggings. He had loaded the carbine and locked a round in the chamber, as prescribed. He had made a quick tour of the guard duty posts while the MP corporal did a little goldbricking. All the guards were present, all their posts secure. At the F. B. I.'s suggestion, their numbers had been augmented by the State Police, one trooper for every two MP soldiers. And one or the other of the two F. B. I. agents here at the Fort would duplicate the Corporal of the Guard's duty. In short, although the possibility of someone forcing his way into the vaults had always been nil, it was less than nil now.

"Everything okay?" the MP yawned.

Joe nodded. Everything, he had to admit, was too damn okay. There didn't seem to be a weak spot in the guard network. Hell, of course there wasn't, yet the gold was missing. "Think I'll take another stroll," Joe said.

"First duty, huh? Eager. You won't find nothing."

Shrugging, Joe went into the corridor. It was lighted almost as bright as day and a guard was stationed at every entrance and exit, although all these were locked. "Inside job, corporal," one of the soldiers joked. "I knew it was them F. B. I. men all along."

"Or the Post Commander," said Joe, going along with it.

"Or the Preserdint of the United States," said the guard.

Joe grinned, inspecting the soldier's rifle only half-heartedly. A single M-l didn't seem very important in the face of what had been happening. The thieves, whoever they were, hadn't stolen the Fort Knox gold by overcoming any guards. They had stolen it by circumventing the guards, by entering through an unguarded area, which Joe told himself for the tenth time, was impossible. For there were no unguarded entrances to Fort Knox.

"Or Harriet Fuller," said the guard. "Man, what a piece!"

"You know her well?"

"Well, I—"

"I hear she can arrange guard duty for you out of turn," Joe said on impulse, and wondered if he would regret it for Harriet's sake.

"Aw," said the guard.

"No, really."

"I didn't mean nothing," the guard protested almost paranoically. "A guy I know over at Headquarters Detachment said my name was popping up any day on KP roster. But I foxed 'em, pulling guard instead."

"With Harriet's help?"

"Aw...I ain't supposed to tell."

"With Harriet's help?"

"Yeah. Aw...so what?"

Before Joe could answer, a voice cried: "Corporal of the guard! Corporal of the guard!"

Joe sprinted in that direction, his boots slapping loudly on the stone floor, unslinging his carbine as he went. Overt trouble, for the first time? His heart raced. He hoped so. He had absolutely nothing to report so far.

Two guards were supposed to be stationed before the vault door, an enormous round steel door that wouldn't yield to a charge of TNT big enough to blow a destroyer out of the water. Two guards should have been stationed there, but Joe saw only one.

The soldier's eyes were very big, very round, and full of terror. He was trying to stand at parade rest before the vault, but his knees wouldn't quite support him in the necessary upright position. His hand on the M-1 barrel was trembling. Sweat beaded his forehead and got in his eyes and made him blink. He stared at Joe very solemnly and some of the terror left his face. He said two words. He said:

"In there."

"In there?" Joe repeated. "You mean, in the vault?"

"In there, corporal," the guard said, and nodded slowly.

"Well, what about it? And where's the other guard?"

"In there," said the guard.

"But that's impossible. You couldn't open the vault even if you wanted to."

"From the outside, you couldn't," said the guard stubbornly.

Joe frowned. "Now, what's that supposed to mean?"

"Five minutes ago," said the guard in a frightened voice. "We was standing here, me and George. Just like me an' you are standing here. It don't make no noise. It just opens a little, slowly, kind of an inch at a time."

"What does?"

"The vault door," said the guard.

"Now, wait a minute!"

"I was here," pleaded the guard. "I seen it with my own eyes, corporal. It opened slow..."

"But it's on a time mechanism. It can't be opened except by the timer, even if you wanted to open it."

"From the outside it can't," said the guard.

"You mean it opened—from the inside?"

"Got to be that way, in case somebody accidentally gets hisself trapped inside. Poor slob might starve to death before the timer got him out, so he don't have to wait—if he's on the inside."

"Nobody was inside there and you know it."

"I'm tryin' to tell yuh," said the guard, his southern accent coming thick once more as terror crawled back into his eyes. There and then Joe decided to let him talk, although what he had heard of the story sounded incredible. There was something about the guard's eyes...

"All of a sudden, George's face goes white. George is like that, see? George can blush like a beet if a pretty girl much as grins at him, or George can go white as chalk if he's scared. Well, George was scared. I look behind him, and there's the vault-opening.

"George points. He don't say nothin'. He don't have to say nothin'. He just points. A inch at a time, the vault is opening. I looks at George but George don't look at me; he can't get his eyes off of that door, I'm tellin' you. Well, it keeps on opening while George is watchin' an' I'm tryin' to git my heart from stickin in my throat so as I can holler.

"Then," the guard finished quickly, gazing about fearfully, "it comes out and grabs George and goes inside again. Lord!"

He looked at Joe. He shook his head. He was still sweating.

"What came out?" Joe asked. "And you mean, out of the vault?"

"Yeah. Out of the vault. George, he's still in there."

"Tell me what you saw. It's very important. Tell me what came out."

The guard shuddered. He clutched the barrel of his M-1 and his knuckles were white as bleached, fleshless bone. "Well," he said, his voice hardly more than a squawk now, "it didn't come all the way out. Just far enough to grab George."

"What? For crying out loud, what was it?"

"All I saw were the arms."

"A man's arms?"

"N-no."

"Not a woman's?"

"No, corporal."

"Well," Joe said after a silence, "are you going to tell me?"

"They was green, corporal."

"What was green?"

"The arms was."

"Wearing green clothing, you mean? Green sleeves?"

"Nakid, corporal. Scalylike. And green."

"The *arms?*"

"The arms. They reached out and took George in there."

Joe said, "You realize what you're saying? You'd repeat it under oath?"

"On a stack of Bibles."

"And you weren't drinking?"

"Not me," said the guard.

"George? Was he drinking?"

"George?" the guard laughed for the first time. It was a strained sound and it seemed to frighten him. "He don't drink at all, George don't."

Joe went to the vault door, tugged at it. He grinned, then shook his head. It was like a flea trying to move a grand piano. He lifted his whistle to his lips, feeling the slight pull of the lanyard around his neck. Leather against flesh, something he could understand. He wished it wasn't the only thing he could understand. Because he considered himself a good judge of human character and had already decided that the guard was telling the truth—at least, what he *thought* was the truth.

Joe blew the whistle, and waited. When a relief guard came pounding down the corridor, Joe told him, "Get the O. D. This is urgent."

Five minutes later, the Officer of the Day came trotting down the corridor. He was a first lieutenant, pink-cheeked and baby-faced, with a petulant mouth but the hard, arrogant eyes of the R. O. T. C. officer who considers himself infinitely superior to all enlisted men, most regular officers, and all civilians.

"Well?" he said. Everything looked very peaceful. His eyes said: whatever your story is, I don't believe it.

Joe said, "There are usually two guards on this post, lieutenant. One of them is missing and the other one's got a story to tell. I think you ought to hear it."

"Naturally," said the O. D. condescendingly, "or you wouldn't have sent for me. Go ahead, soldier." The O. D. wore finance brass. The brass was very bright; his uniform starched and immaculate. He had probably been, Joe found himself thinking, a wolf scout.

He listened while the guard repeated his story. He did not interrupt, as Joe had interrupted when his credulity was taxed. But his hard eyes became bright with suppressed laughter. He was thoroughly enjoying himself and trying not to show it, at least until the story was finished.

Finally, when the guard had lapsed into nervous silence, the O. D. looked at him and looked at Joe and said only two words. He said, "Green arms?"

Joe shrugged. The guard nodded solemnly before the O. D. told Joe, "Corporal, in the future please don't summon me on such obvious fabrications. That's why you're here. You're supposed to be adult enough to deal with them." He chuckled. "Green arms..."

"You're forgetting one thing," Joe said.

"Corporal, really—"

"A man is missing."

"Did it ever occur to you that his buddy is trying to cover for him because he slipped away from guard duty without permission? Did it, corporal?"

"Cover for him—by shouting for the corporal of the guard? You tell me, lieutenant."

The O. D. grunted something under his breath, then asked for the missing man's name. He took it down without much interest, told Joe he would report it through channels and was about to leave when the guard said:

"But, suh! He's in there. He's in *there!*"

"Address your remarks to the corporal, soldier. He'll forward them to me—when they merit it."

"But suh—"

"That's enough," snapped the lieutenant, and acknowledged a pair of salutes halfheartedly, turned on his heel, and marched away down the hall.

Joe told the guard, "I'll send a couple of relief men. You've had enough for one night. But listen, fellow, if you change your story, somebody's name is going to be mud."

"Don't worry about me, corporal," the guard promised. Ten minutes later, the relief came and Joe returned to the Corporal of the Guard's office.

CHAPTER THREE

The next day, George was listed as AWOL. He wasn't the only one: Harriet Fuller also was absent without leave, this despite the fact that the base had been sealed off with all gates barred and watched. Joe could make nothing of it, but knew that the two events were not necessarily connected.

Meanwhile, the guard's story went up through channels and was known to the Chief of Intelligence, the Post Commander, the C. I. D. Colonel and the two F. B. I. agents by the time the vault timing mechanism was to open the vault. Joe was given a routine interrogation by the Intelligence Colonel, a Colonel Fullbright, who seemed a sensible man. Nevertheless, Joe did not reveal his identity as a Counter-Intelligence agent, mostly because there was no indication as yet that Counter-Intelligence was needed. Colonel Fullbright could hardly accept the guard's story, but did not reject it outright as the O. D. had done.

"Remember the Brinks case," he told Joe. "Halloween masks! Maybe it's green arms this time. Who knows? Who knows, corporal?" Abruptly he asked, "Do you know anything about P. F. C. Fuller?"

"P. F. C. Fuller? Oh, Harriet Fuller. I had lunch with her once. I don't know much about her, sir."

"Where's she from?"

"Pennsylvania, I'd guess. Why?"

"Because somebody's face is red in personnel, corporal. I oughtn't to tell you this, but you know as much about what happened last night as anyone and I think it's a good idea for you to know whatever's pertinent."

"What is it, sir?"

"Personnel has no Form-20 card for a Wac named Fuller, Harriet."

"Colonel?"

"You heard me. As far as personnel is concerned, Harriet Fuller does not exist. That's a problem for the Wac detachment, isn't it? If she doesn't exist, how can they list her as AWOL? But it's a bigger problem than that, corporal. Who is Harriet Fuller? Is she really a Wac? Then why haven't we a record of her assignment here? And if she's not a Wac, then why the masquerade? You see what I mean, corporal—a first rate problem."

Just then a master sergeant entered the office and said, "Vault timer's set for ten minutes from now, colonel. You wanted to be told, sir."

The colonel thanked the sergeant, and dismissed him. "Well, you'll have to excuse me, corporal," he told Joe. "I'll have to be going down there right away."

"I'd like to come, sir," Joe said. "I mean, to get the rest of the story."

"Rather irregular, don't you think?"

"But you said—"

"Bait, boy!" beamed the colonel. "You're not just a corporal of photography, are you?"

"I want to go down there, sir."

"Well, are you?"

Reluctantly, Joe showed his identification. The Colonel's face sobered and he said: "C. I. C., eh? I thought it would be something like that. They figure it's a job for Counter-Intelligence in Washington?"

"Not necessarily. They want me here, just in case. And Colonel? I wish you wouldn't reveal my identity. An Agent works better if—"

"I understand," said the intelligence officer, and Joe respected him for it. Often, G-2 officers saw red when they saw C. I. C. operatives. But the Colonel seemed cut from a different bolt of cloth, almost as if he were relieved to have Joe working with him.

"You'd want to come downstairs, of course," he said.

"Of course," said Joe, and they went down together.

The enormous vault door swung open at precisely 3:04, as scheduled. The Post Commander, the G-2 Chief, the two F. B. I. men, the C. I. D. officer, the Post Provost Marshal, their aides, and Corporal Joe Grange, Counter-Intelligence Corps, were on hand.

What they saw was to make headlines all over the country—and the world—that night.

The vault—one of fifteen at the Fort—had held half a billion dollars in gold bars. This made it the smallest of the vaults, but half a billion dollars was a lot of money, even to the U.S. Treasury.

There was no gold in the vault when the huge door swung open.

The shelves were empty, but there were streaks and splinters and smudges of dull yellow on the floor where some of the heavy bars had been dragged across it.

There was a hole in the center of the floor.

A perfectly round hole, four feet across. It went down. It was very dark inside. The dragging marks led toward it. On the lip of the hole were two uniforms, a soldier's and a Wac's. The G-2 colonel's aide, a second lieutenant, rushed to the uniforms and went through the pockets for identification. One belonged to a private named George Murdock. The other, the Wac's uniform, belonged to Harriet Fuller.

General Brandon Burress, Post Commander, had a normally red face. It was redder now. "Gentlemen," he said slowly, distinctly, gazing at the perfectly round hole which led to blackness in the center of the floor of the empty vault, "Gentlemen, Fort Knox is an impregnable fortress, as you all know—except for entry from one direction. No one ever considered that direction any kind of a threat. That direction, of course, is from below. Gentlemen, you all see it with your own eyes: we have been invaded from below!"

Invaded, naturally, was an overstatement, and brought a deflating remark from Colonel Fullbright. "Yes, sir," he said, "invaded by men with green arms."

"Now, colonel!"

"Well, sir, I don't know if their arms are green or not, whoever they are. But this is not an invasion. It's robbery."

"Half a billion dollars," said one of the F. B. I. men, softly, devoutly.

"What's half a billion!" the C. I. D. Colonel thundered. "Don't you understand what this means? If they attacked here, they can attack any of the vaults the same way. Of course, we can station guards in each one, but in the first place we won't be able to do that until the timing mechanisms open them and, in the second place, look what happened to these two guards here."

"Only one of them was a guard," the Provost Marshal was quick to point out.

"Visited while on duty by his girl friend? That's even worse."

The argument might have gained in intensity, but Joe said: "What about the hole? You gentlemen each have your area of interest—but what about the hole? Whose baby is that?"

"Being responsible for the security of this post—" began the Provost Marshal.

"Investigating the theft of gold from Fort Knox—" began the C. I. D. colonel.

"I'm Agent Grange of the C. I. C.," Joe admitted reluctantly. "My rank is corporal, but as you know I can assume the rank and privileges of any officer up to and including full colonel. Therefore, with General Burress' approval, I'd like to take over this investigation—for the C. I. C."

"But why Counter-Intelligence?" demanded the Criminal Investigation Detachment Colonel, passionately believing that his own province was being invaded.

"I'll tell you why," Joe said. "Because the mere theft of gold isn't what's really important..."

"Mere theft!" snorted the Colonel, but his G-2 counterpart said:

"Hear him out, will you?"

"We all have our jobs, don't you see?" Joe said. "Provost Marshal, to safeguard the rest of the gold. G-2, to double-check every employee and soldier on this base. C. I. D. to assume responsibility for investigation of the theft itself."

"What about the Bureau?" one of the F. B. I. men wanted to know. "Where are they slated to fit in, sir?"

"I don't know about the Bureau, but I'm all alone here and could use some help. Now, the reason Counter-Intelligence ought to take over is an easy one. Whatever came through the hole, wherever it came from—don't you see? If it can enter Fort Knox it can also enter White Sands proving grounds and Brookhaven and Oak Ridge, and who knows where else? We've got to find out what it is and how it got here and who it's working for, and find a way to stop it. And that's a job for Counter-Intelligence."

The others expressed their doubt, but General Burress said, "That makes sense, Agent Grange. You talk, they'll listen."

"Thank you, sir," said Joe. He took a deep breath and plunged in. "First off, I want the post engineer summoned. I want a thorough study made of the hole. Look at the edges. They haven't dug mechanically! they're perfectly smooth." He got down on hands and knees near the lip of the hole. "They look almost fused. I'm no engineer, but they look like they've been heated. Well, don't they?"

No one said anything. They were all listening breathlessly. Joe took a pen-knife from his pocket. "Everybody watching?" he said. "Let's get some idea as to its depth, shall we?"

General Burress nodded. The others crowded around. Joe dropped the pen-knife, and they waited. The seconds fled reluctantly. Someone cleared his throat. The C. I. D. colonel cursed softly. An awed look came to General Burress' face.

No one heard the pen-knife strike bottom—if there was a bottom.

"We'd better get the post engineer," Joe repeated.

This time, there was practically a race to the door to carry out his wishes.

CHAPTER FOUR

Before noon on the following day, a post engineer report was forwarded to Colonel Fullbright's office. It was typed in the standard Army subject-to form, beginning—

Subject: Hole of Unknown Origin, Vault 15. Fort.

To: Richard Fullbright. Colonel. AG. G-B.

The Colonel read it while Joe waited politely across the desk from him. The Colonel grunted once or twice, and Joe watched the pattern of wonder made by his thick eyebrows. Finally, without a word, the Colonel handed the report across the desk. Joe all but pounced on it.

The report said many things, in inconclusive Army jargon. The report was of such a fantastic nature that no one wanted to put himself out on a limb calling a spade a spade. The hole, said the report, had been bored by no known method. Bored, it suggested, was the wrong word. The hole, apparently, had been caused by great heat: the granitic and metallic rocks at its lips had been fused, and such fusion could not occur ordinarily under the heat of friction alone.

The hole, said the report, went down to an indeterminate depth. It suggested, however, that instruments adequate for measuring the depth were lacking. It gave the dimensions of the hole and reported traces of gold on the lip. It made no suggestion as to the nature of the hole's origin. All this was interesting, but the bombshell came last. The bombshell said:

Controlled dropping of articles of various weights had been attempted. These articles did not fall in accordance with the laws of gravity. This was worded as if the violation of said laws was somehow punishable by the code of military justice. But the fact remained: gravity was violated. The dropped objects, permitted to fall freely but attached to ropes so their speed of descent could be measured, began by falling at the theoretical speed. Then they slowed—and slowed. By the time they reached the end of their recording ropes (the longest were five hundred feet) they were drifting downward slow as feathers borne on a faint breeze. This happened to every object dropped—without exception.

"My God," said Colonel Fullbright softly. "What does it mean?"

Joe shook his head. "Anti-gravity, colonel. We don't have it, but that hardly means no one does."

"But anti-gravity...?"

"Well, look at it from the pragmatic point of view. If the gold were merely dropped down there—wherever down there is—those bars would splinter. So, they rigged up anti-gravity and then—"

"But Joe! Merely because something is needed doesn't mean it's going to be invented. Necessity mothered a lot of things, but this..."

"Besides," Joe went on, unperturbed, "there's the Wac, and George Murdock. They went down there."

"They might have fallen."

"First taking their clothing off?"

"Can you explain why they stripped?"

Joe shook his head. "No, but it probably means they didn't fall unexpectedly. Colonel, someone ought to go down there."

The Colonel's eyes widened and he said, "You mean, just sort of fall in?"

"No. I mean on a rope. On the longest rope we've got. If he's still falling fast when the rope is all played out, he can yank at it and be drawn up. But if he's not falling at all and if there's something down there that needs exploring, he can just unfasten himself and keep going."

Colonel Fullbright lit a cigarette, inhaled and let a long plume of smoke out toward the ceiling, and shook his head. "This is the G-2 Section, Joe, but I can't ask any of my men to do that."

"I'm not asking you to," Joe said softly.

"I don't understand what you mean, then."

"I'll go down there myself, colonel."

"But you—"

"Someone ought to. It's what I'm paid for."

"But there's no telling—"

"I've made up my mind, colonel. Have Post Engineer rig up some kind of a pully device in Vault 15. I'm going down, yes; but if I want out in a hurry, I'll want to know it can be done."

Without a comment, Colonel Fullbright got the Post Engineer on the phone. But he was shaking his head slowly from side to side while he made the necessary arrangements.

"All set, fellow?" a captain of engineers asked Joe an hour and a half later. The captain stood near a winch around which a five hundred-foot length of sturdy rope was winded. The played-out rope had been fastened about Joe's middle in such a way that he could get rid of it in seconds if he had to.

Joe was standing on the lip of the hole, looking down. He could see nothing, as before, but felt compelled to look. He wore a combat uniform, helmet, green herringbone-twill fatigues, trooper boots, a slung carbine and a .45 automatic, and a cartridge belt for the carbine's .30 caliber ammo around his waist and one for the .45 across one shoulder like a bandolier.

"I still think you ought to take a walkie-talkie," Colonel Fullbright said.

Joe shook his head. "Too heavy. Too encumbering. I want to be able to look around."

"*If* you can see anything."

"Well, I've got this flashlight." It was a big three-battery model and it hung at Joe's left hip, balancing the .45's holster on his right. "I feel like a one-man Army," he said, and grinned.

No one grinned back at him. Everyone thought they were seeing Joe Grange for the last time alive, which was hardly the sort of thought worth grinning about.

"Remember now," the Captain of engineers was saying, "we let you down slowly. No rush. Slowly, we speed it up. According to what we found yesterday, that shouldn't be possible. That is, even if we speed your descent, whatever anti-gravity agents exist down there should serve to slow it proportionately. You understand?"

"Yes," Joe said mechanically, dutifully. Now that he'd made up his mind to go down, all this delay, all these explanations, seemed patently unnecessary. He stood at the edge, looking down. The sides of the hole were silvery, but the depths were black. He could not see very far.

"It may or may not be bottomless," said the Captain. "As you know, we haven't attempted to send anything beyond five hundred feet. As for sonar—" he looked at Colonel Fullbright, who shrugged. "As for sonar, we get a confused picture. One theory: there is a bottom, hardly more than five hundred feet down, but somehow it's masked."

"Well," Joe said as if it hardly mattered, "if they have anti-gravity they also could have some kind of anti-echoing device that swallows up the sonar without letting any of it bounce back."

"Do you think so?" the Captain challenged pedantically.

"I'm going to find out," Joe said.

He shook hands all around, wishing the formalities could be dispensed with. He did not know if he were afraid or not. A strange lassitude always gripped him in the face of danger, but he knew it was deceptive. It was a lassitude out of which he could spring into violent activity, when the occasion demanded.

"And for God's sake," Colonel Fullbright said, "if there's any kind of trouble at all, give a yank on the rope and we'll withdraw you."

Joe nodded, and stepped to the very edge of the hole. Then he threw Colonel Fullbright an informal salute, and stepped into nothingness.

CHAPTER FIVE

"He went without a word," Colonel Fullbright told the Captain of Engineers unbelievingly.

"I saw him, sir."

Fullbright watched the slow, steady unwinding of the winch, watched the inch-thick rope being played out into the hole. "How deep is he, Captain?"

"Fifty-five feet. Still going."

"Fast?"

"As fast as I'll let him. If there's any anti-gravity down there, I'm not aware of it."

Fullbright swore softly, wondering if Joe would admit defeat and have himself drawn up. "Depth, Captain?" he demanded, pacing uneasily.

"A hundred feet."

"Falling—?"

"As fast as I'll let him. There isn't a thing slowing him down, sir."

"Is it safe?"

"Reasonably, but only because we've got the winch acting as a brake."

"Umm-mm. Depth?"

"A hundred sixty-seven. Still going."

"Let me know every fifty feet, please."

"Yes, sir... Wait a minute!"

"What is it, Captain?"

"The rope. It isn't checking his fall, sir!"

"You mean he's falling out of control?"

"No, sir. I mean he's slowing down—of his own accord."

"Anti-gravity," said Colonel Fullbright, and breathed easier. "But how can you explain it?"

"I can't explain, sir. I can only report it... Two hundred and fifty feet. Why sir, you could walk a straight line as fast as he's falling."

"That's incredible," Colonel Fullbright said.

He had no idea how deep he was now, but knew he was moving slowly. He could not sense the motion at all, and became aware of it only when he switched on his flashlight beam and saw the glazed walls moving upward slowly.

For the first few moments, though, the rope tugged almost painfully at his middle. This was a pretty good gauge of the gravity, he knew. It meant his hundred and seventy-five pounds were pulling downward with all their weight. Then, suddenly, the tugging was gone—he couldn't believe it. He reached over his head, pulling at the rope. It was barely taught now, as if something were pushing back from below, slowing his fall. He switched on the light again and was surprised to see the walls disappearing upward at apparently the same rate of speed, until he realized that the rope had previously been checking his fall and so his rate of drop had not altered.

All at once, he wasn't falling. Five-hundred feet, he thought. He'd come to the end of his rope, and it wasn't figurative. He dangled there—over nothingness. He pointed the beam of his flashlight down, and it was swallowed by darkness. Slowly, he spun back and forth like some laggard pendulum in the few feet of room he had. For, down here, the hole was wider—ten feet across perhaps.

Cut the rope?

The thought occurred to him. There was nothing else he could do. He didn't think the rate of fall would increase again, but his only indication of that was the fact that Harriet Fuller and George Murdock had come this way before him, apparently of their own free will.

But the sonar didn't clearly indicate a bottom.

He smiled. That meant next to nothing, and he knew it. Whatever invisible force counteracted gravity might absorb sonar echoes as a side effect. Still, once he cut the rope, he was completely on his own. There would be no turning back—

Which hadn't seemed to bother Murdock and Harriet.

He toyed with the bayonet that they had given him. All he had to do was place the edge, honed almost razor sharp, against the rope, and apply pressure. He'd drop clear and—

And what? He didn't know. But dangling here he wasn't going to find out. He smiled grimly, trying to imagine Colonel Fullbright's shock when he was told by the Captain of Engineers that the rope had suddenly gone slack. He hung there, swinging slowly, and checked the magazine of his carbine and the clip of his .45. He hardly knew why. The weapons seemed almost superfluous. Bullets, in the face of anti-gravity!

But anti-gravity hadn't stolen the gold bars. Antigravity had made the theft possible. The bars had been stolen by—by whom, he thought. People with green arms?

Green arms?

Somehow, the thought annoyed him—and called for action. With one deft motion, he cut the rope. He barely felt the strands part, for their pressure was very slight now. But his pendulum motion ceased and he became aware of drifting gently downward. Without his weight at the end of a rope to keep his fall straight, he found himself drifting back and forth, bouncing gently as a feather from wall to wall. It was the oddest sensation he had ever experienced, and he had no doubt about anti-gravity now.

And then, abruptly, he reached bottom. He fell easily, softly, rolling once and coming to rest against the fused wall. It was almost completely dark, although directly overhead a faint patch of light—from the Fort Knox vault far above—shone down on him. He got up and switched on the flashlight.

On three sides of him, blank wall, gray, silver-mottled, glazed almost to the polish of glass. On the fourth, a passage! It cut out at right angles to the tube through which he'd dropped, forming the base of a letter L for which it was the stem. And deep within the new passage, so faint that he had to cut the flashlight's beam to assure himself he actually saw it, was light.

Almost jauntily, he set out down the passage. He tried the flashlight again, and received another surprise. For these walls seemed different. They were not glazed, but rough-hewn from the soft rock. And somehow Joe got the impression that they were very old, and quite possibly a natural rock formation. After all, the soft Kentucky bedrock was honeycombed not infrequently with caves and caverns, from gigantic Mammoth Cave on down. Had Joe stumbled on the outskirts of a cave system that might extend for miles into the subterranean rock? He hardly knew—but knew he was going to find out.

He stumbled on an outcropping suddenly, and fell forward. All he suffered was a scraped knee, but when he tried to light the flashlight afterwards, it would not work. Up ahead, though, the unknown light seemed brighter, and the loss of the flashlight hardly seemed important.

Shrugging, Joe went ahead.

CHAPTER SIX

"I'm hungry," George Murdock said. The light was blue. From head to toe he looked a pale blue color. "We've been here a long time already," he complained. He was utterly naked, but it was warm in the cavern.

Harriet Fuller, who also was naked and who sat a couple of paces from him, said, "Stop complaining, will you? Take a look at yourself, why don't you? We haven't begun to change back yet, have we? We've got to stay here until the job's completed."

"And meanwhile," George went on bitterly, "the others go on ahead with the gold."

"You're talking like a human," Harriet scolded him. "What in earth do you want with the gold?"

"Well, that's true," George admitted. "Maybe I liked being a human, Harriet."

"Please don't call me Harriet."

"That's your name, isn't it?"

"*Was* my name. It won't be much longer."

"You're very beautiful," he said abruptly, and edged closer.

"There's that, too," she told him acidly. "Beautiful—by whose standards? Human standards. It should mean nothing to you. I'm very much afraid that you're going to be a readjustment problem, George."

"There, you see! You called me George."

"Habit," she said, and yawned. "How does your skin feel?"

"Still smooth," he said happily.

"Still smooth," she echoed, but not happily. She longed to feel the first signs of roughening, see the first darkening of color...

"I hear something," George said.

"Naturally. Do you think we tucked the hole in after us?"

"You mean—"

"I mean the hole wasn't seen until all the gold was taken because the stacks of gold bars hid it. But the hole's been seen for some time now. I imagine they've sent someone after us."

"We're unarmed!" George squawked.

"So what? Even if whoever's coming down after us is armed like a walking arsenal, do you think he came down to kill us without finding out what's going on?"

"Well, no," George admitted in a whisper. "Listen. He's coming closer. What shall we do?"

"You look like an Earthman, don't you? And not what they would probably call an Under-earthman?"

"Yes, but—"

"So, act like one. We'll have to play it by ear, George, at least until we find out who they've sent and how much he has on the ball."

"See, you're talking like an Earthman!"

"Because of who's following us, stupid. Hey, why did we strip?"

He stared at her in surprise. "Why, in order for the blue rays to take effect rapidly, changing us back to our own kind, and—"

"I know that, stupid. I mean, what are we going to tell *him?*"

"Compulsion?" George suggested brightly. "I mean, why did we come down here in the first place?"

She admitted, "That's a point. All right. The whole thing was a compulsion and—shh! here he comes!"

"Harriet!" Joe cried a moment later. He looked at her and liked what he saw but couldn't tell if she were blushing or not, thanks to the blue light. She stared back at him, though, then turned away and covered her nakedness ineffectively with her arms and hands. Joe removed his fatigue shirt and tossed it to her and she got into it swiftly, buttoning it and straightening the tails along her flanks. The heavy shirt covered her from shoulders to mid-thighs.

"I think you've got some explaining to do," Joe said.

"I guess I have," Harriet said.

Joe looked at George Murdock and said, "You would have to be Murdock, of course. Mind explaining what you're doing down here?" While speaking, he tossed his shirt at Murdock, who fashioned it into a rough loin cloth which, under the circumstances, would have to do.

"Compulsion," said Murdock doubtfully.

"What he means," Harriet explained, "is that we don't know what we're doing down here. We don't even know where we are. Do we, George?"

"No," said George obediently. "We don't know what we're doing down here at all. We don't even know how we got down here."

Joe frowned and said, "But you both used the words 'down here,' so at least you know that much—that you're down somewhere."

"I guess we did," said George. "I guess we do."

"Listen," said Joe. "We found your clothing up—"

"It was a compulsion!" blurted George. "Leaving it up there at the lip of the hole."

"Oh, so you knew that much too," Joe said. He looked at them suspiciously and added, "Let's be frank. I was hoping I'd find you down here—and hoping when I found you I'd find you alive. I had no reason to be suspicious of you—but I'm suspicious of you now, and I don't know why except that your story sounds phony. Want to start over?"

"Not really," Harriet said.

"Suit yourself. What did you intend to do, just sit here until you starved to death or died of thirst or something?"

George looked at Harriet and cleared his throat and said nothing. "We were lost," Harriet said.

"Then you've been exploring?"

"A little. There isn't much to see. Caverns. We stayed in here because there's light in here."

The light seemed to seep from cracks in the wall. The light was blue and not very bright. "If I went back down the tunnel and shouted, they could probably send down a rope for us," Joe said. "Would you want that?"

"Yes!" George cried.

"No," said Harriet. "I mean, since we're here, ought'nt we to find out exactly where we are and what this place is?"

"That's my job. I'm going to find out. But you don't have to."

"We're soldiers too," Harriet said. "We want to help. Don't we, George?"

"Yes," George answered dully, dutifully.

Harriet told Joe, "You have a bayonet and a couple of guns. Want to divvy the arsenal up a little?"

Joe considered this, and shook his head. "Not just yet," he said. "Don't see why we need the weapons anyhow. What do *you* expect to find down here?"

"I don't know," Harriet said at once.

Joe looked around. Two passageways besides the one through which he'd entered led out from the blue-glowing cave. "Any preference?" he said. "It's going to be dark, I might as well warn you, because I broke my flashlight."

"That's all right," George said. "It gets lighter up ahead."

"Oh, does it? That's interesting."

"We were exploring there before," Harriet said. "Weren't we, George?"

"That's where we were exploring," George said, and pointed.

"Which passageway?" Joe asked.

"That one," George said, and pointed. But Harriet had already pointed to the other dark opening.

"I guess one of us is a little confused," she said.

Joe looked at her, suspicion back in his eyes. "I guess somebody is plenty confused," he said. He went toward the passage. "You two go first. Come on."

And he followed them into the darkness.

CHAPTER SEVEN

The Bajii of Urpadu paced back and forth in indecision before the row of gleaming crowns. Each of the cavern cities supplied him with a crown—solid gold for Ukana, gleaming silver for Toz, ruby-platinum for Holgg, and so on. Which crown he wore hardly mattered to the Bajii of Urpadu, but mattered to his subjects. Make Ukana happy today? But what had Ukana or the Ukanese subjects done to deserve it? Toz, then? But the Bajii was not partial to silver, although he did not actually dislike it. Holgg! he thought. He snapped his fingers and performed a jubilant little jig before the crowns, snatching up the ruby-platinum crown of Holgg and placing it at a rakish angle on his bald head. Holgg, of course!

For now he remembered. Curse his memory, it wasn't as good as it had once been, but he'd been ruling the joint caverns of Urpadu for a great span of time. Still, the Bajii had never married and had no issue and, as far as he was concerned, would go on ruling in Urpadu till the crack of doom.

Thanks to the magic-worker from Holgg, this was entirely possible. Bless the Holggian magician, whose name the Bajii had forgot! For it is a tenet of Urpadu—the people are restless and need diversion, since nothing ever happens in the caverns of Ukana, of Toz, and of Holgg. There is no weather, not that the Bajii knew what weather consisted of. There are no changing seasons, no light-dark fluctuations of night and day, no storms, no sun, no tropics, no arctic, no desert and no jungle, no oceans and no tundras. There is only Urpadu—changeless caverns and generation on generation of the Bajii's green, scaly-skinned people.

Divert them! Amuse them! That's the way to keep your crowns!

The Bajii sighed. He had almost run out of diversions, and that would have been fatal, for wasn't it true that the royal heart surgeon opened the chest of whatever monarch ran out of diversions, to see what blight lay heavy on the moribund king's heart? And, shortly before the Holggian magician had made his discovery, hadn't the royal chest surgeon been sharpening his flint tools and eyeing the Bajii appraisingly? The chest operation, naturally, was fatal, but a new coronation always followed it, providing the folk of Ukana, of Toz, and of Holgg with some diversion.

Magician! thought the Bajii. Long may you live! May you prosper! But not, of course, he hastily added, at the Bajii's expense.

Perhaps, the Bajii suddenly thought, he should have placed the gold crown of Ukana on his head. After all, the gold crown was in a way symbolic. For, weren't the first fruits of the Holggian magician's discovery a cavern full of gold bricks? Hadn't the heat borer and the anti-gravity machines developed by the Holggian magician led to all that gold? And wasn't gold the color of Ukana's crown?

No. Let it be Holggian ruby-platinum, in honor of the magician. The Bajii, deciding thus, took a ruby-studded cloak to match the Holggian crown, and fastened the clasp over his thin shoulders. I'm old, he thought. Old! Then he grinned, realizing that both the royal chest surgeon and the Holggian magician were still older. True, they might form league with one another; they would have to be watched. But the Bajii of Urpadu had a distinct hunch he would outlive them both.

The long cape trailing in a train behind him, the small bent king went on his bowlegged way into the throne chamber, where the aristocracy of Ukana, and Toz, and Holgg, were awaiting him. As he entered the chamber, throwing his scrawny shoulders back and with an effort even straightening his shanks somewhat, a great cheer went up from the onlookers.

"The Bajii! He diverts! The Bajii!"

He diverted, all right, the Bajii thought. But almost, he had run out of diversion—which would have been fatal. His latest had been the semi-nudity bit. It was warm in the caverns of Urpadu, so why wear clothing? That is, why wear clothing if clothing had been worn since time immemorial? Wear a cape only, like the Bajii's cape! The style had quickly caught on and had proven very diverting. But it was absolutely the last diversion the Bajii of Urpadu had felt himself capable of—until the thrice blessed magician of Holgg had come forward.

This magician was seated now on the final step leading to the throne, his magician's cape draped across a body more ravaged by age than the Bajii's own, an emaciated, hard-skinned, loose-scaled body of the gray-green color of mouldy bread. Despite his infirmity, though, the magician of Holgg was smiling.

"I see your majesty wears the crown of Holgg," he observed with an octogenarian cackle.

"Ruby-platinum!" cried the Bajii, playing on the chauvinism of the Holggians, who were singled out for praise since he wore their crown. "I love ruby-platinum!"

The magician grinned, and bowed, his forehead scraping the top step as the Bajii settled his skin-and-bones on the throne. Then, in the utter silence that followed, while the hundreds of aristocrats from Ukana, and Toz, and Holgg, awaited for word of the latest diversion, the magician said, "They're coming back, majesty. My agents inform me they have now entered the outskirts of the Tozian domain and are marching on the palace."

"Yes?" yawned the Bajii, not wishing to show his eagerness. "Who? Who is coming back?"

"Why, majesty! The two agents I sent to upworld, of course."

"If upworld exists!" a Tozian noble cried. Naturally, the Tozians were jealous of the Holggian magician's seat of favor on the uppermost step.

The Holggian magician cackled, revealing blackened gums and two teeth, like fangs, one upper and one lower, on either side of his mouth. "Oh, upworld exists!" he cried, still cackling. "Does it not, majesty?"

"Upworld exists," said the Bajii, and yawned.

"Gold!" screeched the Holggian magician. "The new symbol of Urpadu! Pure gold!"

"Calm yourself," suggested the Bajii.

"Upworld," the magician went on, "consists of caverns and caverns of pure, pure gold."

A groan escaped the assembled nobles from Toz and from Ukana. They did not hide their disappointment, nor their jealousy. It seemed a time for Holggian crowing, all right.

The Bajii sighed. If the magician from Holgg didn't watch his step, his own carcass under the flint instruments of the royal heart surgeon might be an object of diversion before long. For the Hollgian's ethnocentrism could be dangerous. There had been ethnocentric wars before, hadn't there? The Bajii, who was old and past the age for bearing weapons, had no great liking for war. The long campaigns had a way of dragging out interminably.

The Bajii sighed, but the Bajii also said, "No, magician. You are wrong there. You see, while you have your agents and your agents made a swift, admittedly daring entry into upworld, the royal agents—"

"You sent agents to upworld, majesty?"

"Indeed," went on the Bajii in a friendly voice. "They merely observed, however, and they have long since returned. Their report indicates that upworld is a region of immense diversity, although, sadly, a region where we can never dwell, thanks to the deadly actinic rays of an enormous ceiling light which seems to alternate with periods of darkness. At any rate, I merely point out that the caverns of pure gold are not the whole story of upworld."

"No, majesty," went on the magician doggedly, "but there is much gold in upworld, isn't there? Haven't we taken our share? And haven't my agents..."

"Yes, man of Holgg! Yes, we have taken our gold. For distribution among all the people, not for the coffers of Holgg!"

"But, majesty..." groaned the Holggian magician.

Much shouting and huzzahing went up, however, reverberating from the roof of the throne chamber, as the Ukanian and Tozian nobles realized their sovereign was enriching them at Holggian expense. The Holggians, on the other hand, couldn't actually complain, for hadn't the Bajii worn his ruby-platinum crown and honored the top step with one of them? The Bajii clucked happily. A long life of rule had yielded this secret to him: make no one deliriously happy, make no one intolerably sad, make everyone mildly satisfied and play the kingdoms off one against the other, and the royal chest surgeon will keep his distance...

"Where is the people's gold?" demanded the Bajii in a loud voice.

"Majesty!" squawked the magician defensively. "It has been cached in a Holggian store-cavern. I never dreamed..."

"Do not dream. Work magic."

The assembled nobles tittered at the magician's expense. The royal chest surgeon, seated cross-legged in the first row, as was his right, looked at the crestfallen magician appraisingly and at the Bajii hopefully, but the Bajii shook his head. Still, the surgeon fingered his bag of tools lovingly, as if his time would come soon.

Well, thought the Bajii, perhaps it would. Keep the people guessing—that was another thing. Keep them off stride—expectant, confused, suspenseful! For example, if the Holggian magician fell entirely out of favor, the people would expect the Bajii to summon the royal chest surgeon with a crook of his finger. Well, then, he would not! Only as a last resort would he ever yield to the expected. True, it would anger the royal chest surgeon, but the Bajii had survived his anger before. The key was ennui—or, a lack of ennui. The deadly ennui of the caverns; if somehow the Bajii could prevent the dreaded ennui from gripping his people and making them do desperate things, such as fomenting revolutions, everything would be all right.

"...while my magic is for all Urpadu, for the Bajii to dispense in the three kingdoms as he sees fit, it nevertheless," declared the Holggian magician, "is Holggian magic and therefore ought to benefit the kingdom of Holgg first and foremost."

"I am not aware that Holgg had its own Bajii," the Bajii said coldly, referring to the magician's use of the word, kingdom.

"I spoke figuratively, majesty."

"And you wish Holgg to keep an inordinate share of the upworld gold?"

"I merely suggest that in all fairness to Holgg…"

But the shouts of the nobles from Ukana and Toz drowned out his words and the Bajii raised both hands for silence. Momentarily, the royal chest surgeon misinterpreted the gesture, scooped up his bag of tools and headed up the steps happily toward the Holggian magician, but the Bajii waved him back.

"Silence," said the Bajii.

It grew silent.

"Archers!" called the Bajii, stentoriously.

Two dozen archers, their bodies greased and naked and unencumbered by any capes, male archers to the left of the throne and female archers to the right, filed from behind the throne-steps. The nobles from Ukana and Toz roared and shouted their approval, but the nobles from Holgg were silent. The Holggian magician stood up quickly, shooting desperate glances in all directions. In the instant it took him to rise, sweat was streaming down his face. He opened his mouth to talk, but his jaw flapped loosely and he said nothing.

The nobles of Ukana and of Toz roared again. The royal archers, who lived, and ate, and slept, and played, and loved in a small cavern behind the throne, awaiting the royal summons, had not been seen in a long time. The archers, if not overused, were always a diverting joy.

"Archers, ready!" said the Bajii.

Arrows were notched to bowstrings by the dozen men and dozen maids and the archers dropped motionless to one knee, awaiting the royal decree. They were like statues of green jade.

The Bajii raised the royal right hand, held it up. Two dozen bowstrings were drawn back in unison, the muscles rippling on two dozen sleekly oiled shoulders. The Holggian magician screamed and screamed, but the Bajii merely smiled, his hand poised. The Holggian magician ran down the royal steps, but the Tozian nobility closed in on one side, the Ukanian on the other. The Holggian magician fled back up the steps, waving his arms desperately, the sweat pouring from his face.

And the Bajii pointed the royal right hand—at the royal chest surgeon!

The dozen right hands opened. Two dozen bowstrings thrummed together. Two dozen arrows sped whistling to their target. The royal chest surgeon leaped up as if he had been struck—as, indeed, he had. He flung the bag of royal instruments high and leaped up one step toward the throne and fell there, pierced front and back and both sides by two dozen arrows.

The bag of royal surgical tools was fought over by the chest surgeon's acolytes, the archers filed back behind the throne and disappeared, and the Holggian magician collapsed from fright. The Bajii gave vent to a deep-throated, royal sigh. He knew from experience that whichever surgical acolyte succeeded in winning the bag of tools would be so grateful for the royal appointment that it would be a long time before he even thought of opening the royal chest.

Even the Holggian nobility joined in the waves of cheering that engulfed the throne. True, their champion of the moment had been humbled and now quaked in fear before the royal throne, but hadn't the hated chest surgeon been done away with unexpectedly? Wasn't that something to cheer about? Besides, the royal archers were splendid specimens, male and female, and the Bajii purposely kept them under wraps most of the time. And further, the royal archers were usually summoned in cycles. That is, one unexpected execution was often followed by another. The Bajii, it seemed, liked things in pairs. Thus the nobles cried their approval, awaited developments.

"Then I'm to live, majesty?" croaked the Holggian magician.

"For the moment, yes," said the Bajii magnanimously.

The new royal chest surgeon, a young fellow with the vivid green scales of recent maturity, held up his bag of tools and looked questioningly at the Holggian magician. The royal shoulders lifted and fell in a shrug, the magician shuddered and wished he had never discovered upworld, and the nobles roared their approval of the whole diverting show.

Meanwhile, the Holggian magician's agents approached the palace-cavern.

CHAPTER EIGHT

"I wouldn't go that way if I were you," George said a little desperately.

"Why not?" Joe Grange asked him, heading for a brightly-lit passageway.

"I don't know, I just wouldn't."

Harriet said, "Now, really, George." The passageway in question led to the cache of gold, she knew, but that wasn't too important. The upworlder Grange was important, and Harriet wasn't at all sure what to do with him. They still had some time, true; they were some distance from the palace. But Grange was a problem, all right. Bring him on to the palace, to divert the Bajii and his court? Possibly, but Harriet had known such diversions to backfire fatally. For the whims of the Bajii and the whims of the royal court were unpredictable and Harriet had no desire to bare her chest to the royal chest surgeon. Still, they couldn't let the upworlder Grange prowl around down here much longer. For one thing, he might decide to take some kind of drastic action after he saw the missing Fort Knox gold. For another, George and Harriet, already having bathed in the blue light, were in the process of changing back to their true forms. *Some* kind of explanation would be necessary, Harriet thought with a grim smile, if the upworlder were suddenly to see his two companions grow scales and green skin!

Then, kill him?

They could hardly do that, for the Bajii might learn of it and the Bajii would have wanted at least one interview with the real, live, breathing upworlder. For diversion, naturally. Well, a pox on the Bajii.

But that, naturally, didn't solve Harriet's problem. And George? George was a problem, too. The trouble was, George had swallowed the royal line about diversion being what made life worthwhile. So, when George had seen the manifold diversities of upworld, he had naturally preferred that world to his own. Result: a mildly mutinous fellow agent who actually desired to return to upworld.

Joe was saying, "Well, are you coming with me or aren't you?"

George looked at Harriet, who shrugged. "Lead the way," she said, and Joe stepped through a ten-foot long passageway that opened on a large chamber roughly the same size as Vault 15 at Fort Knox. And, like Vault 15, it was filled with stacks of gold bars.

"The missing gold!" Joe cried, running forward and examining his find.

Before Harriet could stop him, George rushed forward too and got both arms around Joe's neck, then freed one hand as they stumbled to the floor of the cavern, picked up a large rock with it, and bashed it across Joe's head. George got up, shaking. The rock was matted with blood and hair. Joe lay very still.

"You fool!" Harriet cried. "Oh, you fool! He didn't really suspect us, don't you see? You didn't have to kill him. What will the Bajii say? Do you think upworlders hang from ceilings like stalactites? Where are we going to find the Bajii another one?"

Harriet got down on one knee next to Joe, examining him. His pulse throbbed regularly, heavily. His scalp was cut, bruised, and bleeding, but the skull had not been smashed. Harriet stood up. "You're lucky," she said. "He's still alive. If the Bajii ever found out... Listen, George. He needs a doctor, and—"

"You'd better not report this to the Bajii or any of his officers," said George sullenly. "I'll claim you were in on it with me and got cold feet, see?"

"I'm trying to help you," Harriet said coldly. Joe groaned. Harriet added, "I said he needs a doctor. Very well, we'll get him to one. Remember that nice young fellow—what was his name?—one of the royal chest surgeon's acolytes..."

"Nellafello?"

"That's the one, Nellafello! I once—well—diverted him. So he owes me a favor. Suppose we take Joe to your cavern, it isn't far from here so we ought to be able to carry him. I'll watch Joe and you go find Nellafello. All right?"

"I didn't know you diverted him," George said coldly.

"My goodness, what's the difference? There's no such thing as sexual jealousy down here, and you know it. Prestige jealousy, that's all. You certainly have picked up some bad upworld habits, haven't you?"

George scowled but held his silence.

"Here's the rest of the plan," Harriet said. "While Nellafello is repaying his debt to me by healing Joe, we'll seek an audience with the Bajii and tell him we've brought back something even more diverting than the gold—a real, live, honest-to-goodness upworlder. We'll keep the Bajii on a string, though, until Nellafello tells us Joe's healed. We can tell the Bajii he's had an accident or something. How does it sound?"

"All right, I guess," George admitted reluctantly.

"Well, let's go, then. And don't forget where to find Nellafello. He's an acolyte of the royal chest surgeon, in the royal chest surgeon's quarters."

George lifted Joe's shoulders, Harriet took hold of Joe's feet, and off they went with their unconscious burden.

CHAPTER NINE

Nellafello couldn't believe his luck. He hadn't let them see this on his face, of course, for it never paid. Still, it was really wonderful luck and it might even prove more diverting than Harriet's happy form of diversion.

For Nellafello, erstwhile acolyte second-grade to the chief royal chest surgeon and now royal chest surgeon himself because he had caught the defunct surgeon's bag of tools, was alone with an upworlder. Knowledge of the upworlders had been common for some time now, although no one had ever been this close to an upworlder before. Why, Nellafello could reach out and touch the unconscious, pale-skinned, scale-less creature if he so desired. And, best of all, Nellafello was alone with him. He had waited, feigning indifference, until the two Holggian agents who called themselves George and Harriet—outlandish upworld names!—had gone to seek an audience with the Bajii after summoning the new chest surgeon here.

Waited—and now, alone! With a creature only slightly human, a creature whose insides were a mystery to magic and to medical science.

For example, Nellafello asked himself eagerly, did the unconscious upworlder actually have a heart, as we humans have a heart? Was it in the same place? The same size? Of the same muscular construction? Early external tests indicated it was, but what were external tests to the new royal chest surgeon? Hadn't he won his position through strength and bravery? But, on the other hand, couldn't the Bajii have him slain if he didn't prove diverting?

What better diversion than to open the chest of the alien upworlder and pluck out the still-throbbing heart and rush with it, hot and red, to the royal throne chamber, there to present it, as proof of Nellafello's devotion, to the unsuspecting Bajii?

Of course, there was no predicting the Bajii. Quite possibly, the Bajii might have other plans for the upworlder. That was why George and Harriet had gone to seek an audience with him. They thought he had other plans—or would develop other plans—didn't they? And certainly, George and Harriet were both somewhat older and far more worldly than Nellafello. Still, the prospect of opening the upworlder's chest was mighty inviting.

Eagerly, Nellafello got his bag of tools and opened it. With loving care, he fondled the sharp instruments, the pinching instruments, the sawing instruments. The blades were of flint and he'd re-chipped the edges himself, sharpening them to perfection. A deft cut, a swift plucking apart of the flesh, bone and membrane, and the upworlder heart would be bared. See? The upworlder was unconscious still. His death would be painless, in the interests of medical science and of Nellafello's career.

Am I overly ambitious for one so young? Nellafello wondered. He thought the answer was no. An overly ambitious new chest surgeon would have made an attempt on the Bajii's chest—and probably wound up with two dozen arrows pricking his carcass. This of the upworlder, though, while it was ambitious, was not *overly* ambitious. Deciding thus, Nellafello brought his bag of tools over to Joe Grange's unconscious form.

Of course, George and Harriet would be angry. Well, upworld take George and Harriet! They'd left their prisoner with Nellafello, hadn't they? Nellafello was a free agent, wasn't he? Besides, George and Harriet looked positively repulsive at the moment, precisely like upworlders, so if it came to a royal judgment, Nellafello was confident the Bajii's decree would be in his favor.

He approached Joe with a flint-bladed cutting instrument. Having given his fatigue shirt to Harriet, Joe was bare chested, but the bandolier of ammo was in the way. Nellafello removed it, noticing that another similar item went around the upworlder's belly. Deciding it was some charm or other, Nellafello wrapped the bandolier around Joe's waist over the cartridge belt. At least the upworlder would die with his charms and amulets to protect him…

Nellafello leaned over Joe, the knife-edged surgical instrument inches from his chest. Nellafello took a deep breath, and sneezed. He lifted the scalpel-like instrument again.

Joe stirred and groaned.

The royal chest surgeon jumped back as if stung, watching the upworlder roll over sit up and gaze in a stupefied fashion across the room. Swiftly, the royal chest surgeon came up behind him, raising the haft of a pincer tool, a heavy instrument used for peeling back ridges of chest bone, and brought it down on the upworlder's already injured head. The upworlder slumped, rolled over again, and stretched out on his back.

Now! thought Nellafello, and returned to the upworlder's bare chest with his scalpel, making a few practice cuts in air before he was ready to plunge the keen blade home. He regarded his subject with keen interest.

"You fool, you see?" Harriet told George as they headed for the latter's cavern. "Did you ever see the Bajii look so delighted?"

"Well, no," George admitted.

"Oh, it will be a great day for Holgg and a great day for us, all right. But no thanks to you. *You* wanted to kill the upworlder! Tell me, did you ever see the Bajii look so genuinely diverted, so expectant?"

"No," admitted George, wishing Harriet would stop her infernal crowing.

"Even the magician knew his own agents had wrestled him out of the limelight. Did you see the look on *his* face? He's torn, that poor man. I really feel sorry for him. What we do is for the good of Holgg, and so he ought to be happy. But he's no longer directly responsible, and therefore he…"

"Here we are," George interrupted, sliding the entrance stone back from the mouth of his small living cavern and politely stepping aside so Harriet could enter before him.

He was aware of a swift, lithe-limbed blur and a startled cry as Harriet went flying into the chamber. He followed behind her and saw the blur, which was Harriet, swoop down on Nellafello, who stood over the unconscious upworlder, a flint-bladed surgical tool poised to strike. He saw the blur strike the scalpel from Nellafello's hand and in the same motion strike Nellafello's cheek stingingly. He saw Nellafello fall back with a frightened cry as the scalpel went clattering to the floor.

Nellafello slapped a hand to his stinging cheek and whined, "Why did you do that?"

"Are you crazy or something?" Harriet asked him. "You—you were going to kill the upworlder!"

"To divert the Bajii, yes."

"I'll give you 'divert-the-Bajii'!" cried Harriet, but Nellafello ducked behind the upworlder's body and George said:

"That's enough, Harriet. He didn't know—"

"But we trusted him and he tried to pull a stunt like this. Nellafello, didn't you know we'd gone to the Bajii to arrange an interview before the entire royal court for the upworlder? Didn't you know if the Bajii wanted him killed the Bajii could have the royal chest surgeon or the surgeon or the royal archers do it?"

"I," Nellafello said proudly, "am the new royal chest surgeon!"

"You are?" gasped George.

Quickly, Nellafello explained what happened at the last meeting of the royal court, then smiled smugly at Harriet and George.

"That doesn't change a thing," Harriet said. "The Bajii now expects an audience with the upworlder, and he won't be disappointed if I can help it. George, whose side are you on?"

"Now, wait a minute..." George began, but the new royal chest surgeon interrupted him, saying:

"I'm not opposed to what you say. How was I to know? If the Bajii wants an audience with the upworlder, far be it for me to kill the upworlder first. Nevertheless, I shall be at the audience and I shall have the royal surgical tools ready."

He was thinking: to pluck out the upworlder's heart and offer it, red and steaming, to the Bajii.

CHAPTER TEN

Oh, the life of a Bajii, thought the Bajii of Urpadu. He had a headache. Didn't the nobles of Ukana, and Toz, and Holgg, realize that Bajiis got headaches too? The pain drummed like an anvil between his temples, seared like hot needles behind his eyeballs. Oh, he would be cross and unpredictable today, the Bajii thought.

Naturally, he wouldn't inform the court of this. Why should he? In the first place, his mental state, now unpredictable, offered more diversion. In the second, if he told the court of his temporary weakness there was no telling what they might do. He remembered with a sigh— then a shudder—his lost youth. Once, when he was very young and not Bajii yet, the old Bajii of Urpadu had attended his court with a head cold. Things hadn't gone right for the poor old Bajii. He had lacked the necessary sharpness and responsiveness to keep his subjects under control. Result? The old Bajii had been given over to the royal chest surgeon, recently defunct, and the royal chest surgeon, while four strapping nobles had held the old Bajii down, had plucked out the royal heart and tossed it at the nobles first-grade. The current Bajii, a mere stripling from Toz then, had caught the warm royal heart and had, on the spot, been proclaimed Bajii of Urpadu. Ever since, he'd kept on his toes and managed to remain Bajii—and alive.

He selected the Holggian crown of ruby-platinum for the second day running. There was no choice, he told himself, it had to be the ruby-platinum crown, for weren't the Holggian magician's two agents bringing the upworlder before him? Hadn't Holgg won the field a second court-meeting running? But he'd have to watch that, the Bajii knew. His subjects of Ukana and Toz wouldn't like it and, besides, the Holggians in their power would remember that the Bajii himself was originally from Toz while, obviously, it was time for a Holggian native to reign.

The ruby-platinum crown felt heavy, oppressively heavy. It was his headache, the Bajii knew. Usually, he liked the feel of a crown. Then he thought suddenly of the upworlder. Would the upworlder prove as diverting as the two Holggian agents had indicated? The Bajii hoped so, for perhaps diversion would take the Bajii's mind off the Bajii's headache. And besides, if the upworlder were sufficiently diverting, the royal court might never realize their Bajii was indisposed and, as such, ripe for dethroning. Or, if the upworlder proved disappointing, on the other hand, the Bajii might order his death either in an unexpected way or at an unexpected time, thus saving the day for himself.

His royal ruby-platinum cape trailing, the Bajii of Urpadu made his bow-legged way into the throne chamber. There was a buzz of excitement out there, and the buzz did not subside when the Bajii made his entrance. This confused him at first—it had, in fact, never happened before—but then he realized that the two Holggian agents and their upworlder had preceded him into the court. Naturally, all eyes were on the newcomers. Hadn't they all white skin, soft skin, scaleless skin? Hadn't they that loose, stringy stuff on their heads instead of flesh-shocks? Hadn't they, in short, the look of complete alienness?

But, decided the headache-plagued Bajii, this wouldn't do. Not for a minute. For the Bajii knew his office demanded the center of interest for himself. Lacking that, all would be lost.

The Bajii raised both hands over his head as he sat down on the throne. Instantly, the two dozen royal archers filed out from behind the throne, the dozen males on one side, the dozen females on the other. The archers strung their bows, arched their bows, and looked at the royal arm for a signal. By now, some small number of the nobles from Ukana, from Toz, and from Holgg, had turned from the three alien-looking creatures to the throne, but their numbers were insufficient.

Divert them! thought the Bajii of Urpadu. Perform the unexpected! Astound them!

He lifted his hand. He pointed.

Two dozen shoulders went back, two dozen hands loosed the feathered shafts. A loud thrumming filled the air of the throne-chamber. Noble ladies screamed, not knowing where the fatal twenty-four shafts were speeding.

"…the Bajii up there," George said to Joe Grange, and died.

One moment he stood next to Joe, talking, explaining. The next, Joe heard this sudden strumming sound and saw George's eyes go big and round with fear before a sound, as of many hammers striking something hard, but not too hard, was heard. Then the whites of George's eyes rolled back and George fell at Joe's feet, his body riddled by two dozen arrows.

Women screamed…

"The Bajii wants attention!" Harriet cried. "Quick, Joe! Fling yourself on the royal steps! Prostrate yourself before the throne, if you value your life!"

Joe's head was still numb. He had a lump the size of a big egg, which hurt excruciatingly when he touched it. Until this moment, he had taken the meeting with this underworld king as a kind of joke, although they told him it was serious after they'd revived him. They had not told him, however, that his life might depend on it. Nor had they known George would be killed almost upon entering the throne room. Apparently this Bajii of Urpadu fellow...

"Joe! Prostrate yourself!" He shook his head stubbornly, wondering if his refusal were instinctive and hence irrationally foolish or willful but foolish nevertheless. Because any moment might be his last moment if he didn't bow before that madman up there.

"Joe? Aren't you going..."

"No," Joe said. "I didn't come down here to kow-tow to any underworld royalty, if any. I came down to find out about the gold." He looked up as he spoke. The archers had notched fresh arrows to their bowstrings, for gaily dressed page boys were carting George's corpse from the chamber, and the Bajii of Urpadu was leaning forward from his throne, staring straight at Joe. It seemed a fine time to kow-tow, but Joe didn't.

Bluff? he thought. It was all well and good to speak softly and carry a big stick, provided you had a big stick to carry. But if you were all alone in the enemy camp and had no stick at all, let alone a big stick, and still had to speak, it sure as hell didn't figure to speak softly...

"Hey, you Bajii!" Joe called suddenly. The archers tensed, the nobles became instantly silent, and the Bajii leaned forward still further.

"He can't understand you," Harriet whispered in a frightened voice. "Now that George is dead, I'm the only one here can speak English."

"He understands the tone."

"That's what I'm afraid of. Are you determined to go through with this audience?"

"Determined? Are you kidding? That's what you brought me here for. The king expects it and all the people expect it. What am I going to do, back down? Besides, I want that Fort Knox gold back and I want assurances such theft won't occur again."

"You *want?*" hissed Harriet. "You'll be lucky to get away with your life. You want, do you?"

Joe nodded, walking toward the throne. The points of the two dozen arrows followed him, and George's swift death had been a sobering warning. This Bajii fellow didn't fool around. If Joe displeased him, Joe was a dead man.

"Well, mostly," Joe said grimly, "I want not to wind up the way George wound up. Is that reasonable enough?"

"Reasonable? With the Bajii reasonableness doesn't matter? Quite the reverse, but you…"

"Harriet!"

"What is it?"

"Why, you're—turning green."

"Naturally. It's about time, don't you think?"

"But I never realized you actually were one of them."

"Sure. It was easy to counterfeit Wac papers, to learn your language, to…but that doesn't matter now. In a few minutes my scales ought to be visible again too, and… Forget it, Joe. Take a look at the Bajii. He's staring at us. He's growing impatient, and so are the archers."

Joe reached the first step of the little stone pyramid below the throne. "You'll translate for me?"

"I guess I'll have to."

Trying not to think of the two dozen archers surrounding him, Joe stared up arrogantly at the Bajii of Urpadu. "Are you the bird who got away with the Fort Knox gold?" he asked in a voice as insolent as he could manage under the existing circumstances.

CHAPTER ELEVEN

Harriet translated and the Bajii said, "We have the gold, yes. Do you truly live in a world with a huge light that would wither our skins shining half the day?"

"We do," said Joe. "But I didn't come here to discuss the meteorology of my world. If you want to send us an ambassador later, you can do so. Right now, I want the gold!"

Harriet looked at Joe, shaking her head. Joe nodded and, reluctantly, Harriet translated.

The Bajii laughed and laughed and Joe saw a young fellow—it was the doctor, Nellafello—raise his small black bag hopefully in the first row. The Bajii looked at him, smiled, shrugged—as if to say, not now, my friend, but soon, very soon. Joe wondered what Nellafello's function was. He hadn't been told.

"Okay, we'll get back to that later," Joe said, and Harriet translated. "Mind telling me *why* you took the gold? Is gold a medium of exchange down here?"

"Not exactly," said the Bajii.

"Not exactly? What's that supposed to mean?"

"Careful!" warned Harriet.

"We like gold, but it is not why we stole it. There is much gold in Urpadu."

"Then why?"

"To see if we could do it!" answered the Bajii at once. "At first, my Holggian magician had in mind a bank, any bank, because he knew your world regards its banks as all but burglarproof and, if we could but enter one of them, then we could enter at will in your world, anyplace we wished, for any reason. So..."

Joe interrupted him with a harsh laugh, trying not to see the ready archers. "Is that so?" he demanded, Harriet translating reluctantly. "Do you know the population of upworld?"

"Several hundred million," guessed the Bajii.

"Over two billion!" Joe corrected him. "And yet they sent just one man down here on this punitive expedition."

"Punitive?" gagged the Bajii.

"Punitive, yes. Does that give you some indication of our strength?" Joe hoped it gave a mistaken indication, for the Urpaduse, capable of boring through rock or metal with their heat borers, capable of negating gravity, might become a serious menace if they remained aggressive before they learned the ways of the world.

"We don't fear you," said the Bajii. "We fear no one."

"I don't want fear. I want respect."

The Bajii clapped a hand to his head. His archers misinterpreted the gesture, arching their bows. Nellafello came forward eagerly, black bag ready.

"Anyhow," the Bajii said, "I was telling you about the gold. After my magician determined that the theft of gold or currency from any bank would be a blow to your prestige, I next determined that if we could find the bankiest bank—" that was how Harriet translated it with her greener and greener lips— "your prestige really would suffer. Since Fort Knox is the bankiest bank in upworld, I sent my Holggian magician to Fort Knox."

An old white-haired fellow standing a dozen feet from Joe cackled and danced a little jig. This, Joe assumed, was the Holggian magician.

"I see," Joe said. "Well, you can send him right back. With the gold."

"Joe," Harriet said.

"Translate it."

She did so, shaking her head.

The Bajii listened, and frowned, and clapped a hand to his head, and squinted, and let a groan escape him—as if he were suffering, Joe thought—and shouted, "Flea! Flea on the belly of a flea on the belly of a flea! You dare to talk to the Bajii of Urpadu this way?"

There was no answer to this one. Joe remained silent.

"Well, let me tell you something," the Bajii said, still clutching his head. "Let me tell you—"

"Talk, just talk!" hooted one of the nobles, and Harriet quickly translated for Joe's benefit. "We don't want a Bajii who sits there talking!"

"It's a Tozian," Harriet said quickly. "Even though the Bajii is a Tozian himself, or was originally, the Tozians and the Ukanians probably feel left out in the cold because Holgg—"

"And you're a Holggian?"

"Yes."

"Loyal to Holgg, whatever Holgg is?"

Harriet shrugged. "I'm loyal to—myself. I'm a woman, Joe."

He nodded. The Bajii seemed distracted. Acting like a man with—with a painful headache! And the nobility was restless. Therefore, if the Bajii could be flattered and befuddled into talking, into bantering words when the nobility craved action...

"Oh noble Bajii!" Joe cried, and prostrated himself before the throne as Harriet translated. "Oh, most noble king of kings! If you could forgive this worm in the intestine of a worn..."

"What's intestine?" Harriet hissed, and Joe tried to explain while the Bajii said:

"In my magnanimity as Bajii of Urpadu, young man, I can forgive you, but—" clutching his head—"I'm afraid you can see that my people are beyond forgiving and crave only the special sort of diversion I can give them. As Bajii—yes, as Bajii..." Clearly, his head was in a whirl. "...I know exactly what, how—where were we, young man?"

"Holggian lover!" an Ukanian noble shouted. "We've had enough of your talk."

"Down with the Bajii!" cried another voice.

"Favoritism!" shrieked a woman. "Twice running, the ruby-platinum crown! Are we Tozians to stand for this, from a turncoat Tozian?"

"No!" roared a dozen voices.

"Now, wait," said the Bajii. But half a dozen nobles rushed to Nellafello, who, Harriet now explained, was the royal chest surgeon. She did not, however, inform Joe of the royal chest surgeon's duties. The nobles crowded around Nellafello and spoke rapidly and he tried to run away from them, but found himself surrounded. Once, angrily, one of them grabbed the black bag away from the young royal chest surgeon and would have flung it in the air, but Nellafello got down on his knees and begged, and so the bag was returned to him.

"Divert!" screamed the Bajii, "I must divert them."

Trembling, Nellafello began climbing the steps toward the throne.

"Archers!" screamed the Bajii, but Harriet told Joe:

"It is written that the royal archers cannot stop the royal chest surgeon in the performance of his duty."

"But what's going to happen?"

"Why, the royal chest surgeon will open the Bajii's chest and pluck out his heart and hurl it among the nobles, whoever catches it becoming our new Bajii. And it's about time!"

Joe was too startled to answer her. For the moment, he could only watch, but he knew that the new Bajii's first act would be to have Joe slain—for, hadn't Joe triggered the revolution?

Up the steps slowly went the royal chest surgeon, opening his black bag.

"Archers!" screamed the Bajii again, and pointed his finger tremblingly at the Holggian magician. "That man is responsible for my ruin!"

The two dozen backs bent, the two dozen hands opened, the two dozen arrows whistled to their target. The Holggian magician leaped, and was impaled, and died. By then, Nellafello had reached the throne. Several nobles joined him, flinging the Bajii over on his back and pinning him there. The royal chest surgeon's scalpel rose, an utter silence fell on the throne chamber, and the Bajii kicked and thrashed in his death-throes.

Then the flint blade struck and the Bajii screamed once and was dead.

"Come on!" cried Joe, and grabbed Harriet's hand, tugging her upstairs toward the throne.

Joe reached it a split second before the royal chest surgeon could perform the traditional rite of plucking the royal heart. Joe flung him away from the Bajii's body and fought off the astounded Urpaduse nobles.

"Joe!" Harriet screamed. "They'll kill you."

He laughed, and it was a wild laugh. "Don't you want to be a queen?" he cried, and kicked two of the nobles downstairs. He grappled with a third, then lifted him bodily and flung him at the fourth. They went tumbling down after their fellows and the royal chest surgeon made a wild swipe at Joe with his dripping scalpel. Joe lunged to one side and struck the royal chest surgeon in the face with his right first. Nellafello sobbed and slumped to the floor.

"Quick," Joe said, and nudged the Bajii of Urpadu's corpse from the gilt throne. He took the still-protesting Harriet by the hand and sat her down in the Bajii's place, putting the ruby-platinum crown on her hairless green head and the ruby-encrusted cape about her fatigue-shirt.

And miraculously, Harriet's uncertainty vanished. She stood arrogantly and pointed at the royal archers and, trained to obey whoever sat in the gilt throne, they strung arrows. She pointed again and the archers unleashed a volley of arrows over the crowd's heads. Silence and order fell on the throne-chamber.

"I am the new Bajii!" cried Harriet, who was now green, and scale-skinned, and flesh-shocked.

"Bajia," someone corrected. "Our first Bajia, ever."

Harriet grinned at Joe. "It ought to divert them for a good long time, thanks to you. I guess I owe you plenty."

"I want the gold," Joe said.

Reluctantly: "You'll get it."

"And I want no more horsing around with upworld, understand? It's why I made you queen, Harriet. Sure, you can get away with a few thefts, thanks to your anti-gravity magic, but you know our strength. Right?"

Reluctantly: "Right."

"Would you want to establish diplomatic relations with us?"

The new Bajia considered, then shook her head. "I'm an absolute sovereign down here. I'm going to like it, I think. But intercourse with that crazy democracy of yours—"

"I understand," Joe said. "Will you have the gold delivered to the anti-gravity shaft for me?"

"Yes."

"And give me a guarantee of safe-conduct?"

"Yes, Joe. Oh, Joe, if only you were green and scaly—" She sighed. "How we could rule together!"

"I'm not, and I have a job to do."

"Yes, Joe. You may go now. We won't bother your people again."

Joe walked from the throne chamber without looking back Already he was thinking of the brass-hats and how astonished they would be and wondering what story he could possibly tell them. Well, he'd think of something. It didn't really matter. What they wanted was the gold, and he would give them the gold. Beautiful yellow gold.

As he left, he heard the roar go up behind him, spontaneous, full-throated, thunderous:

"Hail, Bajia! Hail! She diverts! Hail, Bajia!"

Joe smiled. The colonels would, as colonels generally did, miss the best part of the story.

THE END

If you've enjoyed this book, you will not want to miss these terrific titles...

ARMCHAIR SCI-FI & HORROR DOUBLE NOVELS, $12.95 each

D-61 **THE MAN WHO STOPPED AT NOTHING** by Paul W. Fairman
TEN FROM INFINITY by Ivar Jorgensen

D-62 **WORLDS WITHIN** by Rog Phillips
THE SLAVE by C.M. Kornbluth

D-63 **SECRET OF THE BLACK PLANET** by Milton Lesser
THE OUTCASTS OF SOLAR III by Emmett McDowell

D-64 **WEB OF THE WORLDS** by Harry Harrison and Katherine MacLean
RULE GOLDEN by Damon Knight

D-65 **TEN TO THE STARS** by Raymond Z. Gallun
THE CONQUERORS by David H. Keller, M. D.

D-66 **THE HORDE FROM INFINITY** by Dwight V. Swain
THE DAY THE EARTH FROZE by Gerald Hatch

D-67 **THE WAR OF THE WORLDS** by H. G. Wells
THE TIME MACHINE by H. G. Wells

D-68 **STARCOMBERS** by Edmond Hamilton
THE YEAR WHEN STARDUST FELL by Raymond F. Jones

D-69 **HOCUS-POCUS UNIVERSE** by Jack Williamson
QUEEN OF THE PANTHER WORLD by Berkeley Livingston

D-70 **BATTERING RAMS OF SPACE** by Don Wilcox
DOOMSDAY WING by George H. Smith

ARMCHAIR SCIENCE FICTION & FANTASY CLASSICS, $12.95 each

C-19 **EMPIRE OF JEGGA**
by David V. Reed

C-20 **THE TOMORROW PEOPLE**
by Judith Merril

C-21 **THE MAN FROM YESTERDAY**
by Howard Browne as by Lee Francis

C-22 **THE TIME TRADERS**
by Andre Norton

C-23 **ISLANDS OF SPACE**
by John W. Campbell

C-24 **THE GALAXY PRIMES**
by E. E. "Doc" Smith

If you've enjoyed this book, you will not want to miss these terrific titles…

ARMCHAIR SCI-FI & HORROR DOUBLE NOVELS, $12.95 each

D-71   **THE DEEP END** by Gregory Luce
TO WATCH BY NIGHT by Robert Moore Williams

D-72   **SWORDSMAN OF LOST TERRA** by Poul Anderson
PLANET OF GHOSTS by David V. Reed

D-73   **MOON OF BATTLE** by J. J. Allerton
THE MUTANT WEAPON by Murray Leinster

D-74   **OLD SPACEMEN NEVER DIE!** John Jakes
RETURN TO EARTH by Bryan Berry

D-75   **THE THING FROM UNDERNEATH** by Milton Lesser
OPERATION INTERSTELLAR by George O. Smith

D-76   **THE BURNING WORLD** by Algis Budrys
FOREVER IS TOO LONG by Chester S. Geier

D-77   **THE COSMIC JUNKMAN** by Rog Phillips
THE ULTIMATE WEAPON by John W. Campbell

D-78   **THE TIES OF EARTH** by James H. Schmitz
CUE FOR QUIET by Thomas L. Sherred

D-79   **SECRET OF THE MARTIANS** by Paul W. Fairman
THE VARIABLE MAN by Philip K. Dick

D-80   **THE GREEN GIRL** by Jack Williamson
THE ROBOT PERIL by Don Wilcox

ARMCHAIR SCIENCE FICTION CLASSICS, $12.95 each

C-25   **THE STAR KINGS**
by Edmond Hamilton

C-26   **NOT IN SOLITUDE**
by Kenneth Gantz

C-32   **PROMETHEUS II**
by S. J. Byrne

ARMCHAIR SCIENCE FICTION & HORROR GEMS SERIES, $12.95 each

G-7   **SCIENCE FICTION GEMS, Vol. Seven**
Jack Sharkey and others

G-8   **HORROR GEMS, Vol. Eight**
Seabury Quinn and others